Distant Music

Distant Music

LEE LANGLEY

MILKWEED
EDITIONS

Published 2003 by Milkweed Editions
First published in Great Britain by Chatto & Windus 2001
Printed in the United States of America
Cover and interior design by Christian Fünfhausen
Front cover painting, detail, Francisco de Goya, *Señora Sabasa Garcia*, Andrew W. Mellon Collection, Image © 2002 Board of Trustees, National Gallery of Art, Washington.
Lisbon aqueduct photograph courtesy of Phil Wood / Apa Publications.
Faro cathedral photograph courtesy of Pedro Correia, www.portugal-book.com.
Author photo by Theo Richmond
The text of this book is set in New Baskerville.
03 04 05 06 07   5 4 3 2 1
First Edition

Special underwriting for *Distant Music* was
provided by an anonymous donor.

Milkweed Editions, a nonprofit publisher, gratefully acknowledges support from the Bush Foundation; Joe B. Foster Family Foundation; Furthermore, a program of the J. M. Kaplan Fund; General Mills Foundation; Jerome Foundation; Dorothy Kaplan Light; Lila Wallace-Reader's Digest Fund; Marshall Field's Project Imagine with support from the Target Foundation; McKnight Foundation; Minnesota State Arts Board through an appropriation by the Minnesota State Legislature; National Endowment for the Arts; Kate and Stuart Nielsen; Deborah Reynolds; St. Paul Companies, Inc.; Ellen and Sheldon Sturgis; Surdna Foundation; Target Foundation; Gertrude Sexton Thompson Charitable Trust; James R. Thorpe Foundation; Toro Foundation; United Arts Fund of COMPAS; Lois Ream Waldref; Brenda Wehle and John C. Lynch; and Xcel Energy Foundation.

Library of Congress Cataloging-in-Publication Data

Langley, Lee.
Distant music / Lee Langley.—1st ed.
p. cm.
ISBN 1-57131-040-1 (acid-free paper)
1. London (England)—Fiction. 2. Jews—Portugal—Fiction.
3. Catholics—Fiction. 4. Portugal—Fiction. I. Title.
PR6062.A5335 D57 2003
823'.914—dc21
2002151111

This book is printed on acid-free paper.

For Prudence Fay

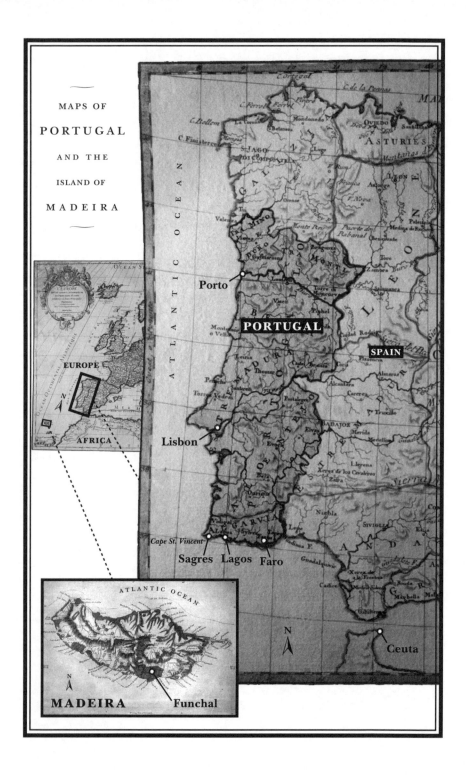

MAPS OF

PORTUGAL

AND THE

ISLAND OF

MADEIRA

Distant Music

Distant Music

LONDON | 2000

No search results. Please enter more information.

The cursor waits, blinking. She enters a request.

"Search for me."
Click.
No search results. Please enter more information.

She tries again.

"Begin search."
Click.
No search results. Please enter more information.

She tries. The keyboard clatters. The cursor skates across the screen. The words fly, free of paper, on a web that links the world.

"Search."
Click.
No search results. Please enter more information.

Information. Information needed: how to decode, unravel, make sense of it—

"Search."
Click.
No search results. Please enter more information.

MADEIRA | *1429*

MADEIRA | 1429

The island is tantalizing: on old maps it vanishes and reappears so that it seems untrustworthy, not quite corporeal. Small and inconspicuous—no more than thirty-five miles long—it offers narrow, glancing angles to the wind. The Romans knew it as one of a handful of islands off the coast of Africa, Pliny's Purple Isles. In 1351, on a Genoese Medici map it is clearly marked: Isolad della Lolagname—*the Island of Wood—but on a map drawn forty years later the seas lie blank, untroubled by its rocky presence.*

Concealed by clouds, shielded by the surge of the sea, the island's green and gray shape mingled misleadingly with the haze, an unclaimed prize. Earlier seafarers mistook the solid land for the mist that hung over it: the sea boiled against the cliffs, sending up a spray that billowed into a cloudy vapor. They saw it as an evil portent and kept away.

On the new maps, drawn after 1420 when an exhausted mariner limping home, blown off course, stumbled on the reality

7

of the island, the dot had reappeared, named afresh, once again the Island of Wood—a ilha da Madeira.

Ships landed and fires began.

Then, trees and clouds covered the island. Now, flowers cluster on its slopes. Also tourists. Flames are reserved for festive occasions when flat round loaves and spatchcocked chickens cook on open fires, the smoke rising above the statue of Henry the Navigator and the big wheel at the funfair, drifting with rock music that pounds like a sledgehammer, buffeting the very air, floating away, smoke and syncopation melting against the steep hillsides above the town, where villas stand in place of trees.

On the Portuguese mainland, the mother country, fires can still be seen, when developers burn swaths of woodland to clear a stretch of coast for hotel blocks and holiday villages. Fire has always been part of what is called progress here. Autos-da-fé of one sort and another.

THE FIRES BURNED for seven years.

No one realized, at the beginning, how deep the burning went, the hold it took, drying the earth, igniting roots that ran below the ground, sending the flame traveling on hidden paths to surface unexpectedly elsewhere, breaking out like the plague. In time, they learned to live with it.

Restless, the straw mattress rustling beneath her as she moved, her sister's weight pulling her toward the sagging center, Esperança felt the warmth from the dying embers in the fireplace and, on the edge of sleep, recalled the heat of those first fires, the muffled roar as the engulfing force swept through the undergrowth and the trees. The moment of unease like an indrawn breath, the awareness of movement beneath her feet, a tremor that rose from the

8

ground like the trembling on the surface of a pan of water not yet quite at boiling point. Then the crackling of flames. Too young to understand the reasons, she had been frightened by the red wind that swept through the forest. Trees and bushes burned, trapped animals roasted, and the dew was sucked from leaves a mile away.

It had been necessary, at the beginning. But no one realized how deep the burning went.

She could remember the time before the fires, but perhaps what she recalled was drawn from hearsay: she had been barely eight when it began and it was hard, sometimes, to disentangle what she had experienced from what she had been told. For so long the persistent, shifting furnace had been part of their lives. That, and the men and ships that came and went, the great logs loaded onto them still warm from the fire like overbaked loaves of bread holding heat from the oven.

Offshore, the ships rose and fell in the dark-blue water. The land stood tall out of the sea: unwelcoming cliffs of basalt crowned with trees, their massed green cushioning the volcanic rock.

The men shouted and called, and the girl watched as they loaded the ships with wood. The superstitious among the sailors occasionally wept and moaned as they headed for the line dividing sky from sea, convinced they would not return, but most knew that death was more likely by shipwreck or disease than a plunge from the earth's rim. They knew this less from acquaintance with Pythagoras and Aristotle than from common observation. Esperança, too, accepted that there would be no falling off the edge, that the world was round. The boy off the ship had explained it to her.

He plucked one of the bitter oranges from a branch overhanging the path and placed an ant on the dimpled surface. After a frozen moment the ant moved on and the boy turned the fruit, slowly, steadily as the insect crawled. See, he said, how the surface curves onward as the ant advances. The ships are like that ant. The line dividing sky and sea, he said, is just a way of seeing, not the end of anything.

She watched him closely, a thin, sticklike figure such as her mother set up in the field to scare the birds. His hair was black and tightly curled. He had long hands and juice dripped from his fingers as he peeled the orange. To her surprise he put a segment in his mouth, chewing rapidly. The islanders did not eat their bitter fruit.

By now she had fed him cherries, which were plentiful, and some hoarded bread, and shown him her secret island paths, the ones that followed the goat tracks from harbor to hilltop, avoiding the areas worst affected by the smoldering fire. He had shown her how to write the name of the Lord, scratched on a stone.

In time, antlike, ships will crawl across the curving sea. Wide-keeled caravels borne up on the turning tide will float free of the motherland toward the low-lying sun, past unsuspected islands, round great capes, and disgorge their cargo on another shore.

Straw huts and age-blurred stone temples will be overshadowed by raw new churches, the multitude of old gods nudged, if not successfully supplanted, by a surprising Trinity. The carved Son, hanging from a wooden cross hewn from smoke-warmed slabs of mahogany, will have pale, European features. Men create God in their likeness.

Meanwhile the fires burn.

She first saw him on her way down to the harbor one morning. He was sitting on a broken cart by the side of the path, staring at an object held in his hands: a square block, something she could not quite make out. Thin, pale, he was scraped looking, his eyes huge, shadowing his face.

The path, rubble strewn and slippery underfoot, dropped down the face of the hillside like a ladder hewn from the rock. Crisscross routes had established themselves, as is the way with much used paths, the passing feet marking out the convenient turning point, the short cut, the shallowest descent. Donkeys were useful, their small, fastidious hooves tamping down the mud, sounding out the firmer ground.

She picked her way carefully, bare feet gripping the earth, the mud squelching silkily between her toes. Her eyes were fixed on the boy hunched against the cart, head lowered, like someone at prayer.

When she reached him she paused, expecting an upward glance, even a scowl, as could be the way with boys, but he remained unmoving, no flick of the eyes or shift of muscle to acknowledge her presence. She stopped. Took a cautious step closer. Craned her neck. A bundle of stiff sheets, fastened together in some way, lay in his hands, warped and creased by much handling. Their surfaces were stamped with black marks that curved and writhed, covering them, as though dark, wafer-thin bracelets lay on the surface, one below the other. Esperança moved closer, fluid as a cat, her eyes fixed, catlike, on the stranger, moving one step at a time, holding him in her gaze, as if in this way she might advance unseen.

A yard away she paused, stooping a little to check that he was actually awake and not slumped asleep where he sat, like her father on a heavy roofing job, snatching rest when he could. The youth's lowered lids flickered and

11

then, unexpectedly, he turned one of the sheets, left to right.

She called, hoping the stranger would understand her, "What are you looking at?"

He glanced up at her, surprised, and lifted the bundle. "This."

"Why?"

"Why?" He frowned. "I'm reading."

"What does that mean?"

"Reading?"

Perplexed, she waited for him to say more.

"These"—he touched the marks—"are words—"

"How can they be? Words are what we speak—"

"And write. Words are like bricks. Put together, they make different things. Like bricks make a building. Each word tells us . . . something."

She stared at him, astonished. The stranger could peel away the mystery of those black marks, so that they spoke to him, passed on messages—

"Tell me some of the words." She tested him, suspicious, pointing. "What is this word?"

Her finger, the nail rimmed with black, rested beside a short cluster of marks on one of the sheets. He did not reply for a moment. Then:

"That is the name of the Lord."

"Lord Jesus?"

He frowned, hesitated. "The one and only Lord."

"God the Father?" she said. She studied the word. "Go on."

His fingers followed the baffling shapes and his mouth gave voice to them.

Esperança shrugged impatiently when he stopped. "Tell me some more words!"

12

His finger moved, right to left:

> "Terror, and the pit, and the trap, are upon thee, O
> inhabitants of the earth. And it shall come to pass
> that he who fleeth from the noise of the terror
> shall fall into the pit. And he that cometh up out
> of the midst of the pit shall be taken in the trap.
> For the windows on high are opened, and the foun-
> dations of the earth do shake; the earth is broken,
> broken down, the earth is crumbled in pieces, the
> earth trembleth and tottereth; the earth reeleth to
> and fro like a drunken man and swayeth—"

Esperança marveled, her eyes moving from his mouth
to the bundle he held. She became aware of a pain growing inside her, the ache she felt when food was running low
in winter. She folded her arms, pressing tightly against herself, to push away the pain. "Teach me to read."

"I cannot."

"Teach me," she repeated. It was not a request. She
said fiercely, "I know nothing! I want to learn how to name
things, don't you see? I can't name things."

"Of course you name things: you name everything
around you. We only write down what we know already—"

She brushed that aside, contemptuously waving away
her familiar territory. "I want the words that give you the
names of what you *don't* know. What you *haven't* seen!
Words can show you the world. Isn't that so?"

Next day she brought him bread and a scrap of cheese.
Someone so thin must be in need of food. There was no
need to tell him it was her own portion she gave him.
"Teach me to read."

"It would be difficult—"

But already she could recognize the shape of God,
picking it out from the maze of others. He had shown her

13

Adam and Eve and the Garden of Eden, day and night. Good. Evil. She acquired the words jackdaw-like, picking them up one by one, admiring them. She felt she was stepping through a doorway to a room furnished with unsuspected treasure.

They exchanged names. When she heard his, she repeated it, questioningly.

"You can find it in the Bible." He showed his name among the curling patterns—"See here it is, in Isaiah."

In bed that night she looked at the shape of his name, traced with her fingertip the pattern he had scratched on a flat gray pebble. Emmanuel. Like everyone else, she called him Manuel.

Far away, on the outermost edge of a continent, in a place once named Lusitania, later Portugal, children cry as men and women burn. But that time is still to come, thirty thousand dawns away and more, spinning towards them. Meanwhile tides turn. Suns rise and set. Fires burn.

THE FIRES HAD been necessary, at the beginning, to clear the territory, to allow the men to get at the trees, the timber to be felled and shipped out, as the new owners energetically ripped the island apart. For Esperança the fire was less interesting than the plants it destroyed. She showed them to Manuel, leaping ahead of him up the path, pinching fragrant leaves, crushing milky, unripe nuts between her fingertips, stroking the bark of trees—the juniper that the carpenters used for the ceiling of the church, its pale wood as aromatic as its berries; trees with tough, pink trunks used by the fishermen for the keels of boats. Sometimes her father carried the pink wood home for a special bit of furniture—not for their own home, but for sale to those who could afford it. There were candle-berry trees with branches that could be hacked and sharp-ened into stakes for the vines, and lily-of-the-valley trees with white, sweet smelling flowers. There were palms and bamboo clumps, golden *musschia* and tall ferns. Below them, bunched low, the strange, spiky dragon trees. And towering over all the rest, the mahogany, its wood red and hard. The names she learned later, with other, more diffi-cult lessons.

Manuel's ship, standing out in the harbor, waiting for timber to be loaded, had brought sugar canes from Sicily. Esperança showed him where they would be planted, next to earlier crops, in the flat places. At present, alongside the paths and spreading across hillsides, good for neither food nor fuel, a swath of wildflowers swayed in the breeze. She thought of it as a coverlet spread over the hard black rock of the island. All this was away from the fiery slopes, though even here the heat could reach her: a scorching breath car-ried on the breeze to burn her cheek; a column of smoke rising from the trees across the ravine.

He was startled when she led him to the steaming bur-rows, the sulphurous deposits, the rocks so hot that she could cook a stolen bird's egg on their surface. The fires no longer surprised her; and in any case she had some-thing new to think about.

"I can read!" she exulted, plucking word after word from the perplexing tangle of black shapes like someone picking her way on stepping stones, feverish to move on.

"Why do you read?" she had asked him that first day, puzzled.

"In order to ask questions."

She thought for a moment. "I don't know *how* to ask questions—not real questions. And who would answer them? I know nothing about anything. I can do nothing."

Nearby, a goat picked its way toward a chosen bush, munching steadily.

"Can you milk a goat?"

She shrugged. "Yes. But that's—"

"Bake bread?"

"Yes, but—"

"This skirt." He plucked at the rough cloth. "Your mother made that, I suppose—"

"I made it, of course! There's no skill to stitching a hem."

"I can't stitch a hem. Look, my clothes are torn, here. And here. I can't sew."

"I know so little," she said. "How will I learn?"

She knew how her father set about thatching a roof, what weight of reeds he needed, where he would start, what he would be paid, in cash and kind. But there was an emptiness inside her head, like an unfilled bowl, nothing to sift through, nothing to be kneaded and shaped and baked into a new form.

"Teach me," she said again.

She felt the restlessness flowing into her, the itching in her feet and hands, the breathlessness, a sense of being trapped, her world too narrow. It got her into trouble sometimes, this seething discontent, the blood jumping in her veins, driving her to try too hard, to attempt tasks beyond her capability.

She stared at him resentfully. She sensed that he had secrets. He seemed foreign, although he spoke much the

same as other mainland men who visited the island. She
had become aware that his life was marked by mysterious
rituals, one of which was the conjuring of words from small,
stiff sheets marked with black symbols. He read daily, sometimes swaying gently back and forth, the way a woman might
rock a baby clasped to her breast.

"Why are you here?" she asked, when they first began
to talk.

"I work on the ship, that one anchored down at the far
end of the harbor."

"Why?"

"Why? Why not? I need to eat."

She shook her head. "You're not like the sailors; you're
more like a priest. What are you doing on a ship?"

Usually he retreated into blankness when questioned by
strangers, eyes dulling and slithering away from confrontation. Usually he managed to look stupid or sleepy and the
interrogation would lapse.

The ships had many such boys, orphans or unwanted
at home, willing to scrub decks and struggle with ropes so
harsh that the soft young hands were scarred, bleeding, as
the twisted hemp snaked through their fingers. Boys agile
as cats, sent clambering into rigging on cross masts slippery
beneath their bare wet feet. Sometimes, when the ship
keeled over and the wind snatched at the sail, the climbing
boy would fall, a faint cry carried on the wind, crashing to
deck or plunging too deep for rescue as the boat plowed
on. This, in exchange for poor food, cramped quarters and
pitiful wages. They lasted as long as their strength held out,
or until a casual brawl got out of hand and cut them down.
Some jumped ship in a port that offered hope of something
better.

A few proved natural seafarers, signing on for expeditions that took them farther than the charts into the cloudy void, terra incognita.

Manuel could have attempted his practiced withdrawal in answer to Esperança's question, but she pushed her small face forward, her eyes unwavering.

"Why?" she asked.

<hr />

MANUEL WAS FIVE years old when Prince Henry, with time on his hands as is the way with the sons of kings, was drawn to the idea of seafaring and conquest. In 1415 the princely navigator and his father's fleet crossed the Mediterranean and battled their way past Barbary pirate ships to take the port of Ceuta. Triumphant, Henry savored the warm winds of Africa, and the itch to explore got under his skin like a speck of sand, an insect bite.

In a narrow cobbled street in an insignificant town in the southwest of Portugal, Manuel heard the story; he, too, felt the sting, tuned his ears to catch the words murmured by cousins and uncles at the family table, listening as they talked of charts and tides and the winds that could scatter a flotilla, crack a mast, leave one vessel becalmed or lost, draw another along sea routes as surely as roads led men across great plains and through mountain ranges. And there were mountain ranges beneath the sea, too, sierras that rose from the ocean floor, their peaks sharp enough to pierce hulls and tear flesh from bone.

The men in the small, airless room in Lagos were finding ways to measure the seas, redrawing the charts, refashioning the instruments that would guide Portugal's mariners, giving them the height of the sun, calculating latitude. Henry drew on their skills, equipping his vessels with their designs, plotting the shape of an empire with the charts they created.

With a sense of disloyalty, Manuel recognized, when he was old enough to understand, that the royal navigator sent men on journeys while he himself remained at home, dreaming of what lay beyond the ocean. Henry, the proxy explorer, the vicarious voyager, never got any farther than Ceuta in Gibraltar's straits, its elbow nudging Tangier, barely more than a nod across the Mediterranean. The queen's troubadour, Black Juda, sang of the triumph, spreading the fame of the royal navigator—something of a private embarrassment, since it was Henry's only expedition, that exhilarating victory over pirates, waves, and infidels. He studied, encouraged, paid the costs; his pointing finger sent others into the wind, his own hand rarely on the helm.

Manuel's uncles, with their pale, soft hands and tired eyes, talked with disparagement of the Phoenicians, the Carthaginians, the Greek and Roman sailors who looked to the skies and hugged the coastline. The Portuguese now would be the first true navigators, Henry's vision driving them. But—the uncles and cousins permitted the question only when talking among themselves—without his Jews and Moors to tease out the secrets of water and wind and sky, to draw the maps, do the calculations, and reach the necessary conclusions, how would Henry's sailors find their way across those uncharted seas?

Manuel had squirreled the stories away, squatting by the door, a wary, well-mannered child, conscious already that he was an outsider, not just as a Jew in the bigger world, but as an orphan within his uncle's house, fed and tolerated, nothing more.

19

1415. A year of gain and loss: Henry captured Ceuta, Manuel lost his parents. The bubonic plague, the Black Death, slithered unstoppable through the city streets and claimed the customary payment. Packs of dogs scavenged the filthy byways, clearing the debris flung from kitchens. The rats were already there. The stars were blamed, malign influences drifting from the skies, tainting the very air, and fires burned at crossroads and in village squares to purify breathing space.

The king was fed rare remedies—a powder made from the blood of a badger filtered through wine blended with gold, seed pearls, and coral and mixed with cinnamon, saffron, and a scraping from the horn of a unicorn. No one had actually seen the unicorn, but scrapings from its horn were available—at a price.

The people relied on divine intercession with variable success. Jews, like Moors, tended to escape the plague: ritual bathing and dietary restrictions usually proved more effective than Gentile prayers or superstitious ceremonials. But this time the grim visitor was less discerning, no houses were passed over. Famine, drought, and evil weather were the heralds, and then the wolf was loose.

Manuel watched his mother across the small, bare room they had been given by the uncles after his father succumbed. Watched as the flesh loosened on the bone, shriveled. For a while the brilliance of her eyes remained: the fever kept them shining. Strangely, she seemed sometimes to be smiling, her lips drawn back from her big white teeth. She was all he had now, and he cared for her like a mother tending an infant: he fetched water, which she rejected, and scraps of food, which lay uneaten on the dish, summoning flies. He wound a cloth over his mouth and nose, blocking nostrils only partially—he still needed to breathe—but trying to filter out the smell, rotten and sweet-ish, that drifted from her body as he fanned her with a palm leaf, watching the black sores on thighs and arms deepen, grow crusty, suppurate. She coughed weakly, spitting blood. Beyond the door, others rotted and died in the street.

Whether the purification by fire was effective, or whether the cleaning of sewers, cesspools, and dunghills helped, the pestilence passed on, leaving funeral pyres, empty spaces, and the corpses of animals piled outside city gates. Unremarked, the rats came and went.

Manuel buried his mother.

His uncles were busy, called on by Henry, bent on con-quering the Moroccan Mediterranean. Henry placed his Jews with care: here a physician, there a scribe. Not cap-tains themselves, they hovered at the right hand of the cap-tains, guiding the ships, reading instruments their fellow Jews had invented.

Later Henry sent his captains and his caravels beating down the coast of Africa, drawn by tales of treasure and bounty, of the gold mines of Solomon the King. But all that lies ahead.

Manuel's uncles made mathematical guesses and created models in wood and metal for new ways to measure the heavens and the seas. And all the while they talked. While the child listened. He stared at the maps with their draw-ings and their words of warning: here be dragons, lying in wait behind coasts and reefs; and here, mountains and wide rivers, great birds with the wingspan of a man's out-stretched arms, and elephants, and mysterious beasts whose skin hung like armor plating and who grew their own daggers on their snouts. But what Manuel sought was not on the map: he was drawn to the world beyond the known world. He wrapped his father's holy books in a prayer shawl, tied them in a neat bundle, and waited.

He was twelve when he ran away to sea.

"Why?" Esperança asked, again.

"Because of the voyage—the search."

"And is it as you thought? Full of wonders?" Esperança demanded.

"Wonders," he said.

"Tell me one!"

"Well . . . think of a fish so big that it could be a floating island. Shipwrecked sailors, tossed about in a storm in their little boat, are flung up onto what they take to be a barren shoreline. In fact, it's the fish's back. They give thanks for being saved, pull the little boat up onto dry land, and light a fire. When the heat of the flames begins to burn the fish, it rears and plunges to the ocean floor, leaving the terrified, half-drowned sailors trying to swim back to their craft—"

"That cannot be true!" she cried.

"Probably not," he agreed. "But it makes a nice picture in the mind. The fish lying peacefully on the surface, the fire warming the wretched sailors and then—"

"And can the storms truly be terrible?"

"So terrible that you cannot tell what is air and what is water. Something that is at once both wind and sea boils up around you, hurling itself at the ship. All you see is the gray inside of the wave coming for you, like the open mouth of a great fish . . . cataracts of icy water clutching you, pulling you off the deck, towering above you, dropping away so that the ship is left in midair as though a mountain had borne it up and vanished. And then the fall, and the hull hits the water, a surface as hard as steel, jarring your teeth.

22

You're flung to the deck, maybe break a bone or two . . . and the wind roars in the rigging, the lightning stabbing holes in the blackness. What you fear most is the spite of the storm. The wind has teeth and you know you are helpless. The ship is a slave to the wind. . . ." He fell silent.

She offered him cherries. "Go on," she said.

THE PRIEST KNEW Esperança's family. Father Oliveira had blessed her First Communion and occasionally he glimpsed her coming and going in the streets above the harbor, fetching water for her mother or carrying bundles of kale. Today, as he came out of one of the cottages, calling a farewell blessing to a sick woman, he saw Esperança in the distance. It had been raining and the dirt road was slippery underfoot. He trod carefully, as always comparing in his mind this uneven path with the well-paved streets on the mainland. Even after seven years he still thought of himself as a visitor: one day his replacement would arrive and he would carry his few belongings onto the next ship. In Lisbon—or possibly Porto—he would once more find himself among civilized people. There would be invitations to dine with the well-to-do; wine in fine glasses, lamb cooked with herbs, food that could be eaten slowly, with relish. He was not a gluttonous man, simply one who had been grateful for refinements that lay beyond his means.

On the lower slopes, by the shore, makeshift structures were spreading. Soon they would have proper buildings— two-storied, brick and stone, perhaps tiled roofs instead of thatch triangles.

He knew that before long this place would be a proper town. There were several families living higher up in Santa

Maria do Cailho; artisans: carpenters, stonemasons, iron-workers, weavers, fishermen. The houses in Funchal were bigger and strung out toward flowing lanes that one day would be hardened into streets, or so he prayed. Already one or two of the thoroughfares had names, and there were shops, a butcher, a shoemaker, and a dark, airless room where wine and salt were on offer.

But these peasants, the dregs of Lisbon and the south, brought over to settle the island along with convicted criminals—the people here were little more than cattle, nothing required of them but strong legs and arms. Even the landlords were made of rough stuff. There could never be anyone with whom he could share a real conversation. Not, in truth, that there had been many of those in the past: just the one evening of fine wine and food, rich fur-nishings, and music. It was in his dreams that the event was endlessly repeated, to form the fabric of a life.

He heard a sound and glanced back to find that the girl was following him at a distance. Nodding a greeting, she caught up with him, her long stride easily matching his painful hobble. Father Oliveira's shoes were old and stiff, city made, brought with him from the mainland: they kept his feet dry but their shape made walking difficult on these potholed dirt paths. He was not yet forty but he moved with the caution of an old man.

"Good morning, Father."

He grunted. His bowels were locked and he was in discomfort.

Esperança kept pace with him, flicking glances up at his face. "Been visiting the sick?"

"What?"

"Have you been visiting someone in distress? Adminis-tering Last Rites—"

He pressed his abdomen. A twinge.

"Father . . ."

They were almost at his door. The girl skipped ahead and turned to face him, blocking his way. She tried to smile, but it was no more than a nervous stretch of the lips. "Father, I need to speak to you."

Ah. He felt the usual tiredness.

The child must be, what? Sixteen? He waited for her to speak. The form was familiar: a request for a private confession, something to be kept from the family.

Father Oliveira could remember seeing beautiful women in Lisbon and was aware that, for a peasant, this girl was pleasing: small, compact, her face the shape of a lemon, a plump oval given unexpected grace by a small pointed chin. The long black hair lay close to her head, smooth as a raven's wing. Almost certainly some local boy would have to be taught his responsibilities. "Yes?"

"I want to learn to read."

His eyebrows shot up. He was not often surprised by these people. "Read?"

"Yes. Will you teach me?"

"Why would you want to do that, child?"

"So that—" She hesitated and he saw a change of expression. This was the way, when they trimmed their responses to fit the occasion of a "conversation" with the priest. "So that I can read the Holy Book."

He frowned at her, his expression severe. "That could be considered a heretical act."

A look of puzzlement. A frown. The girl had a stubborn set to her lips. "But surely, to be able to read God's words—"

He reached for the door handle, easing himself past her, aware that a certain churning was beginning in his guts; perhaps the licorice twigs had been effective. He took off his mud-caked shoes, slid feet into cloth slippers. "It is not for you to read, but to hear, to listen and obey. You know your catechism, the prayers, and responses." He stepped through the door, making to close it behind him. "No need for reading—"

She burst out, "I can read some words already!" She was hopping with excitement. "I can read 'God' and 'Emmanuel' and 'Adam and Eve'—why don't you let me show you? Then you could teach me more—"

The girl was becoming a nuisance. Her mother cleaned his rooms and cooked for him. As a cleaner she was adequate. As a cook . . . too often the minced meat was sour with overuse of vinegar seasoning. There were subtler spices she could have used, cinnamon, ginger and cloves, but either chose not to, or was unaware of them. It was her dry mince that lay hard in the coil of his guts, unmoving. In his old parish he had enjoyed freshly made sweetmeats and cow's milk, but Father Oliveira was beginning to acknowledge there was small chance he would see any of that again.

He did not believe the girl's claim, of course, but she stood so eagerly, gazing up at him from across the lintel, that he found it difficult simply to shut the door on her.

He became brisk. He waved her in impatiently, aware that her feet were spreading pale mud patches on his dark wooden floor. Her mother would have to clean that tomorrow. "Very well."

He unlocked the door of a rough mahogany cupboard made by a local artisan, took out a bulky manuscript, and laid it on the table. Then he nodded at the girl. "Open it. Read me something."

"I know only a few words—"

"You said you can read 'God.' You can find God on every page," he said sternly.

Esperança opened the leather-bound manuscript and bent closer. Slowly she turned the page. Stared at the writing. She looked up at the priest and he saw fear in her face.

"Well?"

Her finger hovered over the markings on the manuscript page. Then she carefully closed the leather covers. She stood as though frozen. After a moment she backed slowly toward the door.

"Lying is not what I expect from my flock, Esperança!" Father Oliveira, too, was on the move, heading for the outhouse and his defecation pit. With luck he would have something to contribute this time. He called back, "I will not tell your mother about this. But we shall speak privately."

Squatting, relieved as his long-delayed turd unwound and dropped softly into the pit, Father Oliveira wondered what he would have done had the child attempted to fool him by claiming to recognize a few words. He would have chastised her, sent her away with a handful of Hail Marys to fill her idle hours. Put the fear of hellfire into her. He would certainly not have admitted that he was unable to say whether her claim was true. For Father Oliveira, like his parishioners, could not read.

ESPERANÇA RAN, BLINDED, tears stinging her eyes. What sort of trick had the boy off the ship played on her? What had he shown her if not the Holy Book? She was frightened, lost, sick. Rage engulfed her: a wave of shame and anger that poured through her, scalding, shaking her like an ague. She ran without thinking, upward, away from people, toward the slopes thick with trees. The heat from the fires still smoldered underground not far away, warming her feet as she ran, but she climbed, following the goats, through the sugar plantations, the terraced vineyards, the orchards, round the densely wooded plateau, up onto a promontory that overlooked the coast.

Gasping for breath, throat tight with held-in tears, she stood at the edge, the very lip of the rock, clutching a tree trunk to prevent her from falling—though she was tempted to leap. Humiliated.

Dizzy with rage she relived the terrible moment, worse than a bad dream, when she had opened the leather covers, filled with expectation, and stared down at the stiff, yellowed pages. Her eyes skimmed the lines, searching. Her hands shook, her mouth dried. Something was terribly wrong: at first sight there was a similarity, but these were not *words,* not like the ones Manuel had shown her. And the bracelets of thick black marks on these pages were different, the lines broken here and there with fancy shapes like flowers or jewels. And where was the familiar outline of God the Father, of Adam and Eve?

She had been branded a liar by the priest. And *he* must have known all along that this would happen. Looking down on the ships and the people far below, she closed in on the source of the disaster, at work on the deck. Tricking her with his name of the Lord, his black bracelets of words that were not words. He had made a fool of her.

She was waiting for him when he reached the boulder by the path, the place where she had seen him that first day. Her earlier rage had calmed to a cold hostility. "Why did you lie to me? About the reading."

"It was not a lie. I was reading."

"The priest showed me the Bible. The words are not the same."

A pause.

"My Bible is written in Hebrew."

She stared at him wordlessly.

"I am a Jew."

She hunched away from him, appalled to hear the word. In church, the priest had condemned the Jews, the moneylenders cast out of the Temple; Jews were betrayers, the killers of Jesus. Jews had fangs, horns, and hid a devil's tail under their robes. But Manuel was none of those things, surely?

"You cannot be!"

"I should have explained."

But how to explain? How to begin to tell a girl who knows nothing of the matter that you are divided by an unbridgeable gulf?

She cut through his indecision. "Why do they hate you?" she asked. "Now, I mean."

Above them, a tall tree was busy with birds hopping from branch to branch, grooming themselves, seeking food, chirping noisily.

Manuel said, "Think of a flock of birds . . ."

Think, he said, of a people who, like birds swept by strong winds from distant lands, find a resting place. Tired and hungry, they are grateful, make nests, seem to have settled—indeed feel they have settled, with young ones hatched and the tempests that blew them here forgotten. Then, one day, some crested bird, some leader of the local flock will recall their coming, will doubt their suitability for permanence, point out that food may become short with extra beaks to fill, and suddenly local birds will grow suspicious, the newcomers' nests will be smashed, fall from the tree, their defenseless occupants a prey to claws and beaks that rend and kill.

"Sometimes it is a passing threat. Sometimes the flock must move on. They learn to hold themselves ready. Never to make themselves too much at home. Not to trust too much. . . ." Mistrust lay on both sides, it was true. But it was the Jews who got massacred.

So there were massacres. And it seemed they shared one Bible but not the other. And did they come and go, like the birds? Uprooted herself, wrenched away from the mainland, she needed to pin him down to a patch of land to get his measure.

"Where do you come from?"

"Lagos."

"Lagos? Where's that?"

"Between Faro and Sagres, south from Lisbon, what the Arabs called Al Gharb—"

"You're from the mainland! Like us. So why do you say you come from far away?"

"My people—"

Talk of a distant Holy Land, oppression, flight, exile— none of this meant anything to her. He told her his people were Sephardim. "It comes from Sepharad, the Hebrew word for Iberia. We were scattered here and there on the peninsula. Before the birth of"—he paused—"of your Jesus. A long time ago."

Time was something Esperança had never thought about. Time was the difference between light and darkness. You got up at sunrise or before. You worked, you ate when the sun reached a certain point in the sky, you went to bed when another meal had been eaten and certain tasks completed. There were occasional moments of celebration or quiet; there were seasons when the rain was more frequent. Babies were born, some died, some grew.

But as for time . . . ah, yes! There was one measurement she could turn to: *before the fire.*

She measured time by the memory of when there were no flames. But talk of hundreds of years, words like "before the birth of Jesus" and "a long time ago," this language was not for her . . .

From blankness to questioning is a short journey, but a momentous one. With a glimpse of a language she could not share, a life she could only just imagine, Esperança stepped through another doorway to an unknown landscape. She thirsted for more: more strange lands, more discoveries, each story leaving a tiny mark on the empty walls of her mind, marks that added up to a picture of the world.

Manuel was telling her stories that had no endings, that led only to more questions. Stories of sea journeys and quests, of strange beasts lurking in curious foliage, of lands where the sun burned with a force that turned the sand to glass and where fountains of water too hot to touch came boiling from the rocks. There were stories that dealt with the stars, the fiery signposts that led seafarers from one coast to another; Esperança wanted to hear more about the gods who guided the sun and moon across the heavens, who drew the winds over the earth or hurled flame in jagged bolts; but occasionally he would shift the focus closer to home, conjure up for her an instrument of brass and polished wood with which a man on the deck of a ship, surrounded by water to the horizon and beyond, could calculate the height of the sun in the sky and know where he was. Man, he said, was learning to read the elements.

"At his observatory on the cape at Sagres, Prince Henry has created a wind rose—"

"A wind rose?"

Esperança imagined a wind that swirled yellow dust into a whirlpool of petals, a bloom that hung dancing in the air, but the reality he described for her was less attractive: just a big circle of stones on flat ground high above the sea, divided into shapes that could teach a sailor which way the wind blew. Useful of course. For the sailor. But she preferred to dream about the dancing flower.

Henry, too, it seemed, liked to dream. One of Manuel's many uncles had visited him in his clifftop observatory at the end of the world. He found the prince, he told Manuel, gazing out at the sea, dreaming of navigation and exploration and sea routes to undiscovered lands.

"The sailors followed his directions and brought him gold, ivory, and spices. On one ship there were men. Negroes."

"Negroes?" The word was new to her.

"Black men from Africa. Slaves."

The paradox of the good man who brings evil: Henry, a decent man as princes go, leading his people into the slave trade, the ships ballasted with human weight, dark skins losing their gleam, growing dusty, caked with scabs. There will be a slave market in Lagos, built of yellow stone, that early ship the first of many carrying sad human cargoes bound for sugar plantations and sunbaked fields and in some cases unceremonious burial at sea.

But all that lies many dawns ahead, spinning toward them.

"So, they were taken away from their families, these slaves you saw?"

"Yes. But the prince is very devout and had them all baptized. So he could say their souls were saved."

Esperança frowned, dimly unhappy with this conclusion. She had no experience of irony. She thought of the black men, dragged away from their homes: were there forests, bright birds? Flowers, that they dreamed of, on the ships?

"What is it like, in Africa?" she asked. "Tell me."

———•✠✠✠✠•———

MOST EVENINGS ESPERANÇA remained quiet, reaching unthinkingly into the family bowl at dinner, chewing without satisfaction. Her mother was not a good cook. Father Oliveira would have recognized the flavor; the sharp, sour quality of the meat, the gravy too thin to stick to the hard bread she dipped and swirled in the dish.

The dimness of the room was stifling. The sound and smells of people and of animals thickened the air so that she found breathing difficult. There was nowhere to be alone here; at table, sharing plate and bowl; at night, lying alongside her sister, brother nearby, curled into the angle by the fireplace, parents coughing and groaning across the room, the goats moving restlessly beyond the wall, chickens flapping their wings before dawn, the dog snuffling. The room seemed to be constantly shifting, weighing her down: she crouched as though on the sea floor, drowning in her element.

There was a restlessness within her, an ache she could not pin down, that was to do with a different way of living; a cleaner, freer way, not bound by repeated tasks, the drudgery of survival, day after day, a pitiless rhythm that made no allowance for the pull of her newly unfurling curiosity, the longing to explore, learn, fly.

Words. They found their way through your ears, became a part of you. You learned to use them, though what they described you already knew from touching, breathing.

Earth, air, fire, water. Her foot pressed the beaten earth floor beneath the table: she knew about earth. Smoky from the hearth, the air swirled in her nostrils. In the orchard the air smelled of dampness at dawn, later of sunbaked fruit, and, when the weather grew warmer, the smell sharpened, winelike, as the fruit fermented where it lay in the long grass. Fire she lived with daily, flames licking the blackened chimney breast, an inferno rumbling beneath the hillside, crouching under the rocks and soil, until the ground cracked open in a red grin and a hot breath belched out, scorching the living plants. Water was what she loved best; trickling from the high points, twisting and turning in streams that glittered down the mountainside like gashes of light carved into the dark soil, gushing over stones, down to the harbor, widening into the river. Falling as rain that polished the parched leaves. Cold to drink, like a stone in her mouth. And to bathe in, round beyond the headland, out of sight of other people, the clear green blue lapping the rocks, lapping her body, leaving it clean and salt scrubbed.

But the world was full of those other words, words that created patterns, that sang and puzzled and hovered, unreadable. She had reached for them, like one of the poor cripples in the harbor, regularly tormented by the sailors, helpless, unable to seize the offered nourishment that was held tantalizingly out of reach. She longed to learn, to extract from the fragile, baffling block of parchment the words that lay in waiting, like the gold in the mines of Africa. She thought of the boy, the thin, pale face, long hands holding the book that was his alone to possess, holding words that were not for her. And other books, too, it seemed, were closed to her. To read might be—what was it the priest had said? Heretical—

"What does heretical mean?" she asked.

Her mother and little sister were busy scraping out
the last of the gravy from the bowl. Her father cleared
his throat noisily. Her brother spat into the fire. Nobody
replied.

⁜

SOMEONE HAD SEEN them talking; it was hard to escape
from curious eyes. The boy was a foreigner, from elsewhere. A bird of a different feather. Esperança found it
odd that the locals seemed already to have forgotten how
they themselves came to be here.

"We're all foreigners; we all came from somewhere
else, didn't we?" she asked her mother as they carried
water home, the slopping buckets turning the path to a
sludge that covered their feet with a velvety skin of donkey
brown, thick as shoes. But her mother was tired and had
no answer.

So now she and the boy met out of sight of observers.
Between them they had created a hasty chart of the island,
Esperança explaining how one path went, up and across,
forking when it reached the trees, while another hugged the
sea line, round the promontory. She described the curves
and bays of the coast beyond, and Manuel with a blackened
twig drew the map that would guide him, as she hung over
his shoulder, astonished at the way he could pin down her
territory, recreate it on a scrap of paper.

They met outside the village, high above the houses,
on her little shelf of spongy turf sheltered by a spiky fence
of dragon trees, or inland, in a valley filled with tall white
lilies that hung over them, scenting the air, or on the seashore, round the curve of the headland, in a bay too shallow

35

to encourage ships or fishermen; a slip of pebbled crescent between rocks where Esperança lay in the shallow water like a mermaid, her shift clinging to her limbs and swirling into a wavering tail.

Here, floating between shelving rock and air misty with pollen drifting from the flowering trees that overhung the bay, Manuel told her about Dona Ignez de Castro from Spain and the Portuguese prince who married her.

"It was at the time when Afonso was king—"

She interrupted at once. When was this? She was learning about time, which stretched and shrank like a snake: what seemed no farther away than yesterday could turn out to be a story of King Solomon or tribes a thousand years before him; these people of Emmanuel's had long lives. But Dona Ignez had lived a mere hundred or so years before.

It started happily enough: the young girl from Galicia, traveling to Portugal as maid of honor to her cousin Constança who was to marry the heir to the throne. The marriage took place, Dona Constança wedded Dom Pedro as arranged. But all was not as it seemed. Did the young prince fall in love with Ignez at first sight? And she with him? Or was it a matter of small moments, glimpses, glances, a warmth that grew with time? When Dona Constança died five years later, suitable alliances were proposed to the young prince. Dom Pedro refused them all. Finally he spirited Dona Ignez away to a monastery in the hills and secretly married her. Princes can be fickle; Dom Pedro was faithful. The two lived happily together for ten years. It seemed that love had triumphed. But at court, plots were hatched, plans made: the nobles were hostile to the Spanish girl, to what some saw as a dangerous alliance. Finally three eloquent courtiers persuaded the king that his son's unsuitable wife should be disposed of. Certain instructions were given. The three noble assassins caught her alone, unguarded, stabbed her with jeweled poignards and, to be absolutely sure, cut off her head.

The violated body was buried in a monastery at Santa Clara. Dom Pedro did nothing; stony, silent. Waiting. Some years later, when the king died and Pedro took the throne, he ordered two white marble tombs to be built in the church of Alcobaça, one for himself, one for his dead wife. But Dom Pedro had something more in mind: he gave his orders and his men set off in search of the three murderers. Hunted down, two were cornered. And faithful Pedro's instructions were carried out: the hearts torn from their living bodies, one from the chest, the other through the back. Meanwhile, at Alcobaça the body of Ignez was disinterred while Pedro hovered, giving orders.

Dona Ignez, or what remained of her, was reclaimed from the earth, taken to Coimbra and placed on the throne; Pedro himself, it was said, set the gold crown on the grinning skull and watched while the courtiers lined up to kiss the skeletal hand. Then she was carried on a golden litter the fifty miles back to Alcobaça, the roads blazing with wax candles and lined with loyal subjects. At the monastery the cadaver was sealed in the marble sepulchre. The king had honored his queen and exacted a terrible revenge.

Esperança was enchanted, amazed. The killing of the nobles struck her as wholly reasonable, but what dazzled her was Pedro's constancy: why would he bother, with the woman dead?

"For love," Manuel said.

Love was something not much encountered in her experience, beyond the love of mother for child. This . . .

flame, this fire of love was as strong as anger, stronger, it seemed, than life itself.

She felt a sharp pain in her heart, like the blow of a dagger. "Can love outlast death?" she asked.

"'Many waters cannot quench love, neither can the floods drown it.'" That was from his Holy Book, she now knew.

Moving on the tide like lazy fish, lips salty from the surf, they hung in the water, half awake, half in a dream of warmth and waves, sometimes talking, sometimes sharing a silence broken only by the sound of the surf hushing the rocks.

The water was cool, the shifting current so gentle that a linking of hands or one pale ankle laid across a darker one prevented them from drifting apart. But when the swirling water whipped Esperança's shift around Manuel's legs, binding them suddenly together, she felt a heat that warmed her body more fiercely than the hottest sun; a pulse thumping between her legs, breasts tingling as the water flowed over them.

She knew what men and women did together; she had glimpsed her parents at night, their heaving bodies lit by the embers of the fire, and among themselves girls talked. But what she had seen seemed joyless, the grunting desperate, swift, the embrace almost hostile. What she felt now was a fire, a flame like that which had scorched the forest, which had consumed a prince. A burning that melted her bones. The girl and boy turned slowly in the water, flotsam made flesh, and when they stumbled up onto the beach their two bodies merged, blurred against the sand.

❈

38

IT WAS LATE afternoon, and they were curled up, hunched out of sight beneath a canopy of wild convolvulus. Manuel dragged a handful of slender stalks from the plant and crowned her dark head with white blooms. "A crown of snow," he said. "In midsummer you have become a snow queen."

Esperança had never seen snow, she tried to imagine what he described: rain turned into tiny petals, falling softly, cloaking the land in silent whiteness. That was when he told her the story about the Moorish prince who planted a swath of almond trees in what was then the Al Gharb as far as the eye could see, as a surprise for his bride.

A foreigner from some northern country, Norway perhaps, the girl had languished in the hot south, sickened and taken to her bed.

"She dreamed of icicles, blizzards, the blanketing comfort of snow. She closed the shutters and lay in a dark room, growing weaker, while outside, through the mild winter, the almond trees flourished. Then one spring day her husband ordered the shutters to be flung open and she gazed out onto a sea of foaming whiteness, as cooling to the eye as snow. Like a girl in a fairy tale she clapped her hands and laughed with delight. Next day she ventured out, breathed the perfume, walked in the green and white shade."

"Did it cure her?"

"Ah. The books don't say. It probably depended on whether she loved her husband. That would be what really decided it. Did she *want* to be cured?"

Esperança found it difficult to comprehend the frail princess and her dreams of cold, wet fluff. Still, she enjoyed the story, admired the ruse that roused the pampered girl from her sickbed. Envied her the love of her ingenious prince.

"What would you dream of?" she asked Manuel. "What would you long to see?" She waited to hear what wonders he could summon up and bring to life for her this time.

He pondered. "A different sky, perhaps. To see the stars from the other side of the world."

And I, she wondered silently, what would I lie in my bed and long for so cruelly that I would sicken from the longing?

He glanced at the sun, calculating the hour. "I must get back to the ship."

Sent into town for provisions, he would be punished for the time he had taken. Now he leaped, surefooted, down the goat track Esperança had shown him, saving himself the long, curving road the others took to the harbor.

How long had the ship been tied up at Funchal? A month? Or less? This was another trick time played: changing its shape so that, looking back, she saw long days spent in the yawning sun, losing count of how many, whereas what they had were snatched moments between his duties on board and hers at home, the fetching, carrying, washing, chopping; tasks she had not, till then, resented. Meeting early or late, or when others were drowsy at noon, they could create a time within time, the hours coiling tightly, none wasted.

Days slid treacherously, one into the next, and she was lulled. Perhaps a part of her thought Manuel would stay. But how could he? How could he stay when there was an unknown sky the other side of the bitter orange and he the ant?

She could picture his life on board ship: the mending

of ropes, the washing down of decks, the scraping, polishing, sluicing. She accomplished the tasks with him, living through the hours till they next met. She no longer felt alone: she told herself stories that always began with that first meeting— *"Teach me to read!"*—but which took different directions, paths forking so that each time the story took a different turning. One day it led to a journey, the two of them fleeing the island on a ship bound for the mainland. And sometimes they reached it, stepping ashore at Lisbon or Porto, the world full of possibilities. Or they were captured by pirates, enslaved on the Barbary coast, chained in irons . . .

Another path led to a calmer destination: he stayed, joining her father in the roofing work; houses sprouted across the hillsides like bushes as the town grew, and they prospered, building a home of their own, with a proper wooden floor. She had children to care for—two, three?— and learned to cook dishes more appetizing than her mother's.

The days in that story passed slowly, each bringing pleasures of a different sort, and she grew plump, her breasts heavy with milk, then merely heavy, drooping, but he caressed them without finding fault. Now and then he and she slipped away from the children—older by then and busy with their own plans—and they wandered round the headland, much changed, with a wider bridge and grand houses with staircases, and found their way to the slip of beach where the sea washed up onto the pebbles. They lay together in the water, still finding, as one leg brushed another in the swell of the tide, that the heat could pull them together, two becoming one in the way she remembered.

At moments like this, suddenly restless, she would jump

to her feet and fetch water for her mother, or race up the hillside to see if her father needed help with carrying. Or seize her little sister in a hug that startled the child.

There was another path, one that she veered away from, crossing herself superstitiously, muttering incantations the local girls had learned from the village witch. This was a path that ended in the harbor, with a ship catching the evening tide, she the lone figure on the shore watching it leave. Then watching the empty horizon.

But that surely could not be an ending? Not a proper ending.

LONDON | 2000

THE WOMAN IS lost. She is seated at a scratched metal table in front of a computer terminal in a large room filled with plants. To left and right of her are other terminals, people confidently steering cursors from one icon to another. "Nothing serious, just surfing," she hears one say to another. She knows these words: icon, scroll, surf. She knows the shape and sound of them. The meaning escapes her. She stares at the screen: instructions are required. She rubs mouse on mat and clicks.

> **"Begin search."**
> *Click.*
> **No search results. Please enter more information.**
> **"Who am I?"**
> *Click.*
> **Unable to find "Who am I?" Please try again.**

She tries again.

> **New search?**
> **"Cancel search."**

43

Crossing Vauxhall Bridge to the south bank, she observes how the water swirls into patterns, breaking against the pillars of the bridge, flowing fast, surface shining slickly in the sun, a sun without force, underpowered, lying thin on the ironwork, barely strong enough to cast a shadow. Bronze statues that should confer dignity are oddly placed: tucked beneath the span, they turn their backs to the bridge, offering their faces to the approaching boats. Forlorn in the thin sunshine, the bridge has an air of lost hopes. The woman leans on the iron railing, looking down into the water. In the shadow, it is a murky brown that seems neither water nor land, an unsatisfactory element, insubstantial, ambiguous. A body, dropping from the iron above, falling through the air, would it be buoyed up for a while in the soupy stream, or swallowed in its thousand liquid mouths? A body, falling, would test the waters. Unobserved, she is invisible.

Lift a foot—so, grip the parapet—so, and—

"Looks like soup, doesn't it?"

A man, invading her space, bothering her with a pointless question, a man in a black leather jacket. Why, she wonders, would a man wear a leather jacket on a sunny day? She feels cold. Why would she feel cold on a sunny day?

"What?"

"The river. Looks like brown Windsor soup. I always hated the stuff."

She looks down at the swirling mass. She says, "It looks like dirty glass."

A strange substance, glass: the various ways you could handle it—blow it, press it, strain it. The way it changed its shape and form—

In case of emergency break glass.

She says aloud, "At room temperature, glass can be regarded as a liquid so viscous that it behaves like a solid."

How do I know that?

The man says, "Do you know where we are?"

Why does he ask me that? I know nothing—

She finds herself supplying information. "This is Vauxhall Bridge."

"Ugly area, isn't it?"

Blinking, swimming her way to the words, she says, "It wasn't always ugly. This was a pleasure garden once."

Once the walks were shady, lined with feathery trees. Women in silk and men with fine leather shoes took the air, as they did at Ranelagh across the river.

The man in the leather jacket says, prompting her, "Surely not?"

"Vauxhall Pleasure Park on the south bank. There was a Turkish tent of painted canvas. Swags and a crescent moon. Vauxhall Walk, Glasshouse Walk, Lambeth Walk." She speaks mechanically, like a lift announcement for the next floor. The man nods encouragingly. Her hands are clenched white on the parapet of the bridge, a bandage on her right wrist. Thin fingers, nails bitten, the edges ragged. Dark hair falls forward over her face.

"You're obviously an expert."

Farther up the river a helicopter rises from the smog and swings away, tilted drunkenly, toward the airport, rotors whirring. She follows it with her eyes.

"The heliport," she says. "Nine Elms."

Her hands are relaxing, her body slackening.

"Lovely name, Nine Elms," he says. "I wonder why it's called that."

"It was a village. Nine tall trees lined the high street. Now it's nothing but warehouses and wharves."

"And a heliport—"

"There were tower blocks, too. Ahead of their time. They got bombed. In the blitz . . ."

"Yes? Bombed, you say."

"I saw pictures in a book. The buildings burning. Flames leaping from the windows, as though the fire was trying to get out—" She stops. She looks troubled, confused. Shakes her head as though to clear it. "Trying to reach out—" She stops in midsentence—"I must go," she says and walks quickly away from him.

He waits, watching her. When she has moved on a few yards he begins to follow.

As she approaches the road he narrows the distance between them. Lorries roar past, and delivery vans, battered sedans, music pounding from their windows. She stands at the edge of the pavement. He moves closer. A sudden decision, a leap, and she could be under the wheels. When the lights change she crosses the road. Untidy in trousers and a green anorak, her figure looks bulkier than it is. Above the collar he can see her slim neck.

Where the bridge meets the embankment the river changes direction; the traffic is sucked away and over the water by an implacable gyratory system, giving the street a leftover look, a quality of irrelevance. It veers right, past the Portuguese Café, then left and right again, down South Lambeth Road. To the man it seems as if a shadow hangs over the street, even on this sunny day, the brick buildings squat and heavy, their faces dark.

He feels the sour sadness of this place: Vauxhall is the jilted girl at the London dance, the rough edge the city has forgotten to polish. It has not been "discovered" by a Sunday newspaper supplement; chic chefs do not open restaurants here, nor are there corners that could be Chelsea if prettified with a lick of paint. There is a fiercely tenacious community in this corner of exile: outsiders themselves, they do not encourage outsiders, their very apartness nourishing their prevailing *saudade*.

He knows about *saudade,* a Portuguese condition that resists translation, composed of an unspecified yearning: a sense of displacement and solitariness, a longing for the familiar, with a knowledge of the immensity of distance and the fragility of human bonds. It is an ecstasy of nostalgia, an echo of waves beating on a distant shore. He knows what it is but he can never share it.

The woman walks on, past heavy Victorian apartment blocks, office buildings, an occasional outcrop of postwar housing. She glances left and right without checking her stride.

People walk unhurriedly past the woman, past the man following her; couples, families, talking among themselves. Their voices, slightly guttural, clipped consonants softened by a slurred delivery— *"shh . . . shh"*—turn every sibilant into a soothing implication of hush. It might strike a stranger as odd that everyone in this south London street is speaking a foreign tongue.

As she walks, she steps from gloom to bustle, to a parade of small shops, a butcher, a bakery, cafés offering the everyday fare of a faraway country, the warmth of a stronger sun penetrating their windows, as though through a magnifying glass, onto menus offering *lulas grelhadas . . . bacalhau a bras . . .* Outside one, she pauses, as though to push open the door, the glass white with condensation. She stares at the steamed-up surface, gives a little shake of the head.

47

Then she turns and slowly goes back the way she has come. She passes the man in the leather jacket, unaware of his presence. Tears slide down her face unchecked.

The traffic has come to a standstill. A blaring of horns, a flourishing of mobile phones, body language denoting desperation, in some cases, fury. Lights change and change again. The woman threads her way through the vehicles back toward the bridge. He is about to follow when there is a concerted revving of engines and the traffic jumps forward. Hampered by the moving screen of white vans and juggernauts, trucks and hatchbacks, he tries to keep track of the figure in the dark green anorak, sees her stop, look down into the water with a slow turn of the head as though following a craft or some object passing below her, sees her hands on the parapet.

Another brief stoppage, bumper to bumper. The enamel jigsaw of a wall cuts her off from view. When the cars move on, he sees that she is no longer on the bridge.

MADEIRA |

THE OLD WOMAN had a favorite place, shaded by an almond tree high on the bluff, overlooking the harbor, a corner where she sat, often for hours, watching the sea crawl
and nudge its way over the rocks, the foaming tentacles
reaching up, gaining ground for a moment, falling back.
Sometimes a farmer or a woman on her way to pick fruit
would pause and call out to her—"Dona Esperança?"—
thinking she might be sick, dead even, a woman so old,
so frail, up here above the town, squatting under a tree
in the heat of the day.

Usually she sat alone, thoughts and memories companions enough—too insistent sometimes, the old voices clam-
oring in her head. But for a while now she had been aware
of a stranger, another watcher of the seas, sitting hunched
on a jutting lip of rock where the land fell away to the shore.
A thin man with a dark look to him, shadowed, though he
sat uncaring in the sun.

Older than the tree she sat beneath, she recalled the boy, the ship floating free of the harbor. Was she dreaming? And the stranger watching the tides, brooding: was he part of her dream? Like the island, he concealed himself in mist and mystery, both shadow and substance. Like the island, he had several names: Cristóvão Colombo, Cristobal Colón, Cristoforo Colombo— Genoese, some said, or Spanish; though others thought he could be Portuguese, a man of dubious antecedents and secret ambitions, watching and waiting. What did he tell her of journeys planned, shipwrecks survived? And what did she tell him about the boy?

They shared the landscape, neither intruding on the other; an old, scrawny woman and a man of indeterminate years, young but scarred-looking, blue-eyed, with tangled, fading red hair. Sometimes he drew papers from his pocket and studied them, muttering, talking aloud to himself, his finger tracing lines across the surface. Then he would close his eyes and sit, still as an effigy, lost in thought. One day he looked up as she passed, nodding an acknowledgment of her, hand raised in greeting. She settled in her usual place, her face, like his, turned to the sea. In time they exchanged a word or two.

There had been talk about him in town. They said he was a sailor from Genoa. Or Lisbon. Or Venice—the stories varied—who had put in to harbor to buy salt and had stayed on to marry Felipa Perestrelo Moniz, the daughter of the governor of Porto Santo, the sandy tongue of land just across the water. A good catch for an itinerant wanderer. Some put it down to luck. Others thought the stranger was suspiciously clever.

Sometimes he brought food up the hillside and sat chewing as he watched the blue emptiness below. After some weeks, when they had begun to talk, he shared his food, offering her the smaller, easier bits of meat, tearing the bread into pieces, peeling fruit for her. Now and then he sucked at a bitter orange, an old seafaring habit, he said, a way to keep scurvy at bay. She picked up his unpeeled orange one day, holding it at arm's length, turning it slowly. "There it is, the sphere of earth, turning, the surface curving, never meeting the horizon, like the sea. . . ." He had grown used to her abrupt statements, a fragile patchwork often unreliable, sometimes nonsensical, occasionally surprising.

"You remind me of someone I knew long ago," she said one morning. "A boy off one of the ships. He used to sit up here and watch the sea and the clouds. He said he wanted to go beyond the known world. When I asked him why, he said it was for the voyage. What he called the search."

The man with red hair was eating cherries. He threw a pip far out, to arc through the empty air. "That's it," he said, the juice dark on his lips. "Where did he go, the boy?"

She shrugged and waved an arm as finely wrinkled as a dried leaf. The gesture covered the visible ocean. "He said it was a matter of maps. They were the guides."

"Sometimes," Colombo said, "there *are* no maps." His voice was harsh, the accent rough, almost foreign, though he spoke Portuguese like a native. "You make the map as you go, guessing your way across the sea, sniffing the wind, watching the flight of birds, drawing the guideline with the wake of your ship, finding an answer by chance."

She shrugged. "Half of what people do happens by chance. Do you think sailors came looking for an island called Madeira? It didn't even have a name! Chance. Not intention."

Local gossip about Colombo had been fueled by stories from a couple of recently arrived drunken sailors who hinted the stranger was a royal embarrassment—the bastard son of Prince Henry's nephew, the mother a New Christian. One claimed to know his Portuguese birth name. Another suspected him of being a spy for the king, though what could there be here to spy on? Running through the stories, surfacing repeatedly, was the suggestion that the redheaded dreamer was a Jew. Maybe he really was the son of a Genoese weaver. She wondered, idly, which of the stories was true. Not that it mattered to her.

"To make a map," she hazarded, "that would mean writing. Charts, maps, you'd need to read and write for that. Sailors would need to, wouldn't they?"

"Not your ordinary sailor. All he needs to do is master the ropes, get the sails up and down, keep the water out. Too much activity in the thinking area could be a problem. You want your sailor ready for duty. A strong arm, springing to order when needed."

"The ship's boy I told you about, he could read and write."

"Well, he was probably ambitious in that case. Anyway, he may have changed his mind about the sea. There's not much call for scholar sailors."

"But surely you'd need to read to navigate?"

"So some of them think." He was aware that a few of the seamen were outgrowing the old boundaries, becoming meddlesome. He would have to humor them a little, when he made his own long dreamed of voyage—if there was to be a voyage. If he ever managed to raise the money he needed—no, he rejected "if." *When* he raised the money and set off, it might be prudent to keep two logs: one that the crew could look at—those who could read—to lift their spirits, show them how well the voyage was going, reassure them about latitudes and distance covered. The other log would have information he might prefer to keep to himself: questions or second thoughts . . .

"But there's a lot to be said for the stars. Twilight observation, when the brightest stars are just visible but you can still see the horizon. That's your best time. Your true sailor gets a feeling for it."

"Same with vines. You get a feeling for it." She was slumped, eyes glazed, face dark as a prune, turned toward the shadowing west. "Wine growers these days, some of them send for news from overseas, those who can read, they want to be told what the latest thing is, but you need to have the knowledge inside you, feel the growing and the juice in your bones, sniff and rub, chew and squeeze, watch for the pest and the blight. You should see my vineyards . . ."

She knew about vines, she had learned, prospered over the years, through a system of barter and exchange with the men who owned the vineyards, grim transactions bearing fruit, bringing profit, though slowly and at high cost, her brother's face turned away, her mother choosing not to see, as she filled and then enlarged the tiny plot; replacing vegetables with grapes, buying up neighbors, selling to foreigners. . . . What was his name, that Italian, all those years ago, with his fancy clothes and superior attitudes—Cadamosto? Luigi di Cadamosto, yes, he tasted her wine and his eyes went narrow. He had bargained, but elegantly, their conversations so sweetened by flattery that for a moment she thought he might be after more than her wine, but it was just part of his mainland manners, like using lace handkerchiefs and talking about chivalry. And after all, she was no longer juicy, not yet shriveled, but growing thin, shoulders angular, losing their cushioned smoothness. So they had laughed together, but it was business, not lust, that fueled their spirited encounters. "You should see my vineyards," she had said to him one day. "You'll need strong knees and a stick."

The best area for vines was around Câmara de Lobos and she had bought there, modest strip by strip, climbing the steep terraces, sweating, knees and thighs aching, her hands jeweled with glowing calluses, digging the trenches herself, lining them with loose stones to stop the roots going through to the rock-hard soil beneath. She prepared the land through spring and early summer, planting the cuttings. Fed by the winter rains, the roots were sturdy by the following spring. Then came the patience, waiting for the vines to bear fruit three years after planting. It was late summer when Cadamosto followed her round, stumbling in his fine Venetian boots, exclaiming at the grapes that hung in tight bunches from bowers of chestnut posts with cane lattice tops. In the hot, leafy tunnels buzzing with the sound of bees, she sensed that, had she paused and un-laced her blouse a little at the neck, the day might have taken a more leisurely turn. But she strode on ahead of him, pointing to the slopes that best took the sun.

When they drew up a contract she had been saved the humiliation of pressing her thumb mark on the paper, or scrawling a cross, as was the custom on the island. Instead, she wrote her name, as Manuel had shown her long ago.

She studied the Italian contract slowly, eyes scanning the page, and asked for clarification of some general point. Then, with a brisk nod, she signed her name in neat, cramped letters. He never knew she couldn't read.

In her early days she got the pruning wrong. She watched the old men, did as they did, but her eye was unskilled: which were the wood buds and which the fruit buds? Which to cut and which to leave? Mistakes cost her dear at the beginning. She learned to strip leaves from the vine in midsummer, just enough to allow the sun to finger its way to the fruit to improve its richness—but not a leaf too many.

"It's through the foliage that the vine breathes," she told the Italian as he gasped for breath. "Join us for the harvest," she suggested, flattering him in her turn. "You'll see how well we live here on the island."

She had a two-story house by then, and carved mahogany chairs, but no paintings: the big landowners with their gilded furniture wasted money on shiny Flemish paintings to put on their walls. She had no use for expensive paintings when the best pictures lay spread out before her: she could climb to her favorite place and watch the sea crawl and shift far below, the leaves move, and the birds lift and wheel in the unpredictable breezes. What artist could match the glow of a newly opened flower, the sheen on the back of a beetle, the wrinkled velvet of a lizard's back? And at no charge!

The harvest began in mid-August, women and children, and those grandparents still mobile, filling the great conical baskets that the men carried to the carts. First off the vine were Malvasia, Tinta, and Verdelho, then Boal and more Tinta, farther up the slopes, and finally Sercial in the high, chill sierras. Muscatel grew at sea level and for those the picking began in October. Hardly surprising that the bringing in of the vintage had grown from simple labor to general festivities. The harvest was safe. God be praised. Singing and dancing to follow.

Yes, she had learned about vines. But reading, that had proved more elusive.

"Did he have a name, this boy off the ship?"

She opened her fist and revealed a pebble, a flat stone marked with a scratch:

עמכואל

Colombo glanced at it, eyes narrowed against the low sun. "Emmanuel—"

She looked at him sharply: "You read Hebrew."

His face went blank. "I like to read. Words interest me. Latin, Hebrew . . ."

He took the pebble from her hand and turned it in his fingers. "So he was a Jew. Well, that explains the reading—"

"You know about Jews?"

"Who doesn't?"

"The priest, I think. The old one never mentioned them, except in church, denouncing the Jews who killed Christ. Same with the one who came later."

"Jews, Hebrews, *conversos,* Marranos, New Christians. The names vary. Not many here, I imagine."

"None that I know of. I never heard of any on the boats when we came, but of course, there may have been, how would we have known? Anyway, I was too young to notice. And too sick."

The ships had brought them, city dwellers, feeble, pasty faced from the rough journey, the soldiers encouraging them with promises of a new life—

"What was wrong with the old life?" her mother had asked, forgetting the pinched days, the anxiety, the failed crops that brought hunger, the weeks her husband sat by the door without roofs to mend: who could afford to use him? She had named her daughter Esperança in a defiant gesture of hope for a better future—forlorn, as it turned out.

56

Her husband, who had favored Teresa, reminded her
of this later when things went badly. "Calling the child
Esperança! It's tempting fate."

So: a new life, they were promised, on an island with
soil so rich that bird droppings sowed orchards; an island
ringed with sea so full of fish the nets would split from the
weight of them.

Esperança herself remembered nothing of that other,
mainland life, only this place, the new life, the sound of the
sea and then the hidden flames coiling underfoot. There
had been ships, later, that brought plants from other parts,
from Africa, crops that flourished, and seeds accidentally
transported that sprang to life, spreading over the hillsides,
bushes of scarlet twice as tall as a man, succulent curtains
of orange and green that cloaked uncultivated land and
crept over walls and roofs like a brilliant living web.

There had been days, long ago, when she had tried talking to her mother, questioning her, but her mother was always tired, unwilling to cast her mind back to times past.
Esperança watched her working, the hands lumpy, their
skin dried to a papery whiteness by the harsh black soap.
Her mother worked for those who could afford to pay—the
priest, merchants, officers' wives—crouching to wash and
polish wooden floors, her legs crisscrossed with veins that
ran like worms under the skin, bunched here and there
like budding grapes, dark and swollen. She wore the soft,
shapeless boots they had taken to, made in the village, and
in time she, too, had grown shapeless, the slack body shifting inside her clothing like grain in a sack. She worked at
a slow pace, her face blank, occupied by the task in hand.
A lifetime ago she had laughed, her head dropping back,
her golden throat arched, when Esperança, still a baby,
tried to climb her legs. Her mother's limbs were still

smooth then, with fine, silky hairs blurring the olive skin. She had laughed indulgently at childish pranks; she had sung old songs.

Later came the bad times.

—◆⟡⟡⟡◆—

WHEN ESPERANÇA'S FATHER fell from a roof and broke his neck, it was a time of lamentation. At first they were buoyed up by the very excess of it: the priest (who had hardly known him) spoke of his fine character, his noble spirit. Esperança wondered whether they were at the wrong funeral, and he was talking about someone else. Her father had been no worse than the next—he hit her only occasionally—but the priest was describing a hero from an old story, the pride of any village. She would have liked a father such as the priest described. But in any case it was too late. All that was left was to bury him.

Her brother worked down at the harbor when the ships came in; he had never been one for the roofing craft, lacked the feeling for it. The one thing the priest had not mentioned at the funeral was their father's skill: the strong arms, the balance, the quickness of the weaving. The sureness. Sometimes Esperança would squat down the other side of the stony track, screwing up her eyes against the sun, to watch her father at work, the sure fingers that folded and held and bound rough bunches of wet reeds into a covering that topped a house with a thatch as thick and smooth as a merchant's head of hair. But the skill had not been passed on to his son.

Still, there was always work for the young and strong, loading and unloading cargo, and they managed for a while, until one rainy day, the ground slippery underfoot, the sea heaving gray, Esperança's brother was caught off balance between a boat and the makeshift dock of roughly hewn blocks of stone. The bale fell from his shoulders and he flailed, hands gripping the rail. He might have been hauled back on deck, but the ship swung sideways, dragged by the surge of the tide, and pinned him where he hung. He screamed once, a long, jagged cry, and they pulled him free, legs crushed, blood splattering the blocks of stone, to be washed away with the next wave.

So: three women, one old, one young, one still a child. The roof leaked, with no one to repair it; the small plot of land was ungiving. The brother, his mangled legs sheared by the ship's doctor to save him, lay in a cot near the small window, shifting restlessly. He complained of sores on his back. Occasionally he scrabbled his way to the door, to crouch in the sun like an old dog, eyes blank. First he was thirsty, then hungry.

When she brought him a steaming bowl he brightened. "What's this?"

"I made you a stone soup." She attempted humor, trying to cheer him. "Remember the old story about the hungry beggar and the old woman? Well there are always stones. There wasn't any meat or *chouriço* or beans, but I did catch a fish!"

The broth was gray and thin, with one tiny fish floating on the oily surface as though dead in a stagnant pool. He pushed the bowl away resentfully, spilling some, unaware that it had been cooked just for him, with precious shreds of cabbage and the small fish scavenged by Esperança from a net on the waterfront.

Hurrying with her mother from one merchant's house to the next to scrub and polish floors, garnering scraps of food that would have been thrown to the pigs, Esperança saw that simply to keep the family alive would mean the two women and, when her sister was older, the three of them, toiling all their waking hours.

"Can this be right?" she asked her mother as they dragged themselves home one day. "That we slave night and day just to eat, while they"—jerking her head back at the landowner's house—"sit on their big chairs and lift their feet for us to clean under them. And then take our rent. It's unfair. Who gave them the right?"

"They buy the right with their money. Things are different for those people. And you'd do better not to concern yourself with it. Your father told me a story once, of a nobleman who had his own mother sewn into the skin of a bear and thrown to the hounds because she meddled in his affairs. They're not human, the rich. Thanks be to God that we have no more to do with them than clean their floors."

Esperança could have found a husband, settled for a good man with a patch of ground to cultivate, a few animals. The boy who helped the butcher had already noticed her. Duarte followed her with his eyes, watching her from the doorway, and one day he fell into step with her as she walked home. Then he brought her gifts: chops carved from the neck of a sheep, a slab of beef; food they could never have bought for themselves. When Duarte arrived, Esperança's brother summoned up a friendly wave, her mother managed a smile. He was a welcome visitor. But as he handed over the latest offering—meat of one sort and another wrapped in a palm leaf—Esperança was aware that his hands smelled of blood.

Once, he came complaining of a toothache. She put a grain of salt in a spider's web and pressed it to the painful spot. For a moment, as she attended to the tooth, their faces were close, the inside of his mouth pink and clean. He was tall, she liked that, liked tilting her head to look up at him, the firm chin, flat cheeks.

Two visits later—with enough meat to keep the family feeling comfortable for several days—he spoke privately to her mother.

"Talk to the girl yourself," she said with an encouraging smile.

When Esperança refused his offer of marriage he was surprised. His face took on a bruised, angry look. "I thought you liked me."

"I do."

"I'd see your family was all right."

In her position she should take the sensible, familiar road, she knew that, settle for what was available: a pair of strong arms and meat on the table. And never feel that sudden leap of the heart, never lift questioning eyes to the horizon again.

They were standing close, at a curve of the road above the harbor. She looked carefully at the horizon: the setting sun was slowly being engulfed by thick clouds that curdled the light, blotting out the gold with a spreading gray. There was no breeze and she could feel the heat coming off his body. It was like the warmth from a mule or an ox; it stirred no answering heat in her. How could she explain to him that there were questions still unanswered, stories still to learn. How could she explain that she wanted something different? The leap of the heart, the flame—

No, she said, and began to think of other ways.

SHE HAD LEARNED much from the ships that came and
went over the years. She had acquired knowledge of plants
and propagation; she had a working acquaintance with
medicinal herbs and how to use them—one of her potions
had saved a man's leg from the knife when deadly, green
rot was consuming the limb. She could sniff a change in
the weather and had she been a seafarer she could have
guided the boat by the stars—though she also knew that
the stars alone were not enough: the delicate brass instruments fashioned by Jews and Arabs in small workshops in
the Algarve, instruments that calculated the height of the
sun and the position of the celestial pole, were also necessary. She knew the surfaces that surrounded her, could recognize metals and ore; she knew one rock from another.

The island was formed from basalt, an African word,
the boy had told her, for a stone that contains iron. In time
she had become like basalt herself: iron had entered into
her, at first just enough to strengthen her in the fight to
survive. Then more. So that as she stood, dark against the
sun, watching the peasants work her vineyards, she looked
like a statue carved from the same rock that cupped the
shallow soil.

She no longer had time now to pause at the harbor
when a ship came in, to look, with diminishing hope, for
a curly-haired, stick-thin figure.

A storm at sea. Shipwreck. Pirates. Scurvy. Slavery. Murder. There were many obstacles in the way of a safe end to
a journey. In the early days she used to call out firmly to
the newly arrived mariners, asking questions about destina-
tions and cargo and the movements of trade. The sailors
were amused by the small, fierce girl with her imperious
way of interrogating them. They had no news of a particular
ship, but they told her about the vines Henry was importing

and the royal instructions to his wine-growing subjects. There would be new vineyards here, the climate was suitable, the plants would flourish: first, planted near the seashore, the sweet Malvasia grapes from Crete and Cyprus, then the drier Verdelho from the mainland, planted against the hillsides. From these, in due course, would come the wine of Madeira.

She had her own way of listening, a concentration and stillness, as she watched them readying the ship, loading provisions, and setting the sails. When they left on the turning tide, her figure could often be seen on the edge of the harbor, growing smaller, watching them head for the horizon—though of course she and they knew there *was* no horizon, as such. Just a turning and a crawling, globe and ship, as of orange and ant, toward the endless sky.

Eager to earn money for bread, Esperança had been working wherever an extra pair of hands was needed. Small and agile, she worked fast. In time, she moved on: from inside, cleaning floors, to outdoors, making herself useful in the vineyards; these fields were the future. She learned how to train and tie the lateral shoots, when to clip, how to spot the first attack of pest—blackfly, mildew, mold, and worst, oidium, which begins with white, cobweb-fine traces, then grows, chainlike, covering the entire plant with a pale, mealy powder, the fungus consuming where it grows. She worked the vineyards as though they were her own: watchful, tireless, down by the seashore or up on the terraced hillsides, glancing out only now and then to check if a ship might have come in sight, far out at sea. Her skill was noticed.

"You've done well."

Praise, of course, meant more work. And she was strong. Today would be long and hard: she was to be tried out by a new vineyard owner; Father Oliveira had passed her the word: "The wife is with child, they need extra hands." As always, she was careful to show her gratitude—"Thank you, Father." And he was relieved to see her occupied with honest labor: the matter of reading had never been referred to again.

He knew now that there would be no ship back to the mainland for him, no replacement to deliver him from this isolation. Occasionally he unlocked the dark cupboard in his room, took out the Holy Bible, and opened it, taking care with the brittle parchment. He looked closely at the writing, willing it to make sense, to illuminate him. Sighed.

Rain had fallen during the night and her bare feet slithered in the mud. Crossing the bridge, newly built, the wood still raw and moist, she paused and leaned on the rough wooden rail to look down at the river tumbling below her, bright silver where the rising sun glanced on the water. Liquid silver, racing wastefully to sea. Had she the gift of *al kimia,* like the Arabs she had heard about, she might catch it in her hands, mint it into coins. An alchemist might find a way to feed a family from a handful of silver water.

She had left the houses behind and was alone, the birds noisy, the water loud, churning, the sound filling her ears. She felt an unease, a prickling of the hair on the back of her neck, a sense of being observed. She swung round but the bridge was empty. Farther off, just caught by her eye, a movement, a shuffling figure like an ape—she had heard about apes from the boy: manlike beasts in Africa, covered with hair and walking on two legs. No apes here, but from afar this figure, shaggy and crouched in its movements, could have been one of those creatures. She hurried on, crossing herself from habit.

By sunset she had completed half the new vineyard, tying back the untidy laterals. The landlord ran his eye approvingly over the neat green rows. "You're a quick worker."

Esperança did not expect generosity from her employers: their thanks was expressed in the act of retaining her services. Now, though, she sensed that something was different. His eyes appraised her and he reached for her arm, squeezing the dark gold flesh as one might inspect a chicken in the market. Heavy shouldered, squat, he smelled of unwashed flesh and fish.

Esperança stepped back, without haste, noting the yellow crusting round his eyelids, the broken veins on cheeks and nose. He rubbed one hand against his thigh, as though readying himself. She shook her head. He frowned.

"I'll work hard here; I'll do well for you." She paused, unsure how to proceed, knowing the dangers of refusal. Aware, too, that she must conceal from him the fact that she was frightened.

"What, are you asking for money? That's whore's talk—"

To avoid looking into his face, she fixed her eyes on the nearest vine, seeing how the new leaves curved, cupping the young grapes. Then it came to her. "I don't want money. I want a vine. One good vine. For each time." She made her tone brisk, direct. She must think of it as work and work was rarely pleasant.

He gave a rumble of laughter mixed with disbelief. "We'll see—"

"No. One vine for each time. Or I go." Now she stared up at him, the oval of her face sheened with sweat, not showing the fear clenched in her stomach like a fist.

The vines enclosed them, leafy walls with the low sun glowing through the green, turning the fragile leaves into a thousand lanterns. Above them, a bowl of blue, but a fast, scudding bank of cloud was moving down the mountain-side, darkening the sky.

He pulled her down, hauling at her mud-spattered skirt. She felt his fingers, the sharpness of dried scabs and jagged nails, the roughness of his flesh on hers. Inwardly she might shrink, a sour bitterness rising in her throat as his breath invaded her nostrils. But this was just a task to be accomplished. She kept her eyes on the sky: cold, pure. Nothing could spoil that distant beauty. The secret was to remain distant. Unreachable.

Across the hillside goats snickered among themselves as they cropped. A bell tinkled, far off. The vineyard was shadowy now, the sun gone, the smell of damp earth rising as the air cooled. Drops of rain fell but the wine grower was preoccupied, energetically thrusting and withdrawing, groaning, engaged in a brief planting of his own.

She thought of it as her "silent trade." Manuel had told her about the silent trade in Africa, when merchants from Europe loaded camel caravans with cheap goods and trav-eled to the interior. How they spread out the stuff along a river bank, waiting, out of sight. In the night, under cover of darkness, tribesmen placed their offers—small heaps of gold—beside the objects of their desire and vanished. At dawn the traders would return to claim their price, specu-lating where the mines might be found, dreaming of the secret mines of Solomon the King, never realizing that there *were* no mines, that the gold came from the riverbed by their feet.

So Esperança worked her own version of the silent trade: she spread herself in the shadow of a wall or beneath a convenient shrub and, hidden from prying eyes, her trader took her goods. Later, in the proper season, there was the reckoning, and her little vineyard grew. Multiplied.

Tides turn. Suns rise and set. Time spins.

"Did you ever hear of the silent trade," the old woman asked Colombo, "when you were traveling?"

"It's an ancient game," he said. "Herodotus says something about it somewhere." He was busy with one of his charts, looking up now and again to stare out, unseeing, over the flat expanse of blue, and the conversation went no further. They were often silent companions in this fashion, each busy with private thoughts.

Mostly he stayed across the water on Porto Santo, studying his father-in-law's charts. There, on that tiny afterthought of an island, there were no cliffs, no deep harbor, just a flat, sandy shelf that dipped gently to the sea line. The waves lapped and fell back, and hour after hour he watched, going over his calculations yet again, pondering on wind patterns, noting the debris washed up on the beach: enigmatic evidence of life elsewhere, signals from another unknown shore, perhaps.

Possibly Felipa fretted, as wives have always done, when husbands hold their thoughts folded out of sight like secret messages from a mistress, and there *was* a mistress, not silken-limbed or hot-eyed, but incorporeal and the more seductive for it. A mistress who curled inside his brain murmuring of danger and the unknown, who whispered to the red-haired dreamer of latitudes and tides and winds, singing the siren song of the faraway place waiting to be found—the Indies! To reach the East by heading west—that was the dream.

On the days when he shared Esperança's eyrie he brought with him scraps of diagrams, drew some of his

67

own on the flat rock that formed his table, muttering to himself. Nose to the wind like an animal feeling his way, repeating his familiar incantation: the legendary island of Cipangu, the Antipodes, the Orient.

"See how the wind circles, clockwise . . . southeast towards Africa, but on the way back . . . it comes from the southwest—that's how Zarco's ship stumbled on Porto Santo, and then this place. Trying to get home, to Lisbon, blown off course, too far to the east—"

"A lucky accident, that's all!"

She was a fierce old woman and Colombo was cautious about arguing with her. But what she said about Zarco was only partly true.

"Well, he had heard stories . . ."

The island had been talked of—rather *an* island had been talked of, by shipwrecked sailors—"I'll tell you a story about this place," Colombo said. "A love story. A sad one."

He told her the story: two English lovers, a flight from the pursuing family, a storm, a ship on the rocks, a sad end to it, with twin unmarked graves on the unknown shore, before the surviving members of the crew got themselves away to the Barbary coast. "It was their stories of the mysterious island that reached Zarco." And Prince Henry, ears pricked, hearing Zarco talk of it, told the mariner to try and find the place. But it was true that the actual landing had been unforeseen, a navigational miscalculation, a shadowy cloud that turned out to have substance and an unexpected safe harbor.

He offered the old woman a slice of peach. She curled her lip but took it, gracelessly. "I've no need of stories about this island; I've enough of my own." But he noticed that she had listened with attention, her body held still.

Above her head, a leaf dropped from the tree and was

whirled slowly out over the cliff. He watched it dance. "We have to use the wind; it's always the wind that holds the answer."

It echoed something the boy had said to her once: that the ship was slave to the wind. Provocatively, she retorted now, "It's just air; that's all wind is. What answers can it hold?"

He was impatient, snapping at her as he did at the men he sailed with: why could others not see what was so clear to him? "The clash of warm winds and cool, the battle of the hot and cold, that's what pushes the ship forward. And drives the waves onto those rocks down there. The pull of tides, yes, but the wind is the real force; we have to learn its secrets."

"What's the wind like off Cape San Vincent?"

"Filthy. What's it to you?"

"I heard you were shipwrecked there, washed ashore on a plank—"

He looked irritated. "*Washed* ashore? I steered myself. I'd grabbed an oar. The sea does no man a favor."

Washed ashore. This was the way with stories. They took over from the facts, *became* the facts. Clinging to the splintered fragment of deck, holding a course, the oar bending with the strain, his arms wrenched almost from their sockets by the force of the current, he had staggered onto land half dead, lucky to make it alive, dragged by the waves through the brutal rocks and the whirlpools. When, painfully, he clambered up the cliff face, he had come out onto a treeless headland where the wind had the force of a blow, a sharpness that skinned the body like a butcher's knife. Starving, he scratched around for berries and chewed the wild garlic growing among the heather.

"My breath stank for weeks. When I met Henry's men—"

69

"The prince's men?"

"Who else would be at that godforsaken spot? It was one of his map makers, Jehuda Cresques. I was just a boy, not much more than a child, but Cresques treated me like a sailor. We talked about navigation. The Jews have always had a feeling for charts—"

"Did you see the wind rose?"

She had surprised him again. "How in Christendom do you know about the wind rose? Yes, I saw it. But it wasn't as useful as Henry thought. Old men exaggerate. Anyway, he was dead by then, but I met some minor royal who was visiting. We didn't talk for long: the garlic got in the way of conversation. Princes can't take too much humanity at close quarters."

"Lucky you didn't meet Henry then: he'd have been particularly fastidious, wouldn't he? All that soap."

He gave her a look. She had a way sometimes of making comments that sounded senseless, but he had learned to wait.

She clicked her teeth, chewing on some lingering shred of fruit. "The priest told my mother about it. Henry had the profits from all the soap factories in the kingdom—the black soap and the white. They made it from olive oil and ashes then. I used to wonder: does he use the white for his face and hands, and the black for the baser parts of his body? Of course, we could never afford the white. We all stank; I realized it one day when the priest turned his face away, visiting us. It wasn't just the garlic and onions. We wrapped ourselves in animal skins to keep warm at night. Nobody washed much in the winter. If one of those landlords had found himself in our shoes he wouldn't have lasted a week. We were as tough as the meat we ate. Except when the butcher's boy went soft and brought something special."

This time, he decided, she was definitely rambling.

One day he arrived with letters that he read and reread, from some Florentine astronomer, sending him his personal charts, urging him westward to find Asia.

"Charts! Advice! 'Sail to the West'—I need no urging." He often talked aloud to himself, cursing, groaning, taking both sides of an argument, rehearsing perhaps for the royal audition he still hoped for. This particular idea had long filled his head.

"I've done the calculations—the size of Africa, the circumference of the earth." He slammed a fist down on his creased and folded papers spread out on the flat rock. "I have them all here, my estimates. It can be done! I know it!"

He said he had been to Britain and beyond; he said he had reached Iceland. Well, perhaps he had. The boy from the ship had described wonders to her that sounded like the ravings of a madman, but when she retold them, Colombo said they were true.

So, day after day, going over new charts drawn up by Jews in Faro, men he trusted, and with the private maps from Toscanelli in Florence, Colombo contemplated the journey with stubborn confidence. All he lacked was the money.

She heard his mumbled calculations: headwinds and calms, tides, currents, distance . . . his reckoning of the time the journey would take.

A long-buried conversation stirred in her mind and she said, "The ant, crawling across the orange, thinks he knows the destination; but it's always farther than you think, takes longer. Don't underestimate the journey."

"Oh, I'll be sure to take your advice," he said with heavy humor, and may have recalled her words later—too late—when he discovered she had been prescient: he had indeed, and almost fatally, underestimated the journey.

But money, not distance, was his pressing problem: he felt a sickness creeping over him like the sleeping fever; a weariness that weighted his limbs—money. Always money. The importuning, the urging, the trafficking in promises to nudge at the greed of the already wealthy. Why couldn't someone else take on this drudgery and leave him free to check the calculations, to find the ships and the men and go—that moment that lifted his heart every time—take the tide, begin the voyage. All he wanted was the voyage, but between him and the sea stood a line of stony royal faces: João of Portugal, Henry of England, Isabella of Spain. Seductively he worded his proposals. Portugal first: clinging to the outermost edge of Europe, ignored, patronized, and engulfed by its grand neighbor—how fitting it would be for this tiny country to win the prize! If the king would listen, the Portuguese, the sons of Lusiad, should have the maritime glory: Portugal would lead the world. He offered his gift for the taking. And waited.

England, in its turn, was prevaricating, unconvinced. Maybe if he sent his brother to argue the case, two tongues might prove more persuasive than one. Yes, he would send his mapmaker brother.

"They have no imagination," he said, despairing. "The British have no real seafaring tradition; they're scared to get their feet wet."

And Spain?

"Spain is busy getting rid of the Moors." Spain was

proving a slow campaign. Like the sea, he told the old woman, royalty does no man a favor.

"The Queen of Spain," Esperança said thoughtfully. "Has she some aspect of beauty to catch the eye? Some remarkable feature?"

The queen was known to be devout, pawning her own jewels to finance the struggle to throw out the infidel Moors. He had heard nothing encouraging about Isabella's appearance.

"Why?" he asked.

"If she has fine ankles," the old woman murmured, "slender, she will know it and wear elegant shoes to show them off. If you get yourself to court, have a look at her shoes. Honeyed words could trap her attention for long enough to get your paper signed. Admire her ankles."

"It could lose me my head."

"No woman will have a man killed for noticing her ankles, not even a queen. Trust me," she said. "A respectful admirer is always welcome."

He was spitting out cherry stones as they talked. Now he picked three out of the soil and held them in the palm of his hand. "The ancient Greeks believed there were three particular dangers in life," he said. "Fire, ocean, and women."

"Fire," she said, "yes. You can't control fire." And she told him about the men from the mainland who started a blaze to clear the forests a lifetime ago, when she was a child. The fire that burned for seven years.

"As for the sea . . ." The day was cloudy, the water below them invisible, shrouded in mist. She listened to the sound of the surf, reaching them as no more than the threat of a whisper. A tantalizing murmur: withdraw, return, withdraw, return. *Tides turn.* But people did not always return. *I hate the sea*, she wanted to tell him, but even up here, so far above its reach, she kept the words to herself.

"Well, we all know what the sea can do. But why were they so fearful of women?" She reached for a cherry. "What danger do we offer? What power do *we* have?"

"Sometimes power comes in a different fashion, bringing danger with it. A woman can lodge in your heart. Forming a bond can weaken a man. That can be hazardous. But a queen, now. She has real power. Life and death." And, he might have added, her nod of assent can launch a fleet of ships.

He feels shabby. Not the boots, not the cloak, they're still acceptable. He feels shabby inside. Begging rubs at the soul.

"Money," he muttered, more to himself than her. "You know how you make money? You gather shit and pack it as tightly as cargo in a hold; you stretch out on it, make it your mattress; you roll in it, you breathe it. Shit's under your nails, between your toes, in your hair; you cut it in strips and wear it like a jerkin and hose. Then you go cap in hand, and ask for the money you need. And by then, you're just shit yourself. They hate the smell of you. To get rid of you, they give you the money."

"Is that what happens?" she asked.

"No," he said. "What happens is they wave you away. Not now, they say, later. They don't even see you. Not now, they say. But I keep coming back. I'm like the dung beetle, I feed on it: the more shit they throw at me, the stronger I get."

She said nothing. She could have told him how she, too, had learned the lesson; growing stronger, turning into steel; the loss, bit by bit, of the pulpy softness of yourself. Until one day you weren't there anymore.

74

She remembered the day: patches of cloud moving fast down the mountainside like shreds of sheep's wool caught up in the trees, the air moist with approaching rain. She had made it to the bridge and crouched, resting her head against the red wood, her body aching, folded into itself, and tight against her breast a small bundle, a bundle newly arrived, not yet acknowledged, not yet made known.

She heard the footsteps before she saw him, the boots clogged with mud clomping noisily across the bridge, pockets chinking, heavy with coins collected from tenants. He called to her, beckoning, jerking his head toward the nearest of his vineyards.

Sore, still bleeding from the wrenched and furtive birth, the cord severed with the knife she used for pruning the vines, she remained where she was, propped against the crisscross of the wooden railing. She would have answered but her mouth was dry, tongue furred, and no words emerged. She shook her head.

This was one of the newer landowners, a mainlander bent on making a fortune from wine and sugar. He had workers, slaves, a carriage. A civilized man.

Already he was moving away, expecting her to follow. At the sight of a shaken head he looked bewildered, incredulous. He turned back and squatted down close to her, rocking on his heels, the hem of his good cloth coat picking up mud. He said, confidingly, like one passing on helpful information, "You are a peasant. You people, living in huts, feeding on old bread and bad meat, you're not much better than animals—you're like one of those goats there. Our little game of barter and exchange amuses me. But you do not shake your head if I give an order."

They remained, quiet, side by side for a moment. A stranger seeing them might have thought them friends, resting by the riverbank, contemplating the stream rushing by. Exhaustion had crept up on her so insistently that her eyelids drooped, too heavy to hold open. For an instant she fell asleep where she squatted and it was in that instant that he decided to teach her a lesson. Perhaps the closed eyes provoked him.

He rose, flexed his shoulders, then reached down, gripped her elbow, and hauled her roughly to her feet. She was so light that her heels bounced on the bridge. The sudden movement, the wrench, dislodged the small burden. It flew out of her arms, rose in the air, and dropped into the water. She lunged, as though she could claw back what was already out of reach, trying to throw herself after the bundle, into the river, but he had gripped her and she was held fast, struggling. She howled, the sound inhuman, like something from the throat of a wolf. There was no point in struggling now, or flinging herself into the water. The bundle was already far out at sea, swept away on the current, gone.

As THEY PASSED, villagers called out to the old woman as usual—"Hey! Dona Esperança!" The shriveled figure, crouched beneath the almond tree was hardly more substantial than a cast-off bundle of clothes, but a croaked response reassured them she was still in occupation.

She was alone now. The sea lay spread below her like a great blue bird drying its wings in the sun, a bird that was also a god, claiming tribute. It had taken, one by one, everyone she cared about: Manuel, and then the child, swept away, swallowed in the bird's mouth, and now the red-headed dreamer had gone, too, to knock on one royal

76

door or another, hawking his calculations, his great idea, impatient to set sail. Always the sea.

On some days she abandoned the clifftop, hobbling her way along a different path, one that led inland, where once lilies had bloomed and now more of her vineyards marched in green battalions. One long ago afternoon Esperança had mischievously plucked Manuel's Holy Book from his pocket and run ahead, taunting him with it, laughing at his exclamations of dismay as he chased her, tripping over trailing roots that lay like snakes across the path. There had been palms here then, of one kind and another, and leaf climbers with long, thin stems. One of these, with hooks growing from the underside had caught on her clothes, her arms and in her hair, trapping her like a bird in a net until he called to her to stop struggling. While she stood, watching his face, he patiently extricated her, one tendril at a time, freeing her hair strand by strand, prising the tiny hooks loose, his fingers brushing her as lightly as a butterfly's wing. Where the hooks had pierced her flesh he wiped the blood from the puncture mark with a clean rag and touched the wound with his lips, as though to heal it.

"Set me as a seal upon thy heart, as a seal upon thine arm, for love is as strong as death."

She knew, when he spoke flowery words, that they came from one of his books, but she heard "heart" and she heard "love" and "death" and knew that for her the words were true. And with the confidence of youth she knew that something so good must surely last forever. She curled round him like a vine, arms circling his neck, and rested in the warmth from his body.

Years later she learned the names of the palms, *Calamus verus,* which supplied the cane for local furniture, and one, called *Calamus draco,* the Dragon palm, which held a dye that marked her fingers with a dark red stain. She had pressed her thumb to the back of his hand that day, so that he, too, was marked, as though to seal a covenant between them. When long afterward she bought the land, she supervised the leveling and the killing of the palms, noting how the *draco* bled crimson onto the laborers' axes.

She was capable of killing; she had learned that. It was easy. They stood together that day, she and the landowner with his muddy boots, staring at the heave of the ocean, the lacy patches that briefly swirled white against the green. Was that foam or a shred of white cloth that floated for a moment before it vanished? Could that have been her last sight of the living child she had held close for an hour? The man had relaxed his grip on her now, sensing the slackness in her body. All the force had gone out of her. If she had fought off those hard, restraining fingers, plunged into the water, could she have reached the tiny bundle in time? The blame was hers: her arms had not been strong enough to hold on to that scrap of life.

Limp, face stretched like a cat in pain, she clung to the end post of the bridge. She touched the hard ridges of the grain; almost sleepily she rubbed her fingers across the wood. He had thrust his hand deep into the pocket of his good jacket and he jingled the coins, turning them impatiently. The incident had unsettled him; he was uncertain what to do. Best perhaps to let her be for now. As he turned to go, his boot slipped on a patch of wet mud so that he flailed, reaching out for something to hold on to. His fingers brushed her arm and he clutched at her shawl to save himself, but she stepped away, relinquishing the shawl, pulling her arm free. The heels of his boots plowed into the loose, crumbly earth and he slid down the bank, dragging the shawl with him, and was sucked into the current of the fast-moving stream. It was deep here, swirling into a pool that gathered force before it flung itself on toward the open sea.

He cried out, coughing and retching as the water filled his mouth, screaming at her to save him. She stood, watching as he struggled, weighed down by the coins in his pockets, until his head sank below the water. She saw his hands break the surface, fingers clenching the air, trying to find something solid to grip, until the sodden bulk of him was swept out to join the waves. Then, arms folded tightly against the chill, she walked back into town.

Years later, when she was a woman of consequence, she made known her dissatisfaction with the bridge: inadequate, not in keeping with the growth of the town, possibly unsafe at times of flood. Her views were noted and before long a bigger, better structure spanned the river, one she had approved, with a parapet of strong wooden struts set close together. Safer, as everyone agreed.

Later still, when she had shriveled to a gaunt bag of bones, she limped round the headland to a small bay too shallow for fishermen, still undisturbed by visitors, and when the sun hung closest, warming her with a glow like settled embers, she dipped her gnarled toes in the surf and remembered the wash of water on young breasts, the heat and the melting. It was here, she decided, that she would make herself comfortable, propped against a rock, facing the horizon, and crumble, dustlike, into the strand.

⬥

Tides turn. Suns rise and set. Time folds back on itself, what was and what will be, spinning toward the present.

The ship was ready. The day had come.

From where they stood they looked down on the harbor and the ship, its deck piled with baskets, crates, packages, an animal or two for slaughter tethered to the rail. Everything was surge and movement, the planks crawling with activity, the vessel rising and falling, sailors, women, tradesmen moving in purposeful patterns. Birds pecked at grain fallen from sacks, gulls circled, sharp-eyed.

She turned her back on the harbor, pressing her face against the rough cloth of his shirt. The top of her head reached to his throat, his arms were tight round her shoulders. They leaned into one another as though pinned to the rock face by a powerful wind.

He shifted, loosened his hold on her; his fingers touched her neck, her shoulders, arms, wrists. She rubbed her cheek against his shoulder, softly, repeatedly. They stroked, touched, felt the other's skin with a searching intentness, as if by mapping out the area each occupied they were renewing a covenant, a bond to see them through a long night of parting.

There was nothing to dull the pain. She could have said, write to me; I shall learn, somehow, to navigate my way through the words. He had told her that reading was a conversation across space and time; through reading him she could have held him to her. He could have said, I'll let the ship sail without me; I'll find work here, clearing the smoldering land, felling the trees. But the tide was almost on the turn and he would be on the ship when it floated free of the land, they both knew that.

Esperança slashed off a lock of her hair. He wrapped it in two curled leaves and placed it between the pages of his Holy Book. Then he was away down the footpath, vanishing into the trees above the harbor. He did not look back.

She held on to his moving figure when he reached the

shore, tracing its path through the crowd, this way and
that, until suddenly she lost it: he had blended into the
rest, part of a surging pattern. Her eyes were blurred in
any case: she had held back the tears to spare him. Now
she let them flow, allowing herself to cry aloud, the sound
whipped away from her mouth by the wind.

She stood, watching the tilt and billow of the sails. It
had been a gray day, but the sun slipped out from behind
the clouds like a glowing bowl and poured a stream of light
onto the water. She saw that the loaded craft would follow
a golden path to the horizon.

As the ship pulled away from shore there was a sense of
union thwarted, a skewing of time. She felt a pain sharper
than death.

LONDON | *2000*

THE MAN IN the black leather jacket passes the local
police station, a supermarket, a small parade of shops, a
public library with graffiti-scrawled stucco columns and a
portico. He walks on, glancing quickly into shops, scanning
passersby. He paces unhurriedly, but there is an urgency to
his search.

A few yards away, in the muted hubbub of the library, a
woman hangs her green anorak over the back of a chair
and seats herself at yet another computer terminal, enters
her questioning words.

> **Sorry DGD DAT MSG is out of expected sequence.**
> **Please try again.**
> "?"

*What do you do when a message doesn't make sense? What
do you search for when you have no point of departure? Words,*

mere flickers at the corners of your mind, offer no purchase to the scrabbling fingers. You click on Help but that's no help at all. Adopting a matey, confidential tone, the screen suggests you click the Refresh button. Or close down and start again. Why not? Go blank. Cease upon the midnight. Begin again.

A slanting sunbeam fingers its way past the dust-furred window and lights up a stained-glass panel above a room divider. Lozenges of ruby and emerald glow against the shabby white emulsion. She watches the colors waver as clouds filter the sunlight. Glass. That's something she knows about. There are two ways to make colored glass: by adding colored oxides, or by . . . what? Her concentration is slipping . . . Glass could be regarded as a liquid so viscous that at room temperature it behaves like a solid. Glass has properties of both forms.

Begin again? Begin at the beginning?

"Search."
Click.
No search results. Please enter more information.

The cursor waits, blinking.

Information. The first scratching of shapes onto a flat stone. The slow deciphering. The Aztec codex. The Rosetta Stone. The Eugubian tablets, Linear B, Apple Mac, Windows, the program that brings you all you need to know. And somewhere in there, between the tablets and the shilling life, the printers. And then the printouts—

And then a clipboard carrying cryptic data: "Fugue." Define fugue.

(1) A flight.
(2) A musical composition on one or more themes that are harmonized according to the laws of counterpoint.

Labels on small dark bottles. Signs: → *This way out. No Way Out.* IN CASE OF EMERGENCY BREAK GLASS. *Glass can be broken, or it can melt. More information needed.*

The woman in the green anorak knows there is somewhere she has to go. The screen advises her to seek Help.

The people behind the reception desk smile benignly.

"Do you have your library card?"

"Sorry—"

"We'll look you up on the screen. No problem."

"Sorry," she says. "I'll come back another time."

She walks out, down the steps into the sunlight. Around her, people are walking with the purposeful yet slightly relaxed pace that divides work from whatever follows work: heading for the train or bus or wine bar, sniffing the wind. Briefcases, carrier bags, shoulder bags, books, papers, an occasional bun, nobody walks empty-handed. The girls smoke, striding confidently in their clumping, heavy-duty fashion boots and long, clinging skirts. She, too, has somewhere she must go, there is a journey she has to make.

She walks briskly away from the Thames, the cars keeping pace with her, the rush-hour traffic no faster than a walking woman. She turns left off Lambeth Road and left again, into a quiet side street shaded by chestnut trees, the houses prettified with wrought iron. The steps leading up to the front doors have terra-cotta pots holding bay trees; geraniums flower in window boxes.

The street is short—no more than twenty houses. Outside one, she stops. Six steps up to the door. She knows those steps: the third one up has a chip on the left, barely visible to the eye, caused by an abrupt encounter with a roller skate.

She reaches down and the chipped stone scrapes her finger. She rings the bell.

After a moment the door opens. A young woman, hold-ing a baby, her cheek smudged with food from the small fist, looks out questioningly. "Yes?"

"I'm sorry. . . ." Hesitation. Uncertainty. Behind that, something more: the shadow of fear. "I seem to have lost my keys . . ."

"Your keys? What keys?"

"Don't I live here?"

The young face grows sharp with suspicion. "What? What d'you mean? You've got the wrong house."

The door closes. Not quite a slam, but decisive.

Exhaustion creeps up her legs and into her body, weigh-ing her down. She negotiates the steps carefully, one, two, three—at the fourth she feels a melting and suddenly there is no structure, no underpinning, to keep her upright. She has become invertebrate, she thinks to herself, as she col-lapses awkwardly onto the bottom step. She leans her head against the gatepost, her neck, frail as a baby's, incapable of supporting the heavy weight it bears; without the gate-post her head would drop forward on to her chest like a drunken sleeper's.

Eyes closed, she sinks into an untidy bundle, briefly at peace. Here she could stay, quite content. Sleep. Easeful oblivion. People will pick their way past her; she will be no more than an adjunct to the gatepost; in time she will harden into stone, like an oversized garden gnome. Some-thing flickers, a brief picture on the wall of her mind. Not a gnome but a terra-cotta figure of some sort, in a garden. A damaged girl? A fabulous beast?

Clouds obscure the low sun and a small breeze shakes the leaves of the chestnut trees. Chilled, she becomes aware that she no longer has her anorak. She concentrates on her anorak: she sees it hanging over the back of a chair

85

at the library. That much, at least, is clear in her mind. Very slowly she hauls herself to her feet and steps out onto the pavement. The young woman with the baby watches her through the window, a phone held to her ear, lips moving.

She counts her way past the houses, as she always used to. She navigates the paving stones with concentration, taking care to avoid stepping on the lines.

The woman at the library desk is clearing away papers, stacking them neatly. "You're lucky. It's our late opening today."

The anorak is still there, draped over the chair. She draws it on, zipping it to the chin, shivering, colder than the temperature warrants.

As she comes out onto the portico steps of the library she notices, without interest, a man in a leather jacket approaching the building. He stops, looking up at her. "Ah," he murmurs, the word almost a sigh.

She studies him for a moment. "You were on the bridge."

"I was."

"Do I know you?"

"Yes."

She nods. Something, insubstantial as a scarf of cobwebs, trails fleetingly across her mind. She shakes her head to clear her brain of this obscuring mist. She sways, dizzy for a moment, and the man in the leather jacket leaps up the shallow steps, steadying her. He leads her down the steps and back toward the little parade of shops. She feels safe, abandoning herself to the hand at her elbow. She leans on him, aware that they are almost the same height. She closes her eyes and lets herself be guided, drawn along, in the dark.

FARO | *1489*

FARO | *1489*

PACING THE CATHEDRAL square, the youth counts the
windows of the long gray houses and the orange trees set
out like markers between them. He is planning a model of
the square, the houses, and the cathedral. He particularly
enjoys his outlines of the orange trees, neat symbols for
something more boisterous. The trees on his clean white
page are mathematical, circles and straight lines, whereas
in life they are less tidy: branches rustling like shiny green
rags. When blossoms hang on the branches the leaves flutter in the breeze like tiny fans, wafting the scent through
the casements that open onto the square.

He does these drawings in spare moments, in the course
of errands or taking the long way home. Faro is a small
town but the twisting streets, the little squares, the alleys
that lead nowhere are not always easy to traverse. Setting
down the town on paper is a way of creating order out of
muddle. In the workshop his duties are less demanding, a

matter of checking paper stock, replenishing ink, running errands. The older men have acquired the new skills. He is still learning.

A few streets away from the cathedral, behind the high walls of a mansion close by the Arco Vila, a young girl is getting ready for a dance. So many preparations to be made: the new gown for the evening to be examined to make sure the tailor has sewn seed pearls to the bodice and collar as instructed, with stitches invisible to the eye; the shoes—have they arrived with heels at the desired height and in the correct shade? A clash at hem level would be disastrous . . .

Her hair, braided over her ears by the maid, tied with looped yellow ribbon, looks perfect. It will need no further attention before the guests begin arriving.

From the window she can see the shoreline, the light-house, and the masts of ships, bobbing on the tide. She has never been out on the water—an unsettling element that offers discomfort without subsequent pleasure, unlike the experience of plucking her eyebrows or soaking her hair in egg and honey, when she suffers but is rewarded by the re-sulting improvement in her appearance.

Below in the courtyard she glimpses a messenger arriv-ing for her father, a youth somber in brown garments, a scrawny creature with black ringlets. Her father has these odd people arriving all the time, bringing curiosities from Africa, or rare books for his "library," as he calls it. Some-times she thinks he spends too much on paper and vellum and ivory. An entire banquet with entertainers, musicians, and dancing bears could be paid for with what one of these old books might cost. She prefers it when he brings home a new tapestry, a jewel, or an ermine mantle as a present for her.

She does not dismiss books as a source of pleasure: she enjoys a romance occasionally and she has read several of Aesop's Fables in the new translation. She finds the psalms comforting. But a conversation is surely a more fulfilling activity? A way of exchanging news, opinions, and gossip between friends. Still, she knows her father always likes to show her his latest treasure, so she drifts down the staircase and into the study, a dutiful daughter.

The youth was showing Gonçalves some sheets spread out on the desk.

Her father seemed excited, almost feverish. He called out to her, "Printed pages! This is astonishing! I've seen some Italian work, but nothing produced in Portugal before—"

"We are the first, my lord."

She noticed that the messenger was stroking one of the pages with a long, bony hand, fingers barely touching the surface.

"The first! Before Lisbon?" Her father smiled. "They will go mad with envy. Faro ahead of Lisbon . . ." He looked up questioningly. "How long before more pages are done?"

"We work as fast as possible. But a single slip . . . a few pages can take months—"

"And when will the complete work be ready?"

A hesitation. The messenger considered possible responses. The potential customer must be encouraged, but not too much, so that later he grew impatient or irritated. He murmured words pitched between caution and enthusiasm, watching from beneath lowered lids the girl at the table by the window, noting the slender body beneath a long *cota* fastened with intricate laces, the jewels at neck and wrist, the elaborately dressed hair.

She leaned on the windowsill, her back to the men, breathing in the lemon-scented air from the courtyard. She knew her father would have liked her to show more interest and, in fact, she approved of this new idea: the repetition of pattern could be pleasing, as it was on a sleeve edge or a wall hanging. But if there were to be printed volumes, her own preference would be for something useful, like the old songbooks, or the almanacs sold at fairs and markets. She picked out a collection of ballads and comic songs for the evening's entertainment. The two were still poring over the printed pages as she left.

She was sitting under a lemon tree by the fountain, turning the pages of the songbook when the messenger emerged and crossed the courtyard towards the wrought iron gates.

As he passed, his eyes rested on the smooth, lowered head, the book in her lap. Without stopping, he murmured, "So you did learn to read. That's good."

"What?" Her head jerked up. She was not used to being addressed by a worker, who would normally wait to be spoken to. As was the custom, she did not look at him directly: he was part of the scenery before her. "What?"

He paused and gestured towards the songbook. "You can read."

"Well, of course I can read." She shrugged, frowning.

He looked startled and moved on before she could ask what he meant by his absurd comment. She should have been sharper with him—an artisan dealing in ink and paper rather than tiles and wood, made overbold by her father's interest in his work. On consideration, his words were more than puzzling, they were insolent. She jumped up and ran after him into the street. "You!"

He swung round and for the first time they stood face to face. In the house she had gained only an impression, not really seeing him. Now he was within touching distance. He was not tall and on her raised wooden heels she could look almost directly into his eyes, close enough for her to see the thickness of the lashes, the liquid gleam, the contrast between the white and the deep brown of the iris. She stepped back, as though recoiling from a blow, putting distance between them. Because her hands were shaking, she smoothed her hair, her skirt. She found breathing had suddenly become difficult.

"What did you mean? Why should you remark on my reading?"

"I—mistook you for someone else. . . . I should not have spoken. Forgive me." He stammered on, muttering apologies. He looked dazed.

She listened silently to his confused explanation: something about a mistaken idea that they had met before, somewhere, though obviously that would have been impossible, she must forgive his lack of manners, his stupidity . . .

Cruel, she let him continue, able now to look him over: the face pale as ivory, long, thin hands gripping his leather portfolio.

She broke in. "What is your name?"

"Manuel."

Obviously they could not have met, yet there was a flutter of recognition, no more than a fleeting image across her mind, then it was gone. "What were you showing my father? Let me see."

He followed her back into the garden and she seated herself, arranging her skirt so that the folds revealed her pointed shoes. She was proud of her slender ankles. He stood, head bowed respectfully, waiting, but when she looked up she saw that he was smiling for no reason, his eyes amused.

"Show me these—printed pages." Her voice was brusque.

He undid the ribbons holding the portfolio and extracted a page. She took it, wondering why she was doing this. In a moment she would tell him to go. She would be gracious; she felt now that she had been too harsh.

She looked down at the sheet, at the heavy black marks marching across the paper in meaningless curlicues and jagged strokes. A starburst went off inside her head, touching her like an ache in her breast. *Teach me to read!* A meaningless echo of words she had never spoken. Tears sprang to her eyes and she blinked rapidly to prevent them spilling.

He noticed her distress. "You will not be able to read the words." Apologetically: "This is Hebrew."

"Yes. Of course." No need to acknowledge ignorance.

"It will be an edition of the Pentateuch with the Targum paraphrase of Onkelos and the commentary of Rashi in two volumes, quarto."

He might as well have been speaking a foreign language.

"So this is a page from the . . . Pentateuch. I see." Pause.

"The first five books of the Bible."

"Yes." She handed it back. "It is well executed."

He bowed and waited, tucking the page back inside the leather folder.

Esperança hesitated, for once at a loss. She glanced down at her shoes and rearranged her skirt again. She noted that the hem of his gown was frayed and she saw that the sleeve edges, too, were shabby. "You work for the printer . . ."

"Samuel, yes."

"He doesn't pay you enough."

"How do you know that?"

"I can see it."

To this he said nothing and she added, to provoke him, "Why do you work for him?"

"I enjoy my work."

"Even though he pays you so little?"

"He pays me what he can. I'm happy there."

She did not conceal her bafflement. "It must be difficult to be happy under such circumstances."

"Ah." He would like, he said, to tell her a story about happiness. One of his ancestors had been employed by a Moorish king, Abdurahman the Third, who three hundred years before had built a palace at Azahra near Cordova. "My relative was in charge of the royal mint, which produced the first coins of Spain for the Caliph—"

"So he, at least, cannot have been poor!"

"Indeed no. As for the king, his wealth was said to equal that of the whole of Europe. His palace walls were lined with jasper and four thousand columns of marble; a golden swan spouted water in one of the gardens and there were bathing pools of marble with screens of gold tissue. In the pavilion there was a fountain, not of water, but bubbling quicksilver. When the king died, among his papers was a memorandum he had written. He said he had reigned for fifty years, been victorious in war, lived in peace, beloved by his subjects. He meditated on the riches, honors, power, and pleasure he enjoyed. It seemed he lacked no earthly blessing. But he had carefully reckoned the days of perfect happiness that he could recall and they amounted to fourteen. Fourteen days of happiness. He ended his memorandum: Man, appreciate hence the value of splendor, worldly enjoyments, and even of life itself; place not thy dependence on this world."

It occurred to Manuel that this was probably the longest sentence he had ever spoken to anyone. He thought, too, that it was far more than she needed to hear—and certainly not an opinion that would be welcomed by a rich young woman. There were other things he would rather have offered her. In a different world, at a different time, he might have knelt at her feet, touched her ankles, placed rings on her fingers, and lost himself in her eyes. But there was no other world and this was the time. And yet: how did he know the curve her mouth made when she smiled? She had not smiled today. How did his fingertips know that beneath her silken collar, her nape had a bloom like a dark apricot?

The silence lengthened.

"Thank you for showing me the Pentateuch."

He bowed. It was the dismissal he expected.

The shadowy hall was a relief after the brilliance of the garden, the dark leather paneling of the walls cool to the touch. She ran her fingers over one polished rectangle, delicately tooled in dark red and silver. Quite soon, as winter approached and the sun cooled, the servants would be dismantling the wall covers. She would miss the leather, not only because it kept out the heat of the sun and the swarms of insects that would then emerge from the plaster and succeed in sucking her blood, but because she loved the deep, glowing colors, the golden bronze and crimson the tanners conjured out of drab animal skins, thinned and hammered and stretched into delicate leaves as fine as silk. She remembered the way those burnished panels had cast mysterious shadows across her mother's face, shadows that lit up the sallow skin, lending life to the sickly pallor. But the vividness had been temporary.

A slight breeze lifted the drapery at the study windows. Her father was bent low over the table, peering at the pages of a newly acquired manuscript. She paced the gleaming tiles, waiting for him to pay her attention: nine paces forward, four on the woven rush mat, turn, six on the mat, nine across, turn again. . . . Days could be long; she had fallen into the habit of these counting games to pass the time: how many leather rectangles along the hall? How many steps up to her bedroom? How many stitches on a tapestry flower? . . . Finally she lost patience.

"He seems to know a lot, that boy."

"Manuel? He works for Samuel the printer. The old man is teaching him the trade. Wisely. There'll be plenty of work soon. Everyone will want printed books. They will all become readers. Manuscripts will be mere objects of curiosity. Of interest only to collectors."

"So will you buy this—Pentateuch, when it's ready?"

"If I can. And if he isn't prosecuted first."

"Who would prosecute him? What for?"

"Well, the rabbis aren't altogether happy about it, I'm told. He's risking his reputation. They'll seize any error, any blemish, to condemn the work as unfit. Luckily, some of them approve; they call it "writing with a hundred pens," rather a fine phrase. I like that, writing with a hundred pens. Yes, they see God's hand behind it, that's the thing. But there are others who might not be pleased. When Jews start some new thing, people notice them. That's not always helpful. Better for them when they live unnoticed."

"Why?"

She sounded fretful: the heat was beginning to oppress her. All this seemed too much like politics or church matters and she preferred to keep away from discussions of that sort.

He stroked her hair soothingly. Esperança stifled an exclamation of protest: Graçia would have to undo the ribbons, comb out the whole thing, and start again.

"Don't worry your head; it will only confuse you," he advised.

Yes, she thought, as she gently disentangled herself from the paternal embrace, I shall keep my head out of it, but my hair will now need attention.

As she went slowly up the wide staircase she turned over in her mind those troubling words, "How many days of happiness? . . ." How many days?

ABOVE THE NOISE of the jugglers and the music, Esperança heard her father laughing. She leaned forward and watched him signaling for more wine. He looked flushed, laughing too loudly, his coif crooked on his head. He had not drunk too much, she knew. This immoderate behavior was to do with the woman seated beside him, in a green and scarlet gown. She was picking at her food in what Esperança regarded as an artificial manner. There was no reason to bare her teeth, to draw back her lips, to nibble so delicately at the lumps of meat piled before her. Gonçalves looked bemused, his mouth mimicking her movements, his eyes on her lips.

The celebration was a success as they always were. This one in particular had been planned more lavishly than usual, to mark the wedding of a cousin on a visit from Lisbon: it was necessary to demonstrate, when the occasion made it possible, that Lisbon was not the whole of Portugal.

Esperança's Uncle Alberto, who moved in court circles, had advised on the entertainment: "We shall have a mock joust with a maritime theme. It will be amusing. I have some craftsmen who are skilled at painting on cloth and wood . . ."

"Shall we need to demolish any walls? Will horses misbehave in the ballroom?"

To her disappointment, it seemed the young men would manage without horses—though they might themselves very well misbehave.

"Now: as to the food . . ."

Servants circled the long tables, hauling a golden cart filled with the stuff of happiness—whole sheep with gilded horns and hooves, and arranged between the sheep, roasted peacocks, complete with tails, heads, and necks with all the feathers on. Tucked between the peacocks were capons and, above them, wild ducks, partridges, and quails. Small birds perched on larger ones, at the very top a lark whose charred neck was circled with a tiny golden chain.

Esperança saw her father reach out and pluck the lark from the cart as it passed. He lifted the gold chain from the bird's neck and slipped it over the finger of the woman in green. She raised her hand to her mouth and slowly licked the chain, removing the bits of roasted lark that clung to the links. Then she held out her hand to Gonçalves, who kissed the greasy fingertips.

"No more!" moaned a girl next to Esperança. "I cannot find room for so much as an almond."

On the tables, a river of fruit spilled across the taffeta cloth: white and purple figs, green grapes, dried raisins, candied peaches, here and there pots of sweet lettuce preserve standing like rocks in the serpentine flow. A young man not far from Esperança was lobbing grapes into her lap to attract her attention. She saw with slight vexation that one of the grapes—overripe—had split open and left a tiny mark on her skirt. The maid would have to attend to that. He called loudly above the noise, requesting her presence at the dancing later. She nodded a possible yes and reached for a handful of raisins. She squeezed them for a moment, yielding, sticky, clinging to her palm, then let them fall back on the table. She had no appetite tonight.

The sound of viol, lute, clavichord, and harp drifted from the minstrel gallery, almost drowned out by the noise of conversation, the clamor of clowns and dwarfs. Gradually the guests hoisted themselves from the tables, found various corners to empty their bladders, and dawdled their way to the ballroom. With a rattle of drums, the jousting was announced.

"Will you give me a ribbon to tie to my lance, Esperança?"

João was handsome and well built; she had enjoyed teasing him in the past. Tonight she found him plump and overpleased with himself. Indeed, with his fashionably exaggerated shoulders, tight girdle, and tunic so short it revealed his legs to the thigh, she found him ridiculous. She moved away, disregarding his plea. And in any case, it was time to applaud the bridegroom, hauled into the ballroom astride a wooden ship set on cloth painted with great liveliness to look like a stormy sea. More ships trundled alongside. A troupe of musicians banging drums, blowing trumpets and whistles trailed behind. The decks of the ships were brocade, the sails white taffeta, the rigging silken rope. A wooden swan the size of a sheep, with white and golden feathers, glided in front of the fleet and in the prow of the first ship the Knight of the Swan, keeping his balance with difficulty, haltingly read out a speech in celebration of the recent wedding. Polite applause. He bowed and broke wind.

Now it was the turn of Uncle Alberto, comfortably aware of his role as supremo in this entertainment. The slow arm wave was almost regal.

"Let the jousting begin!"

It was high-spirited and good-humored and—apart from the odd serving man who got in the way—no one was injured, but after an hour of the galloping and the flourishing, Esperança felt the need to escape. With a group of friends she wandered out to the courtyard. They circled the fountain, sprinkling their arms with cooling water. From the house came shouts and laughter. The musicians played on. The girls collapsed languidly over stone benches and balustrades, on shallow steps, and along the flat stone edging of the pool. In their delicate gowns, the cloth lighter than their golden skin, they looked like drooping flowers, pale petals glimmering in the darkness.

Idly they considered the guests: the women's clothes, the charms of the young men, one or other of whom they would find themselves married to in due course. They praised, listlessly, the ball and entertainment, the sweetness of the chilled fruit creams, the splendor of the costumes—

"Magnificent," murmured Isabel.

"A spectacle." Francesca sighed.

Marta, not one of Esperança's closest friends, agreed that it was indeed "excellent," but then let fall that the previous month she had attended a "truly wonderful" celebration set in a garden completely covered by a blue silken canopy symbolizing heaven, "and from a high tower window, angels in silver and white feathers flew out, sprinkling fragrant roses and what appeared to be flakes of ice on the heads of the guests below. The smell of the roses! The cool touch of the flakes!"

Nevertheless, Esperança knew the celebration tonight had indeed been splendid. As always.

Why then, this time, did she feel dissatisfied?

"Perhaps we need some new cooks," she suggested, when she saw her father next day. "Or perhaps the players need new music." Perhaps there should have been more guests. Or fewer. Or newer faces. Different faces.

"Do we know any Jews?"

"Well, in the course of business—"

"I mean, do we know any to invite, to see at festivities or dances? To eat with—"

"Eating can be a problem," he said. "All those prohibitions. True Jews would probably not eat in our home. But *conversos,* of course, we could invite; we know a number of New Christians."

"What about the boy from the printer's?"

Gonçalves took a moment or two to recall him. "Ah! Manuel." He smiled. "We don't have artisans to dine."

For the next few days Esperança was busy, seeing to new outfits for the coming winter season. Faro was never really cold; heavy window hangings and fur rugs kept the house comfortable, but she still needed a few gowns. She ordered one in thick Utrecht velvet and a mantle of Lille cloth. Shoes were being worn cut differently at the toe and the truly fashionable had them in a different color for each foot . . .

A week had passed before she felt free to pursue an idea that had taken hold of her. She called the maid. "Graçia, there is a workshop somewhere on the other side of town—" She gave the maid the name of Samuel the printer.

Finding the place should not be difficult. She would take the carriage.

This was a part of town she knew only by name. The narrow, cobbled streets busy with people, voices, horses, donkeys, even a goat or two; filth swept into mounds by the roadside. No elegance here, no leafy courtyards filled with the sound of birdsong and falling water. Threading between the strollers, laborers carried bales or baskets on their backs; the women's skirts were hitched up above clogs and thick stockings. Down curving dark streets were more shops, their counters piled with food, one with birdcages hanging on the outside wall, another with metal utensils piled up, spilling from counter to shop floor and out into the street itself.

Flames flickered at the back of a blacksmith's forge, the master shouting instructions, two men hammering the iron, another plying the bellows. A youth scurried between them, bringing in firewood and coal, stacking up finished horseshoes, piling the cooled nails into boxes. Ringlets of dark hair stuck to their sweating faces.

Esperança felt an uneasy spasm in her belly: this was not her world. These were the unseen people who produced the objects that filled her world—the pieces of furniture sawed and smoothed, shaped and painted; the leather, the kitchen pots, the cloth that hung at her windows or covered her bed—not her gowns, of course: those were of imported silk and fine velvet, too rich for these people to handle.

The printer's workshop was not so easy to find: it lay behind a wood merchant, through a cramped passage, up worn, narrow stairs. The rooms smelled of metal and wood, and something sharp that stung her nostrils. Esperança trod carefully, holding her skirt away from greasy walls and floors strewn with discarded sheets of paper and spattered with hardened bits of metal.

Samuel was deferential. Greetings over, he stood waiting for her to come to the point, assuming she came with some request from her father.

She felt foolish, almost angry: why was she here? What was there to say? How to explain her presence?

She looked about her. "This is where you do your work?"

He gestured to a long bench. "These are the metal prisms for molding the faces of the letters. Placed backward, of course, to print correctly onto the paper."

The shallow boxes filled with prisms ran from wall to wall, a bewildering number: surely, she said, there were far too many?

"They are necessary. We have two forms in which Hebrew letters are printed: the square and the Rashi. Therefore, many prisms are needed."

He picked up a few sheets, to show her the different forms. "Always forty-two lines to each page. And the press to flatten the paper—you will see it is not unlike the presses used in winemaking. Or bookbinding—" He felt he was talking too much and paused.

She made no comment.

"We could do with more room, but—" He shrugged.

"Why not move, then, to somewhere bigger?"

She glanced about, as though looking for some elusive object, some item required by her father.

"Where is the messenger—" she frowned as though trying to recall his name. "Manuel?"

The boy was collecting an urgently needed item; he would be gone some time. (Was there something the youth should have done, an instruction not carried out?) Gonçalves was a valued customer, it must be important, for a rich man to send his own daughter.) Samuel was growing anxious. "We needed something special." He tried a small laugh, "Dragon's blood—"

"Dragon's blood! Where would you find such a thing?"

"In Africa. Or on the island of Madeira . . ." He added reassuringly, "It is merely resin from the dragon palm, much in demand in weaving and dyeing."

"Ah!"

She spun sentences in her head, trying them out for suitability. None seemed quite right. "He was to show me some examples of your work," she lied crisply, keeping her expression remote. "But no matter. Tell him to see me next time he is passing near the house."

To feel clumsy, to be aware that she had not dealt perfectly with a situation, was something new for Esperança. Her cheeks reddened. She felt a prickle of sweat in her armpits. The gown would be stained, ruined. She turned to go and stubbed her foot against a jutting nail, tearing the delicate fabric of the shoe. An exclamation of genuine irritation freed her from the absurdity of embarrassment. "Your floor is a hazard!"

She left, ignoring his apologies, holding herself fastidiously away from the walls, trying not to touch the flaking, dusty plaster, her thin soles slipping on the worn edges of the stairs.

In the workshop Samuel returned to the bench. He wondered how he might have told the foolish girl without causing offense that it should be reasonably clear *why* they did not move to somewhere bigger: that it would be difficult to shift the thousand and one pieces of equipment without damage or loss; that Jews had limited choices in their place of work and needed to exercise caution. Besides, the cost of moving was beyond their means. For a rich young woman these would not have been interesting topics of conversation.

Around him rose a comforting, muted clatter: the familiar noise of the workmen setting out type, banging the platen into place, pressing inked type against paper, folding the sheets into folio, quarto, octavo. The cutting and stacking went on as usual. But he felt uneasy. A curious visit. A puzzling encounter. The nobility were not like ordinary people; they had their whims, their needs of the moment, like spoiled children—a thought struck him, outlandish, laughable, yet unsettling: he hoped Gonçalves's daughter was not looking for a new distraction, a toy to be taken up and played with until boredom returned and the toy was dropped, possibly damaged. He decided he would forget to pass on her message.

SHE ALWAYS ENJOYED Corpus Christi week: family arrived from Coimbra, from Lisbon, from Porto. There were banquets and celebrations; music and dancing. There were, of course, also the services, longer than usual and less agreeable, in the hot, overcrowded cathedral, but she bore the discomfort with fortitude.

When her mother was alive the services seemed less tedious. Then, side by side, arms touching, so close the child could see the fine, almost invisible hairs that lay like a bloom on her mother's skin, the faint scent of verbena sweetening the air, then Esperança had felt happy—

Happy? The word had popped into her head from

nowhere. Why should she not feel happy? Nothing threatened her. She had everything necessary for a perfect life. As had her mother until the sickness took hold, eating away at her; first the spirit, then the flesh succumbing. The doctors had tried various cures: heat, cold, water, tinctures of this and potions of that. Bloodletting had been the last resort: disease, they said, left the body as the blood flowed. But bleeding was a complicated business: you had to know the veins and which should be drained, according to the season. In March they pierced the veins of the head, in the right arm. In April the leeches settled on the arcal vein, though Esperança never knew quite where it was. In September, the vein in the left arm was bled, the time of month carefully calculated: dog days were considered distempered, not offering the necessary heavenly equilibrium. But perhaps the heavenly bodies had not been in the appropriate positions after all. The bloodletting, too, had failed.

She shifted inside her stiff gown, releasing heat trapped beneath her breasts. She had stepped out of her shoes and, hidden by her skirt, her feet were pressed against the cool stone floor. Where her bracelets covered her arms the skin was damp. The church was filled with lights, incense and the sonorous voices of the choir, the Most Holy Sacrament glittering in the wavering light. The congregation perspired gently together, the smoky incense mingling with the sharp smell of sweat.

She caught the eye of a man across the aisle. Now that she was fifteen there was the additional interest of knowing she was being watched and considered by young men and their mothers and, of course, by older men. She drove her maid into a frenzy of preparation before each event and she herself was quite tired out by the extra work of

107

planning her different toilettes, finding new ways to arrange her hair, and making sure that the friends she liked best were near her in church or riding with her in the carriage to and from the services.

She crossed herself and murmured the response. She leaned closer to Isabel. "I swear," she whispered, "the services get longer every year."

"The priests are punishing us," Isabel whispered back, "for sins past and future."

Esperança thought carefully over her life: she had committed no sin that she could think of. Nothing in the past that the priests could condemn. As to the future, that looked as clear as the skies beyond the harbor. . . . The final blessing droned over her head and she turned impatiently toward the huge doors; the immediate future at least was filled with promise. And processions. The congregation shuffled toward the sunlight and freedom. The closely packed assembly broke up and poured down the steps; men, women, and children dispersed like a gushing stream. This was a festival of transformation; the Eucharist bread and wine changed into the body and blood of Christ, and for the next eight days the city, too, would be transformed.

Night and day the town heaved with movement; humanity swirled and eddied round the curving streets, a constantly moving, two-faced pageant where the populace and the performers were interchangeable, the nobility admiring the common people and the performers taking precedence over their betters. To be part of it all was an occasion of shared pride.

After dark a thousand fires blazed through the town, piercing the thick night with candles, flambeaux, and oil lamps in towers and belfries, at windows and street corners. Faces were caught, frozen as in a flash of lightning, a bony nose sharpened by the flare, a rounded cheek caressed by a momentary glow, eyes catching the flames in a thousand reflected points of light.

"Look!" Esperança pulled at Isabel's sleeve. "A dragon!"

The gigantic figure paraded, capering and bowing to the ladies as he passed, the light glinting on his scales and lashing tail, flame billowing mysteriously from his jaws. Esperança thought of the printer's boy, sent off to procure dragon's blood: where had he found it? Not across the seas, surely? The old man would never have sent someone so young to distant places to carry home phials of the special dye. And where was he now? Weeks had passed since her visit to the printer's and he had not returned to the house.

"Dragon's blood," she murmured, eyeing the dangerous claws, suddenly bored by the mock battles between pagans and Saracens, the everlasting juggling acts, the dances.

The ships in the harbor shared the festive fever, bright with pennants and decorations, with no thought of the terrors hidden beyond the horizon: the thirst, hunger, disease, shipwreck, and death by drowning that lay ahead for so many of the sinewy young sailors. Meanwhile, scrubbed and barbered, they took part in the procession.

Behind the sailors, butchers dragged a bull along the street, pulling on brilliantly colored ropes; gardeners and orchard workers created a moving garden, complete with flower beds and vegetables, mounted on a cart. Fishwives, bakers, and street vendors danced past to the sound of fifes. Three Magi crowned with gems rode in a litter veiled in cloth-of-gold; cobblers, tanners, leather bottle makers, tailors, soldiers, crossbowmen, their weapons garlanded with ribbons. Barbers, blacksmiths, cutlers, saddlers, scabbard makers, tinkers. Another litter, this time St. George slaying the dragon, a pool of silken blood lapping his feet. ("There's your dragon again!" Isabel cried to Esperança, clapping her hands.) More followed: wool combers and carders. A figure of the devil bound by a rope. Silk weavers carrying St. Sebastian. Potters, tilers, brickmakers with a life-size Saint Claire on their shoulders. Carpenters, masons, street pavers, bricklayers, and laborers. Candlestick makers with flaming torches in tin holders got an extra cheer: what would Corpus Christi be without its candles?

Goldsmiths and tinsmiths held aloft the litter of St. John; boys were dressed as angels and evangelists. Scholars, scribes, and judges were suitably dignified, conscious of their place. Clothes became richer, girths more impressive as affluent bourgeois merchants of linen and silk and wool ambled past, until, like water after wine, came the austerity of black friars, gray friars, white friars, brown friars—Augustinians, Benedictines, Dominicans . . . seemingly endless knights in the orders of Christ, and then the triumphant Host, released from the confines of stone and stained glass into the warm, heavy air, the golden Monstrance carried aloft in the hands of the bishop, small girls strewing rose petals in his path, walking backward, reverently kissing the petals before casting them beneath his feet.

"Ah!" Esperança crossed herself, carried away by the splendor. She stooped and picked up a white rose petal and put it to her lips. Her teeth closed on the fragile surface, wafer thin like Communion bread. She had expected sweetness, fragrance, but the rose petal tasted like dry, crushed grass.

Now came people costumed as wild or mythological animals: elephants, lions, capricorns, bears, and a tall, improbable creature with an elongated neck and oddly marked hide.

"That is a creature from Africa," a man called to his neighbor above the noise of the crowd. "The Moors call them *zarafah*." Half hidden by a lion, another beast was approaching, very like a horse, but with a horn jutting from his brow.

"A unicorn! Isabel, look!"

The unicorn, prancing past, swings his long head, as though picking up her voice in the crowd. He pauses, executes a curious, half-human bow, then kneels and rests his head against Esperança's feet. Applause and laughter from the crowd: a unicorn seeking out a virgin, they all know the story.

Charmed by the graceful beast, flustered by the attention of the crowd, Esperança feels something is expected of her. She pulls one of her hair ribbons free and ties it playfully round the colorful horn. Around her, people clap approvingly.

"That's the way to catch him! The virgin's the bait to trap the unicorn!"

Some of the young men are calling out, "Let's catch the unicorn!" And the phrase spread, running like a flame through the throng—"Catch the unicorn! Catch the unicorn!" She senses a change in the mood of the crowd. What follows the catching of a unicorn? A killing?

The beast raises his head, seeming to gaze up into Esperança's face; the sky-blue painted eyes are expressionless but she feels a tremor of unease: the unicorn is in danger. He is beautiful, he does no harm but he is different, not quite a horse, not a human. His presence arouses admiration but also hostility. A man nearby shouts an obscenity: the unicorn's horn, white at the base, black in the middle, is tipped with crimson.

"Blood on his horn! So much for the virgin then!"

The joking spreads, coarsens, the voices louder. The crowd seems to press in on her; it is she now who feels frightened, trapped, in danger, though the shouting has not changed—

"Catch the unicorn! Catch him! Fetch ropes!"

The unicorn rises to his feet. His mouth close against Esperança's ear, he whispers, "Have no fear. I would lay down my life for you."

She stifles a scream, frightened by the unexpected voice, the words that echo her own unease. As the unicorn gallops away, she feels suddenly faint, sways, almost falls. Isabel supports her, concerned. Around Esperança the colorful scene swirls giddily, she the center of a spinning top.

SHE HAD RECOGNIZED the voice. It was the outer shell that had tricked her. A traveler in magic lands, bringing back dragon's blood, transforming himself into a fabulous beast; this was the slippery, unsettling printer's messenger who had failed to present himself at the house as requested. She felt angry. Worse, she felt foolish.

Through the rest of Corpus Christi week she looked out for him. She wanted an opportunity to ignore him and, in doing so, rebuke him for his outrageous behavior. But he was not among the processions and it was hardly likely he would be at the services.

She knew he would appear at the house when there was something more to show her father, so she waited, polishing her words till they shone like knives, looking forward to

112

the moment when she would cut him down, send him bleeding back to his proper place at the other end of town. She stoked her irritation and took even more care than usual with her appearance.

When he came she almost missed him. Changing her clothes, she heard voices, her father calling him into the library. She threw on a linen surplice over her skirt and flew down the stairs, still tying the fastenings. She heard the murmur of their conversation through the window. When he emerged she was waiting. Without a word they walked together across the courtyard and out of the gate.

Her feet touched the ground; she was aware of cobblestones pressing against the thin soles of her shoes, yet she seemed to be weightless, her body so light that she floated. Her flesh felt hot, the way it did when she stood too near a fire, the skin stretched tight.

They walked through curving, tree-lined streets to the seafront. On the ships men were busy cleaning, mending ropes, checking sails. Others carried provisions on board, staggering under bales and sacks.

She, who always knew what she wanted, found it difficult now to pick the right words. "Did you get the dragon's blood?" she asked.

He looked surprised. "Yes. It's not a difficult task."

"I would find it so."

"Your life is different."

"How?"

"I mean, easy. Life is easy for people in your world." There was no accusation in his voice; he made it sound like a reassurance.

"And for people in *your* world?"

"Less easy."

She walked ahead of him—this was familiar ground

to her—showing him the way. It was a sheltered corner where the breeze cooled the warm stone and the high wall shielded them from the eyes of passersby. Roughly hewn blocks of stone formed a seat. She sat down, nodding at him briskly to do the same.

She said, "So it is hard, to live as a Jew."

"The hardest privilege I can think of."

"But you consider it worthwhile."

"Yes."

"I would like to know more."

He considered. What could he tell her that would be comprehensible, that could help her to see the way he lived? Should he embark on history—surely not. Stories of ancient battles, of sojourns in desert wilderness, imprisonment, and flight—what would that tell her?

To prompt him, she said, "This language that we cannot read, this—Hebrew of yours, is a foreign tongue. When did you come here?"

He smiled. "Some say we were in Spain, paying tribute to Jerusalem in the days of King Solomon. A thousand years before the Christian era. In Murviedro, in Valencia, on the ruins of a Roman town, there is an ancient tomb with a Hebrew epitaph: *Zeh hu kever Adoniram, eved ha-Melekh Shlomoh, she-ba ligbot et ha-mas, ve-niftar yom.* It means: This is the tomb of Adoniram, the servant of King Solomon, who came to collect the tribute, and died the day. The rest of the inscription is worn away."

"Have you seen this tomb?" she demanded.

"No."

"Then how can you know it's there? How can you know anything about it?"

"Adoniram, son of Abda, the servant of Solomon, is

mentioned in the Holy Bible, in the first book of Kings. . . .
We Sephardim regard this as our home."

"Yet you are different. Not like us."

The sea leaned a blue shoulder against the rocks and
lay, heaving gently, seeming to be listening as he began to
speak.

"We made a covenant with the Lord," he said. "It is a
matter of trust." He was sparing with his words. Sometimes
she had to prompt or nudge him—"Go on!" But occasionally he could startle her: straight-faced, he would tell a story
with a sting of humor in its tail and she, taken by surprise,
would break into laughter and throw pebbles at him. Talking in this way, even within the family, was new to her, and
her father would have been astonished to see Esperança
so attentive. No impatient movement of the head, no little
frown. She followed his words like someone stumbling
through darkness toward a pinpoint of sunlight.

The conversations were misshapen; the two had no
need for the ritualized, tentative exercises that can trans-
form strangers first into acquaintances, then friends. Each
knew the other's essence. What was unknown was the life.
He had at least observed the surface of her daily life, the
mansion, servants, the visible pattern, though without
any idea of the social complexities that underpinned it all.
She could barely imagine his existence in the Jewry. The
rhythm of her year was set by the Church, his by the Jewish
calendar and the Covenant. Through her questions, his
answers, she constructed a chart of his life; she mapped
his thoughts.

One day she came to their meeting place carrying a
small picture wrapped in silk: an image of the Virgin and
Child, to show him that not all Christian iconography was

based on torture, suffering, and death, as he had once remarked.

"Ah yes," he said. "The child Yehoshua."

"No, this is Jesus."

"His name would have been Yehoshua. He was, after all, a Jew."

The priests had failed to draw this to her attention but she saw that it must be true.

"And do you have similar images, of your prophets?"

"Graven images?" he said with mock gravity. "That would be considered not Jewish. With us, the word is considered enough. We have the injunction in Exodus to remind us: 'Thou shalt not make unto thee any graven image, or any likeness of anything that is in heaven above or that is in the earth beneath or that is in the sea beneath the earth.'"

She thought for a moment, crunching the pebbles with her shoe. "No likeness of anything in the earth or the water . . . But Manuel, what about the maps you draw? Are they not a likeness? Are you not breaking the Law?" Her demureness was mischievous, but he was disconcerted. She touched his hand reassuringly. "Of course, a map is not an image, is it? It's just a way of describing something. If they had spent more time in conversation God might have handed down a map to Moses—it could have been of help!"

She was teasing him and he took it well, but still he wondered fleetingly: could a map indeed be going against God's will? To seek to know too much could be dangerous. It was eating of the fruit of the Tree of Knowledge of Good and Evil that caused Adam and Eve to be expelled from Eden.

He put away the thought and said, glancing again at the Virgin and Child, "Charming. Well executed.

Nevertheless"—an apologetic shrug—"in worship at any rate, with us the word is considered enough."

But in both their worlds, words could be instruments of construction and destruction: words built bridges and at the same time kept people apart.

Later, when the darkness descended and life shrank to the span of a held breath; when terror rose like flood waters beneath their feet and hope had been snuffed out, she tried to remember how it had been in the beginning—a time that she had innocently considered hard—and then later, when it seemed that halcyon days followed one upon the other and she was at peace. Was that how it had been? Certainly it had begun with the conversations.

———✦———

HER FATHER BRUSHED it aside when she told him. Others would have dealt with her more harshly, but he treated her declaration of love for a printer's apprentice, at first, as an emotion of the moment. There had been episodes in the past when Esperança had announced her passion for an unlikely goal: achieving skill at a musical instrument, for example, or designing a garden in the English style. This, too, would pass. But he had her watched, kept her busy with banquets, took her to visit an aunt in Silves, exhausted her with social obligations. He reasoned that a few weeks would be enough to purge her of foolishness.

When she stood firm, he became at first angry, then fearful. He saw that this was no matter of a jeweled hat or a new carriage. This was life and death, and he proposed to fight her in order to save her. He himself had little time for matters of the next world: the present world kept him busy enough. But this was no everyday matter. He called in the priest. "Talk to her."

Father Bartolomeu raised his hands in a gesture that blended benediction with boredom: "I shall open her eyes to the horror that could await her. The poor, deluded child shall be saved."

Summoned to his presence, she faced Father Bartolomeu with composure, though she was by no means as calm as she appeared, her silence largely due to an inability to assemble a forceful argument. But when he began to summon up hellfire and the Evil Worm, to describe the terrors of the Pit—"You will burn; the pincers will tear your flesh"—she found the words she needed.

"Is God not God? The Old Testament God of the Jews, is He not also *our* Father? How then can it be so wicked to worship Him?"

He decided to shift the argument onto more personal ground. "To think of polluting your innocence with the unholy embrace of the Jew—"

"Jesus was a Jew."

The priest pronounced her "lost" and handed her back to Gonçalves. "The girl is stubborn. Willful. Perhaps a whipping might help. Women dislike seeing their smooth flesh raw and bleeding; pain can be persuasive. As a last resort," he suggested, "there is excommunication."

Gonçalves found her in the courtyard, cooling her hands in the fountain. "Father Bartolomeu thinks I should whip you till you bleed. I might do as he says."

She ruffled the water with a twig fallen from the lemon tree. "Father Bartolomeu is a foolish man and you are far too good and wise to listen to what he says."

She always knew the right words to deflect his anger. It would be so easy to draw her to him, smooth her hair and grant her what she wanted—that was the pattern. But this time she was asking the impossible. "What has this wretched boy said to convince you that there is the least possibility you can be happy with him? Has he spun you stories to turn your head? Perhaps he imagines this is a way to escape from poverty, share our life, taste the pleasures of ease—"

"He wants nothing to do with our life, as you call it. I would share *his* life."

Now indeed he looked bemused. "You intend to live as the wife of a pauper—"

"Manuel is no pauper, Father. He has a trade."

"Printing? Printing! Who knows where that will lead? The whole thing may collapse. There have been other great ideas that failed. In any case it is you I am discussing, not some youth from the backstreets of town. You have enjoyed a sweet and happy life. You do not comprehend what you are entering into."

She looked down at her yellow shoes, long, pointed, dyed to match her gown. She wanted to try and explain, to tell him about her beautiful life; how everything about it seemed unnecessary. That for the first time something was being asked of her, something hard. She dared not tell him she was frightened, uncertain of her own ability to meet the challenge. If she even hinted at that he would be down on her with the full force of his will, bending her, as he always did. Never so rough that she broke, but with the strength that came of unlimited power.

So she remained silent.

He looked about for causes, for reasons that might excuse her foolishness. He still could not accept that his own daughter, a child reared in Christian values, who could read the thoughts of great men, who had been properly brought up in the fear of God, was standing before him saying what she was saying.

His anger built slowly, stoked by his fears for her. "You have so much," he said.

"I have too much." She twisted the five Italian rings on her right hand. "When you have too much, you do not want what it brings you."

"How do you imagine you will live? A Christian woman is not permitted to enter a Jewry."

"I shall convert to Judaism."

Gonçalves found himself shouting, weeping, overwhelmed by fury that his tender chick, whose knowledge of the realities of life went no further than a muddied hem or a spoiled dish at table, was proposing to embark on a conversion to hell. Not only the hell of the priests—brimstone and flame—but the hell of a life lived at odds with an unforgiving world.

She turned away, looking out at the sea. Far out, beyond the harbor, she saw a small craft rocking and bobbing on the waves. She kept her eyes fixed on the frail vessel as she weathered the storm of her father's rage.

In Lisbon, petitions are presented to the king regarding Jews. It is proposed they should wear the sign, the yellow hat or badge of their tribe. Conditions are suggested concerning their attire.

> *And whereas at present we generally perceive much injurious dissoluteness as well in living, in dress, and in association that is disgraceful improper and abominable. And we notice Jew cavaliers mounted on richly caparisoned horses and mules, in fine cloaks, cassocks, silk doublets, closed hoods, and with gilt swords that it is impossible to recognize them.*

*The king considers the petitions. Changes are made to the law.
There is nothing here of affliction or oppression. But one change
heralds another.*

Gonçalves still hoped to pull his daughter back from the
edge of the precipice. He called her to his room, but let
her remain standing. The conversation was to be formal.

"All I ever wanted was for you to be happy. I can tell
you without the slightest doubt that this will not make you
happy. This is no more than fire in the blood. I blame myself: you are fifteen; I should have arranged matters earlier,
found you a husband. But your presence here was sweet. I
thought we could wait a little—"

He looked at her closely. He knew that expression: the
small chin jutting so firmly, the mouth set in a downward-
curving line. This was Esperança in her mulish, stubborn
mood.

"Shall I paint you a picture of your life, if you do this
thing?"

"I know—"

"You do not. You think you know. You think everyone
has three mattresses on their bed, with furs to warm you
and a purple counterpane. You have no experience of not
having what you need."

She sighed—how well he knew that sound—and began
to pace the room, looking down at her feet, her face set.

"First, of course, you will be dead to your former world;
you will have ceased to exist. You will certainly not be welcomed by the Jews who, very sensibly, do not encourage
foolish outsiders. What do his parents say about this affair?"

She knew he would seize on what she was about to tell
him. "They do not approve."

"Ha! Of course they don't. They will probably sever

121

relations with their son. If you persist in this madness his family will be destroyed. You will be isolated."

"Manuel and I will be together."

"Not for quite some time. It would not be considered proper. You will be placed with some pious family to learn the Scriptures and the Law. You will not spend one minute alone with the ruffian I foolishly allowed into my home. The Jewish community will regard you as a dangerous outsider—they know I could bring an accusation against them of Judaizing." He held her face between his hands. "You will have no life—"

"My present life means nothing to me."

He could have locked her into her room. He could have taken the priest's advice: beaten and starved her into submission; sent her north to relatives and married her off to a suitable candidate when she was too weak to resist. She would have sobbed for a fortnight, suffered for a month, drooped for a season. At the end of nine months or so, with the arrival of the first child, she would have been herself again.

But he was incapable of violence to his child. He believed in freedom to choose. And he still hoped to persuade her. "It will be hard for you, without means." He sounded regretful. "I shall, of course, disinherit you."

She had been expecting something of the kind. "I shall take only my everyday clothes—"

He managed to laugh. "By all means. The everyday velvet and brocade; the everyday Cordovan shoes and silk chemises with Madeira embroidery. An everyday gown of lace perhaps. You might want an everyday porcelain cup for your coffee. A few everyday ribbons of French silk—

"By the by, did you know the king issued an edict after

the last petition about the Jews? They're not allowed to wear silk now. Just wool or cotton. This will not present a problem for you, of course." Savagely he gave her the last thrust: "You'll be in rags, my dear. You'll be lucky to have clogs on your feet."

When the day came she wore her plainest gown, her stoutest shoes—they would need to last. She kept her personal jewelry: the diamond ring, a present from her father; the emerald necklace and bracelet that had belonged to her mother; a gold chain from Africa. . . . These, she thought, could be worn at her wedding when it took place; surely jewelry was allowed on festive occasions?

There was a painful leave-taking, the servants tearful, voices hushed.

Her old nurse sobbed aloud. "Take me with you. I won't ask for wages, just my food and lodging."

How to explain that she herself would be a lodger in a stranger's home, with nothing more than a bed to call her own. They would certainly be unimpressed, her teachers and guides, if she announced that she was embarking on her journey to spiritual enlightenment accompanied by a servant. For a moment, no more than a heartbeat, she had a twinge of regret for the ease that had always been hers.

Her father remained in his library, the door closed. He had said what needed to be said; the rupture was complete.

She had expected his anger. She had known he would find harsh words, persuasive arguments, to deter her. She admired his skill at describing the hardship she faced. The closed door was, strangely, harder to bear. Through that open portal she had run to him since childhood; he was the source of consolation, comfort, warmth. Now she must manage without him.

"MANUEL'S FAMILY IS devout," the rabbi told her. "The father is a silversmith in Évora, skilled though not rich. He had plans for his son. You must understand that they cannot accept you."

"And you?" she asked.

He stroked his beard in a way that had already become familiar to her: it provided a background for silence; it gave him time to think. "I believe you are sincere. You know the difficulties you face. If you are prepared for it, we shall proceed. After all, the Bible says, therefore shall a man leave his father and mother and cling to his wife and they shall become as one flesh. And besides, there are precedents. Ruth . . . Joseph the Patriarch married Asenath, a proselyte."

For a moment she failed to recognize herself in the description: a proselyte.

The food was a problem at the beginning: she missed the daily fruits from her father's orchards, the fat grapes from Madeira, the delicately seasoned pork and game, sweetmeats rich with cream, wine with her meals. Her new diet with its proscriptions and restrictions was tedious. "Why no milk with meat?" she asked Manuel fretfully.

"The Law says 'Thou shalt not seethe a kid in its mother's milk.'"

"But why can we not have chicken followed by flavored cream?"

"Well . . . to avoid any possibility . . . They are called hedges, extra precautions to protect the Law."

"Hedges are silly. Who built the hedges?"

"The rabbis."

"Can I argue with the rabbi?" she asked Manuel one day, after the Sabbath service. Segregated in the synagogue, they could walk together, if not touch.

"Discussion is always possible; examination of words and meanings, looking closely . . ."

"So I cannot argue with the rabbi."

"It depends on the rabbi. And on the argument."

AT THE BEGINNING Esperança had been preoccupied with her own needs; the lessons she must master in Hebrew and Jewish law. Converting had been a duty that occupied her day and night; the particularity of Judaism covered every waking moment and she had to be familiar with each detail. Her existing skills counted for nothing: to the rabbi, secular learning was no learning at all. Indeed, worldly books, she suspected, were better left unmentioned. No Aesop or troubadour songs here. But she did have the Psalms—and rediscovered them afresh in Hebrew, their beauty revealed in a new light.

Still, there were questions that worried her. She had completed her basic studies, the reading of Hebrew, the daily observance of the Law. She wondered sometimes about her own attitude to the task, one of curiosity and a certain peace she found in pursuing it.

A true believer died for his faith, if necessary. It had happened in the past. Which faith, therefore, would she die for, if necessary? The old or the new? Did not casting off one faith for another signify a certain frivolity? She had taken her church for granted: the rituals, the music, the

drama of it a part of her life, the all-powerful presence comforting. When her mother died she had felt less lonely in
the warm and fragrant arms of the church: the wood carv-
ing that glowed in the soft light of the candles; the gold
and silver icons; the suffering Christ. The patient Madonna.
I have lost a son, she seemed to be saying, and you have lost
a mother. We can share the bitterness of that loss and find
new hope, with God's help.

And now Esperança was turning away from that patient
gaze, from the comforting arms of Mother Church, to embrace a new faith, celebrated in yet another foreign tongue:
where it had been *"In Nomine Patris et Filii et Spiritus Sancti,"*
it was *"Shema Yisrael. . ."*

She felt she lacked profound faith and worried that she
might therefore be insincere, a fickle worshipper. She had
put the question to Manuel one day when they sat together
in the rabbi's dark, stuffy room, shutters closed against the
sun, the rabbi's wife busy with preparations at the table, to
chaperone, though not, it would seem, required to listen to
their conversation.

"I feel I lack faith," Esperança said. "I persevere.
But should I not be changed in some way, sense a holy
spirit? . . ."

They sat far apart, a table of holy books between them.
Touching was out of the question with the rabbi's wife
swiveling an eye at any movement.

He said conversationally, "I look at your hands, resting
like two birds in your lap. With my eyes I take your hand and
circle your wrist; I trace the line of your headscarf round
your brow. I touch your throat and smooth your cheek with
my fingertips. I rest on the corner of your mouth, where
your lips curl like a printer's comma. And as to faith," he
went on, "the faith required to do what you have done is

very great. Your determination, your strength of will. You are learning the ways of the Lord and you will live in His ways. We are taught that by your actions ye shall be judged. In mathematics, if the calculation is correct, the result will be so. If the groundwork for a map is accurate, you can depend on it. Faith is part of the equation and will be there when you need it. And your eyes are beautiful."

Through a gap in the shutters she caught a glimpse of a sky so blue and deep it burned like a lamp through the broken wood. The flash of blue recalled for her the scent of lemons and the splash of water, cool stone against her skin. Moments like that were hard; not touching his hand, not sliding her fingers up inside his sleeve, feeling the smoothness of his flesh.

She had known it would not be easy; her father—Manuel himself—had warned her. Still, it was hard.

"Read me a psalm," she said. The sound of his voice washed over her, soothing as the sound of water.

She persevered and, with time, the rabbi's grim skepticism gave way to grudging approval, even softened into something approaching warmth. Teacher and pupil grew a little closer, a little more like father and daughter.

Then came a day that surprised them both. The rabbi huddled in his chair, racked with coughs, shivering with fever, throat too hoarse for more than a whisper. And half a dozen boys waited at the door for their daily instruction.

"We can send them away," the rabbi's wife suggested. He shook his head, opening the book, reluctant to disappoint his pupils. He closed his eyes for a moment, his hand resting on the open page. Then he beckoned to Esperança. She leaned forward, trying to catch his almost inaudible words; stared at him, shocked as he repeated his muttered instructions, gesticulating fiercely. "There is a precedent," he whispered hoarsely. "Beruryah, the daughter of Rabbi Hananiah ben Teradyon. A worthy woman, who discoursed on the Law. You may speak the words for me."

Esperança picked up the book and placed herself by the window, screened by the half-open shutters. In the yard, the rabbi's wife pushed the students toward the window. Inside the house, the rabbi raised his hand and, voicelessly, began the lesson. Esperança, leaning against the window, spoke the words for him, giving the boys their cue. She was by now familiar with the lessons.

For a moment, at the sound of a woman's voice, they remained silent, startled, six pale youths with dark, shadowed eyes, uncertain what was expected of them. Then, hesitantly they began their recital. Unseen, only her voice reaching them, she guided them through the lesson. When necessary she corrected them.

Sun filtered through the shutters, throwing narrow lines of light onto the wooden floor. Warm, thick air flowed between house and yard and cobbled street beyond. The boys' voices rose and fell in singsong harmony. She could see just their covered heads moving as they rocked in prayer. At the end they chanted the blessing in unison. The rabbi nodded, producing something close to a smile. High praise indeed! Tears came to her eyes and she realized that she was happy.

Later, when the nightmare had taken over her life, thinking of that moment she recaptured fleetingly that sweetness and tears came to her eyes again. But not of happiness.

There were fewer days now when she stared at some new task to be learned, a new duty to acknowledge. Mastering Hebrew was an exercise she enjoyed. "How shall I sing the Lord's song in a strange land?" the Psalmist asked. She

added, "How shall I learn His ways in a strange tongue?"
But gradually it all became familiar.

And there was, finally, the ritual immersion, the trip
to the *mikveh* with the women, the windowless stone room,
the prayers, the green water closing over her head. She was
reborn—a daughter of Abraham.

She began to prepare for the wedding.

MANUEL WAS PRINTING maps now: his drawings of
the city, the crowded panoramas of houses, churches, and
clocktowers, had been abandoned for the sea charts that
showed the gradually emerging coast of Africa, the discoveries of new islands, new shapes looming beyond the boiling seas—first the mariners reached the unknown lands,
then they needed to have them drawn, accurately measured and named, for the next journey, the next step.

His dealings were with captains or their officers. Their
roughly marked findings, the calculations that accompanied them, the descriptions and logs and lessons learned—
all went into the construction of a picture of the world,
albeit provisional, one still in the making: the next voyage,
for those who returned, brought with it new information.
Sometimes, boarding a ship in the harbor, he encountered
the ordinary men, the owners of the hands and feet and
eyes that raised the rigging, searched the horizon, and kept
the vessel driving on.

For these men he felt a complicated mixture of compassion and envy; compassion for the privations they endured:
chilled, sick, hungry, and fearful always that the next storm
might bring them a watery burial. Envy, because he would
never share the journey that took them where no man

had yet dared to go. He would not experience the heart-stopping moment of sighting land when hope had all but gone.

The first man to see land on Colombo's first great voyage to what he called the Orient was a relative of Manuel's, his cousin Rodrigo from Triana near Seville. Visiting Faro to collect new charts not long after the ships returned, he made a discreet visit to the Jewry—the Spanish Expulsion had made *conversos* cautious even outside Spain—and gave Manuel his account of the journey, which began with an uneasy encounter.

"We were getting ready to sail from Palos, the last preparations made, when I saw approaching the town a crowd of travelers, some carrying possessions, others helping children and old people. I thought they might be pilgrims, but there was about them such a look of despair, such a dragging of the feet that I was puzzled. Then one of the men coming aboard told me they were Jews, expelled from Spain, making their way to Portugal. I thought of you, how fortunate you are to live here in peace and safety."

Perhaps to dispel the beginnings of disquiet, to stifle premonitions of evil days to come, Manuel turned the conversation back to the boat, to the great journey.

Once again he found himself veering between attraction and revulsion as the reality of the great adventure was unfurled for him like a sail in the wind, a blank canvas on which he painted for himself the life he heard described: the harshness of the sailors' daily existence, the meager diet, drinking water so foul that the wine they added to it could no longer disguise the taste. A thin floor mat to sleep on, sliding and shifting on the groaning planks as the ship dipped and rose with the waves.

A man here was reduced to no more than a beast of burden; there was neither time nor space for anything but the grind of work—no dreams of beauty or the thoughts that might come in the contemplation of the frozen canopy of the stars.

Yet Colombo himself, it seemed, was a dreamer; a man who spent hours gazing at the horizon while he murmured aloud to himself, not always in the same tongue. In the questioning, skeptical eyes of the sailors he might have spent his time more profitably checking his charts—

"He underestimated the distance," Esperança broke in from across the room, startling the visitor and surprising herself with her own words. *Where had they come from?*

"He underestimated the journey, yes. The men were mutinous. But even as each day ended without the promised landfall, he managed to convince us to continue. Sometimes I wondered if the man had secret powers: one day more, he would beseech us, a few leagues more. Journey's end was close, so close. Watch out for land, he kept urging us.

"I was going on watch and I rinsed my eyes with a few drops of drinking water to refresh them—though the water was so poisonous by then that my eyes stung from it. The admiral had promised a personal prize to the first man to call out that he had sighted land: there would be a fine silk jacket, in addition to the purse from the king. So we were all keeping a lookout, I from high in the rigging.

"After a while I saw a bird wheeling above me, followed by a whole flock of birds and what looked like a dark cloud low on the horizon, or I thought it might be a wave, my eyes were weary by then, but a moment later I knew for sure and I shouted land, land! And then everyone was shouting and laughing, and those not too weak or sick, capering about from high spirits.

"Afterward, though, the admiral told us he had himself sighted land, earlier, during the night, when he saw a far-off light moving from place to place. He showed us the log where he had noted this, though most of the men have never learned to read, of course. Well, that was good-bye to the silk jacket. And the purse."

But at least the return journey was more comfortable for the men. Colombo had noticed in the natives' huts woven string beds slung from the rafters, high off the ground.

"As well as gold ornaments from the natives' necks and nostrils, and fresh fruits such as we had never seen before, the admiral had also bartered bells and beads for some of their string *hamacas*—you cannot imagine the difference: how sweetly you sleep, swaying with the movements of the ship, away from the rats and beetles scuttling about the floor below."

But strange fruits and string beds were not what touched Manuel's soul: he listened, enthralled, to what seemed phantasmagoric tales—of the Sargasso Sea as dark as printer's ink, with its floating cloak of gold and green weed, so thick it seemed a man might walk on it, of fish that leaped high out of the water onto the deck, of the sheet of blue flame that hovered on the surface of the ocean by night so that the ship's prow carved its way through cold fire. He heard of painted natives, gentle savages innocently unaware of their nakedness; of terra incognita and the lure of the new horizon—aware that for him the only horizon to be seen was the one he saw from the waterfront.

Esperança, too, had become familiar with the water-front. A place she had once feared—noisy, surging with violence—she now saw it for what it was: a marketplace not only for fish but for men, the seagoing laborers who were there for the hiring, their lives worth no more than their sometimes uncertain wages. They stood about, clustered against the walls in groups, sheltering from the sun in summer, the wind in winter—they were remarkably susceptible to discomfort on dry land—exchanging tales of storms, misadventures, and injustice, while cheerfully offering themselves up for more of the same; waiting for whichever captain's mate was assembling a crew, calling aloud: "Seamen needed! Ship's boy! Cook! . . ." They had personal experience of the eccentricities of explorers, madmen who blithely set off in search of unknown lands, legendary islands that promised wealth and too often delivered death or death's handmaid, disease. So they were well placed to pass on news and gossip or advise a fellow mariner to avoid a bad captain or a jinxed ship.

"God save us," she heard one scraggy wretch confide to another. "Last one I sailed with, we were gone half a year. Went aground on a reef, ran out of water and wine, and ended up slaughtering the sheep we had on board and drinking their blood." He laughed, without amusement. "And we're still waiting for our pay."

But, volunteers or pressed unwillingly to serve, men would always be found. When the ship was provisioned and ready to sail, a full crew would be in place, even though they knew in their hearts that return journeys were always made with fewer men.

As she turned toward home, laden with fish, she noticed a man coming toward her, muttering fiercely to himself, heading for the waterfront: a shaggy, scarred man with pale blue eyes and graying saffron-colored hair—a sailor, she guessed, though dressed more showily than most, a

heavy gold chain draped round his neck, lips moving as
he mumbled his way through some inner argument. He
passed nearby and she felt a shock, like a blow, and thought
for a moment he might have struck her, but she was out
of his reach and he himself was far away, lost in thought.
Words sang in her head, a jumble of new horizons and
shipwrecks and steering by the stars—for a moment she
was lost, too. Head spinning, she turned to call after the
man, question him, but he was out of sight, melted into
the crowd, and the nonsense running through her head—
What shipwrecks? What stars?—faded and was gone. The
fish was heavy; she shifted the string bag from one hand
to the other and walked on.

✦

> Entreat me not to leave thee, or to return from fol-
> lowing after thee: for whither thou goest, I will go;
> and where thou lodgest, I will lodge: thy people
> shall be my people, and thy God my God:
>   Where thou diest, will I die, and there will I be
> buried: the Lord do so to me, and more also, if
> aught but death part thee and me.

The Holy Book could always be counted on for words to
fit the occasion, but Esperança felt that Ruth failed on one
count: it dealt with love, with famine and bereavement—
"thy people" and "my people"—it did not deal with the ones
bent on destruction, eviction, expulsion. It was no longer
death that dealt out the cards: it was men. Men in the uni-
forms of king and Christ, cleansing the land of otherness.

At first it had all seemed rather distant: an edict, conditions imposed, a date. For Jews, accustomed to living with

134

restrictions, interdictions, it was just one more to be dealt with, then lived with, bending to the wind of change like ears of corn, to spring up again when the climate grew calmer. But as the date grew closer, the conditions clearer, the full implications emerged.

How gradually it had come about, first the small fears of those long converted to Christianity: the king's men, walking about the city to sniff out secretly practicing Jews among the New Christians; noting which houses did no cooking on the Jewish Sabbath; climbing the tower to observe which chimneys were smokeless on the day Jews should light no fire. . . . The questions, the visits. Finally the decision that affected Manuel's family: for all Jews not baptized into the Church—expulsion. Why, she had asked one day, why is this happening?

"The king," he replied, "wishes to marry a Spanish princess. For her wedding gift she demands a Jew-free Lusitania. A Catholic princess holds out her hand to be kissed by her neighbor king and the long shadow of her sleeve falls on us, blotting out the sun."

In the synagogue the men discussed, debated, advised moderation; there had been threats before. This, too, would pass. Faro was not Lisbon; there had been no riots here, no Jews massacred. Life must go on. Though for others the Spanish Expulsion was too recent to wave away. If Spain, five years before, could take a broom to an entire community, why not Portugal? At Passover they read from the Song of Solomon as always, "Lo, the winter is past, the rain is over and gone; the flowers appear on the earth, the time of the singing of birds is come. . . ." But as the year advanced and the date approached for all Jews to convert or be banished it was Isaiah, not Solomon, who had the last word: "The harvest is past, the summer is ended, and we are not saved."

❦

IT WAS HER father who made the first move. She had been tempted more than once to creep back to the house, beg forgiveness for the hurt she had caused him, ask his help—for the sake of the children. But she recalled their last encounter, the bitterness, the chill of his voice, the door closed against her. She stayed away.

He came on foot—"No carriage can get down these alleyways," he complained without heat. "How do you manage?"

"It presents no problem," Esperança said dryly. "We have no carriage."

He stood on the doorstep, hot and out of breath, fanning himself. She thought he looked fatter, perhaps the new wife (not so new now) enjoyed feeding him. Did they still have banquets, dine off sheep with gilded horns, a roasted lark or quail decorated with gold and gems?

"Will you come in, Father?"

He stepped in, his bulk making the small room seem more cramped than usual. Seeing it through his eyes, she was aware how stark it was: what she took for simplicity must strike him as discomfort. She offered him one of the plain wooden chairs. He was looking at her, quick little glances, then away. The children played in one corner, rolling a colored ball of felt between them. She had sewn tiny bells to the cloth so that it tinkled pleasingly as it rolled from one infant to the other.

"These are my boys. Isaac. And Benjamin, the little one."

136

For a moment he watched them, his lost grandchildren, greedily noting that one had Esperança's sharp little chin, the other the line of her brow. With a suitable father they would indeed have been his grandchildren: he could have been dandling them on his knee, taking them for rides in his carriage; he would have bought them handmade playthings from Germany, wooden animals and music boxes. Instead they were strangers, like the beggar children he passed in the street.

"Are you thirsty, Father?"

His eyes brightened.

"I can offer you water," she added apologetically.

At home he would have clapped his hands for a servant to bring him cool sherbet or wine, or the juice of pomegranate and sweet plums.

She poured water for him, unaware that his eyes lingered on her hands—work-roughened—and, as she turned away, her body—shockingly thin. A father likes to see his daughter plumply rounded, smooth fingers showing off her rings. He saw with a twist of the heart that his golden girl had become a drudge. She caught his eye and smiled, and his throat contracted at the familiar curve of her lips, the eyes still bright with amusement.

He was brutally direct: "There is no more time to waste. The date is set. Your husband"—he could not bring himself to the intimacy of using the name—"will he accept baptism?"

"Of course not."

"You, as a Christian—"

"Now a Jew."

He glanced at the two small children playing in the corner. "Have you considered them? I have heard stories from

Spain. The king's men will do as they did there: achieve their ends by force. They seize the children, hand them to Christian families, even transport them. Those two could end up slaving on a sugar plantation on an island the other side of Africa."

"It will be different here; we are not Spain."

He was too agitated to remain seated but, having got to his feet, he found there was no room to pace the floor as he did at home. He stood frowning at her helplessly. "You must leave."

He sounded brisk, as though discussing a business arrangement, but then all at once the briskness left him; he pulled her into his arms and held her tightly, as he did when she was a child, when he could soothe her and hush away her tears. But now, though he fought against the weakness, it was his own cheeks that were wet. He could feel the frailty of her thin body. He was not strong enough to contemplate what lay in store for her.

"Let me talk to your husband."

She had been anticipating arguments, resistance; two strong men, each of whom believed he was right. And she would be pulled two ways, her loyalties divided. But nothing went as she expected: formal, even distant, the two men swiftly came to an agreement. She was unaware that Manuel, too, had heard stories from Spain.

He said, "I would stay. But I am not alone. I have a family."

The family now consisted only of a wife and two children. His parents had left Évora without a word to him—no longer their son—but through rabbinical routes of information he heard that they had been welcomed in Florence.

"We should be able to return when it is safe again, once the madness has passed," he told Gonçalves.

Her father and Manuel arranged the details: Esperança and the children would sail to Livorno, with Manuel going ahead of them to find a place to live—a cousin of Samuel's would smooth their path: a printing works was already established in the town. Manuel refused, for his part, the money that Gonçalves was anxious to hand over. For Esperança and the children, however, he accepted the offer of an easier passage. Gonçalves would purchase them a comfortable cabin, buy them privacy and safety.

When Manuel left, it was a hurried parting; they knew they would meet in Livorno before long. She took a flat gray pebble from the shelf and pressed it into his hand. "It shall be our covenant."

He held her close, aware, as Gonçalves had been, how small she was, how lightly the bones were covered by her flesh. For a moment he allowed himself to be filled with a sense of guilty anguish at what her love for him had led to. Had he stopped her first inquiry with an evasive answer; had he left Faro, as he had not had the strength to do; had he, finally, answered her crucial question with thought for her well-being rather than the truth, her life would have continued on its smooth course unchanged.

Without him she would be sitting in a shady garden, hearing the music of a fountain, clad in silk, her children cared for by servants. She might have grown matronly, rounded by contentment with an undemanding life.

But when she had asked, "Do you believe that love is as strong as death? Stronger than life itself?" he had answered in the only way he could: with a yes.

Now he felt terror for them all. The unforgivable sin of

despair engulfed him, but he pushed it away. "It won't be long. We'll be together."

Royal patience is a fragile thing, soon wearing thin. Conditions were already in force—banishment of all Jews not baptized by a stated day. The alternative: slavery and confiscation of all possessions. But as expulsion day came closer, the royal mind entertained what seemed a splendidly humane idea: reflecting on the melancholy prospect of what must surely be thousands of people condemned to perdition, the king decided that the children should be saved.

All children between four and fourteen years of age would be removed from their parents and baptized. After which, for the sake of their immortal souls, they would be separated permanently from their heathen families and given Christian homes.

Far from simplifying matters, this created a new problem for the king: too many Jews, it seemed, were now deciding to leave. Yet another change was announced. All ports of embarkation save one were closed to Jews: only Lisbon remained open.

For Esperança, with one flourish of a royal signature, the calm departure, the comfortable passage to Italy, disappeared. Her father's financial arrangement with the ship's captain in Faro melted like mist in sunshine.

Gonçalves, arriving at her door out of breath and red-faced, found her hurriedly putting a few possessions together. She said shakily, "I'm frightened now. For the children."

He did his best to reassure her. "Take the carriage. It will be ready in an hour and the driver will come for you. In Lisbon, go to Alberto's house and rest there. He will find a ship and arrange everything for you."

Uncle Alberto would arrange everything. Of course. How simple life was for the rich and powerful.

Gonçalves frowned at the bundle she was assembling. "I have a strong leather chest you can use for the journey."

How easily, she saw, her father had banished hardship and fear. And she gave thanks.

The driver came, bringing the chest. While she filled it, she saw him glancing round the room. She saw the look on his face: disbelief that she would choose to leave his master's mansion to live like this.

The chest was filled. He swung it onto his shoulders and she opened the door. She had been aware of noise, voices, the sound of people passing. She was unprepared for the throng clogging the narrow lane: men, women, children, the old and the young, pressing forward like a herd of frightened cattle, stumbling on cobblestones, pressed against the confining walls.

The driver was tall, heavy shouldered. He cleared a path for Esperança and the children, pushing his way through the crowd, knocking some aside as he went. One or two called out angrily after them. Esperança, carrying the younger child, keeping close behind the driver, drawn along in his wake, gripped Isaac's hand, pulled her shawl farther over her face and hurried on. Soon they had left the crowd behind as he led them out into one of the wide boulevards where the carriage was waiting. Esperança lifted the children and thrust them into a nest of soft cushions and animal skins. They bounced on the seats, laughing, enjoying the adventure.

The day was warm but overcast, the sun no more than a glare in a white sky. As the driver cracked his whip and the carriage began to roll, Esperança craned her neck and looked back. She could see the harbor and beyond it a

stretch of water as bright as the blade of a sword. She could
see the curve of the sea wall where she and Manuel had sat,
concealed, for that first conversation. The road crested a
slight rise and the whole town came into view, protected by
its encircling wall. Clustering close against the ramparts,
the trees began—almond and fig and oak. Far out beyond
the harbor a ship lay motionless, sails slack in the still air. A
man stood like a statue, gazing out to sea. The carriage was
moving faster now and the ship and the man on the sea
wall grew smaller. She wanted to cry out to the driver to
stop; she was swept with a certainty that the carriage was
carrying her away from a place of safety.

On the road out of town they rejoined the stream, some
walking, some on donkeys or pushing handcarts, others
driving mule carts laden with bundles and sticks of furniture. She felt a pang: perhaps she could have brought the
shelves of dark mahogany that hung on their wall—even
the little wooden stool she used—to give their new home in
Italy a familiar touch. With more time, she could have prepared for the journey, the new life ahead.

The driver cracked his whip, clearing a way for the carriage, urging the horses on through the crowd. Young men
carried grandmothers on their backs, mothers clasped infants and toddlers, seminarians and rabbis, accustomed to
a life of study, hobbled, awkward on the uneven road. The
crowd parted, unwillingly, as the driver yelled and urged
the horses on, and Esperança shrank back from the windows, mortified to be riding where so many walked, but her
father had been fierce in his warning: "If you offer a place
to one or two, there will be a riot. Think of the children."

It was already dark when they made their first stop, at
an inn where they rested while the horses were fed and
watered. In the sordid upstairs room, mice ran along the

beams, and the walls were smeared with the dried blood of
dead insects, swatted by earlier occupants. When Esperança
drew back the blanket, the bed seemed to be made of some
wavering, shifting substance: bugs, lice, and cockroaches
were on the move beneath the sheets, ready to fasten on
any unwary human hosts. She dropped the blanket and
drew the children away from the bed.

"You will sleep on the table. I shall spread my cloak for
you." She lifted them and they curled up together without
complaint. She sat in an ill-made wooden chair, watching
them, seeing how they drooped obediently into sleep. They
knew without the need of words that they should be grateful even for this.

As she sat, her hand resting on Benjamin's damp head,
Esperança could hear shouts and voices from below, calls
for wine and food, the occasional crash of a bench or table
overturning. Within the room she caught the tiny sounds
of mice and beetles, a whispering like the movement
of dust.

By dawn they were off, the road a slowly moving river
of humanity streaming toward the sea, which was their only
hope. In Lisbon there would be ships. In Lisbon there were
sea captains waiting to take on human cargo and carry them
to refuge and safety.

On the outskirts of a small town, the streets steep and
narrow, the procession came almost to a standstill. The
driver, attempting to force a path through the solid mass,
knocked into a donkey cart and the impact sent the beast
skittering sideways. The cart overturned. Screams of alarm,
shouts, a waving of fists—suddenly the mood of despair was
changed into one of brief fury: two young men pulled the
driver from his seat. Limbs flailing, he was sucked into the
seething crowd. Taking fright, one of the horses reared

143

and backed, and the carriage slowly keeled over onto its side, wheels splintering beneath it. The panicked horses, with no one in control, bolted, dragging the overturned carriage behind them, knocking aside or trampling anyone in their way until they slowed to a halt. Men wrenched open the carriage door, now tilted upwards to the sky, to lift Esperança and the bruised and terrified children from the wreckage.

But the worst had already happened: the driver was lost somewhere in the throng; the chest with all their belongings had fallen from the carriage and was gone. The carriage itself was wrecked. Afloat on a tide of panic, Esperança and her boys were carried along by the crowd. She knew they were heading the right way, toward Lisbon. But once there, what then? Surrounded by strangers, she was frightened and alone.

That night, along with everyone else, she lay down in a field by the side of the road, pulling the children close, wrapping the three of them within her cloak. No inn table this time, no bed to be spurned. Now the field mice and the ants and spiders might explore their bodies if they wished, while bats swooped overhead, blotting out the stars with their wings.

Before daylight they were on the move, people hurriedly crouching by bushes to relieve themselves. Another day, with bread and fruit purchased at twice the true price from townsfolk turned street traders and eaten on the move. Another night beneath a canopy of stars that no one found the spirit to admire.

It was when they reached the outskirts of Lisbon that she was forced to confront the reality of just how disastrous her circumstances were: she had no directions to her uncle's mansion. Her father's letter was lost with the chest.

Her plan had been to find a carriage for hire and simply order the driver to take her to the district where her uncle lived. But when she attempted this, the driver threatened to beat her off with his whip. She could see the situation through his eyes: a bedraggled, mud-spattered woman with two tearful children was not a likely customer. She had become, like the rest of the crowd, a threat to respectable people.

Standing by the side of the road as the others trudged past her, she found she was swaying on her feet and sank to the ground, keeping hold of Isaac and Benjamin, pulling them close. She leaned her head against a wall and closed her eyes, shutting out the sun and the dust. One or two women called to her anxiously, urging her not to get left behind, but their voices grew faint.

She stayed, huddled against the wall, until the last of the footsteps died away. She must find an inn, somewhere to wash and rest, and buy something to eat. With a night's sleep, she would have the strength to continue. Perhaps, if the little family looked cleaner, more respectable, a carriage driver might be persuaded to take them across town.

The inn, when they reached it, was better than she had hoped for: the bed almost clean, the food almost palatable. The children sank into sleep at once, while she paced the room, trying to think how best to plan the search for her uncle's house. Six floorboards across, ten paces, turn, ten paces back . . . with a shock of memory she recalled how she used to pace her father's library, the gleaming tiles, the woven rush mat, nine across, turn, six paces on the rush mat, turn, waiting for him to look up, the scent of lemon blossom drifting from the garden . . .

Stifled, she went to the window and leaned on the sill, looking down into the darkness of the street below, hearing the voices of the passersby: gossip about the price of meat, the celebration of a family wedding, the Jews flooding the city—

"Sleeping on the waterfront, like beggars, waiting to get on the ships—"

"Well, it's almost over"—an elderly woman yawned as she spoke—"I pity any poor souls left behind . . ."

With a lurch of alarm, Esperança counted the days the journey had taken. The night at the inn. The nights sleeping in fields. Tomorrow time ran out for the Jews of Portugal.

Early, before sunrise, she was urging the children out into the street. It was no longer a question of looking for her uncle's house: she must find a ship, a captain who would take them on. She could pay—well—thanks to her father. But there must be many in her situation, possibly too many; some might be turned away. She must not be among the last.

The streets around the inn led on to broader avenues; there were fountains, trees. In the distance a Moorish castle loomed high on a hill to their left, another hill rising on their right, so that the streets between formed a funnel leading to the great quayside described with such pride by her uncle.

These elegant streets were still empty and silent, the well-to-do folk asleep in their soft beds, so she heard the Jews before she saw them—a sound like the humming of bees. As she came closer, she could distinguish voices, calling out, moaning, children crying; the desperate ones trapped by circumstances or lack of money: those, like her, who were still on Lusitanian soil as the last of the sand ran through the glass.

From afar it looked like a field of flowers waving in the wind: people packed close, pushing, gesticulating, trying to find a way through a wall of flesh, confusion, alarm. Then, as the sun rose higher, confusion turned to chaos with soldiers surrounding the throng, driving them toward a large, many-windowed palace on the far side of the square. Here more soldiers, with a sprinkling of monks, were already dragging the bigger children away from parents, herding them into the church, to be baptized as the mothers shrieked in despair.

From the avenue to the right Esperança saw a sudden upheaval. The crowds pushed back as royal guards flourished lances; then cavaliers arrived on horseback and following them, surrounded by more guards, an open coach of gilded leather and gleaming silver wheels: the king had come to inspect his work.

Penned behind the barrier of guards, Esperança stared at the brilliant procession: at the silks and jewels, the furs and fine leather shoes cut in the latest fashion, the hats and elaborate hair. As her eyes reached the circle closest to the monarch she saw with a leap of the heart a face she knew. She screamed out, "Alberto! Alberto!" and he heard her voice, turning, startled, to see who in this crowd could be calling to him with such familiarity. He found her face, stared at her, perplexed, and was turning away when she screamed his name again, "Alberto! Here! It's Esperança!"

At first he failed to recognize her. Then she saw his face crumple and he reined in his horse, urging it closer to where she stood among the heaving throng.

"Help us!" she implored, hands held out like a beggar.

He leaned from the saddle and muttered, "Call out to the king. He can be merciful."

Slowed down, blocked in by the weight of his unhappy

subjects, the king's carriage moved through the crowd like a ship held back by the tide. Where they could be reached, more children were being plucked from the crowd and carried away. Fathers, attempting to intervene, were struck down by the guards. Cries of alarm and the sound of weeping filled the air. Esperança darted forward, ducking beneath the neck of Alberto's horse, and flung herself on her knees beside the king's carriage, dragging the bemused and frightened children with her.

"Your majesty!"

What she cried out she afterward could not recall; entreaties no doubt, begging him to let her keep her babes, so young, so helpless. There was a pause. She saw him murmur a word to his companion, then he waved to the attendants to remove the obstruction. A soldier reached towards them and she struck him aside, clutching the children, screaming at him to keep away. Alberto made one more effort, swerving his horse close to the carriage, leaning forward to observe, "Your majesty, the poor woman—"

"She howls like a bitch when her pups are drowned," the king broke in, amused. "Baptism is the only hope for these people."

As the procession moved on, she saw Alberto, twisted round in his saddle, staring at her with helpless sadness. The guard had fallen back for a moment and she darted through the crowd, bent almost double, close to the ground like a bird, trying to keep out of sight as soldiers continued rounding up people, driving them like cattle toward the palace on the far side of the square. In the distance more soldiers could be seen, lined up, cutting off the streets that led to the waterfront.

The royal plan had been modified once again: advisers

had pointed out to the king that to lose so many industrious, in some cases prosperous, subjects might not be in the best interests of the crown. Indeed, they might join his enemies abroad. Why not extend the forced baptism to the adults? And then prevent the New Christians from leaving. Indeed! A brilliant solution.

One adviser, more closely educated in the conflicting routes to God, pointed out diffidently that there might be drawbacks to this plan: for a devout Jew, baptism was worse than death. There would be many who would choose to die. No matter. A wave of the royal hand: the signal was given.

Now, trapped on the waterfront, the Jews had only two choices: to allow themselves to be herded toward the palace by the soldiers, or to cling to the quayside in the hope of escape. It was a matter of hours, perhaps minutes, of finding a ship before the king's men moved in to take the next consignment. Dragging the children with her, their feet barely touching the ground, Esperança fought her way toward the quay and the nearest ship.

The captain seemed agreeable, eyes bright above his graying beard, teeth gleaming in a smile. His price was high—more than she had in gold—but he accepted one of her rings to make up the sum and lifted the three of them on board. Not all were as lucky, waving purses, begging the sailors to take them, some crying, others in silent despair as the ship pulled away. Some threw themselves into the water, attempting to grab a trailing rope and climb aboard, briskly beaten off by the crew. The lamentations of those left behind trailed like a vapor in the sea breeze.

Esperança held the children close against her body as she watched the land recede. Across the wide square she saw the soldiers bludgeoning resistant Jews, dragging them away from the waterfront. Holy water glittered in arcs as priests baptized the captives like farmers cooling cattle. God was roughly served here.

On every side, it seemed, there was a convulsion of godliness: in Spain, devout women stitched holy tapestries, artists painted frescoes depicting the triumph of the True Faith. Now the Papal arm had reached the narrow slip of land that lay at the edge of the known world.

Portugal, too, had its artists, its voices raised in praise of the Lord. Where could the Church go next? Beyond the horizon, of course; it was a time of great discoveries and the sails of the royal caravels were tilting toward the beckoning sea in the name of God and gold, mariners carrying the Cross and the search for profit ever farther. And as for the king, with the country free of Jews, he was free to marry Isabella of Castile. A celebration was decreed.

In Florence, where Manuel's father was now working with other Jewish silversmiths newly arrived from Portugal, life was calm. But for true believers it seemed that worship was no longer enough. In the name of Savonarola, a cleansing of the Church was embarked on. Works of sculpture that could be considered to have a corrupting effect were being destroyed—in particular, statues of beautiful women—and one day a strange procession made its way through the neighborhood: a bell in the church of San Marco attributed to Verrocchio was taken down and dragged through the streets, condemned to a whipping by the city executioner, and sent into exile for ten years. God was clearly in need of vigilant defenders.

Meanwhile, behind the Vatican doors, plans were being put in hand: Portugal, still seething with sinners despite all its king had done, could benefit from the attention of the Inquisition. The Holy Office prepared to honor the country with its presence.

Men will burn and children cry. God's will be done.

⁕⫷▧⫸⁕

AT FIRST, RELIEF buoyed them up: gratitude for the means to escape. As the ship pulled away from the quayside, those on board gave thanks. Many prayed.

The ship was certainly overcrowded. Esperança saw that she and the children would be sleeping on bare boards below decks, conditions much as Manuel's cousin had described to them suffered by sailors on voyages of exploration. But, she consoled herself, unlike those explorations, this would be a short journey.

On the first day at sea, food and water were available to anyone with the means to pay. On the second day provisions seemed to be in shorter supply—certainly everything now cost more, though no one complained, even when the captain demanded payment for a cup of brackish drinking water, a scrap of mildewed bread.

Esperança settled Isaac and Benjamin in a corner, tucked her shawl round them and sang quietly until they slept. Then she went up on deck. The sun had set and the first stars were visible against the dark blue of the sky. She leaned on the rail, feeling the wind on her face, gazing up at the tiny points of light far above.

Next to her an old man, hunched and frail, studied the

sky, scanning the heavens so intently that he might have been counting the stars.

"You're admiring the beauty of the night," she said.

"No. I'm trying to establish where this ship is going."

He was old, she realized, and probably confused. "We are bound for Italy—"

"I think not. The stars are in the wrong place. We're following a curious route indeed. Last night one direction, tonight another. It would seem the captain is in no hurry to reach land."

Esperança felt a flutter of unease in her stomach. "Have you experience of navigation?" she asked. "Have you been a mariner?"

"I worked with Abraham Zacuto. The mariners relied on our calculations. Abraham should have been with me but he found an earlier ship leaving for North Africa; he had instruments and books to save . . ."

He was staring up at the stars again. "Ah . . ." He turned away from the rail. "I hope you have money for an extended journey." He nodded at the sky. "We have just altered direction."

Later that night, in her cramped corner of the hold, she tried to blank out the stench and the wretchedness around her by thinking back on the beauty of life as she remembered it. The comforts of home, the cherished possessions. And she found that it was not her long-ago silken gowns and shoes made of leather flimsy as rose petals; it was not the mansion with the lemon trees and fountain that came into her mind, but the little rooms she had shared with Manuel and the children. In her mind she revisited them, renewing acquaintance with happiness. Here was the tall cupboard the carpenter had made for her, with the three-legged wooden stool she needed to reach the upper shelves.

Gradually, through the years, with constant use, two grooves had been worn into the stool just where she stepped up to reach for a dish or a bowl.

One day, watching her, Manuel quoted with tender humor from the Holy Book, "'How beautiful are thy feet with shoes, O prince's daughter!'" Wryly she held out a foot for him to observe, clumsily shod in cheap stuff from the market, her soft skin roughened now.

"Still, the feet are beautiful, as is the princess," he said.

There was a carved shelf she had found one day, thrown out by a wealthy family and rescued. Dark, and rubbed to a deep glow with beeswax, it hung on the white wall holding a glass pot of flowers, a lump of cloudy, fragrant amber, and a flat, pale gray pebble that Manuel had picked up on the shore during their first conversation and handed to her. The sea had worn away a hole at its center, and Esperança had threaded a silk ribbon through it, and hung it round her neck beneath her gown: a jewel for her eyes alone. Later, she placed it on the shelf alongside the amber.

There was a narrow chair of mahogany wood from Madeira; the table where they ate and on which Esperança had spread out her books; the silver candlesticks they lit on Friday nights—lost when the chest fell from her father's carriage. So few objects, but by their presence pulling empty spaces into a web of comfort and warmth. If they could have taken their time dismantling it, giving away an item here, another there, selling a few, it might have been less painful. Instead, abruptly dispersed as they were, the loss of the nest left her with a hunger for what she had accepted as naturally as breathing.

Huddled, famished, exhausted, and fearful of what was to follow, she held the two children close to her and sang softly to them until they slept. Unable to sleep herself, she closed her eyes and reached back in her mind, recreating a lost world: the sheen on the wood, the tiny cracks. She smelled the fragrance of the amber with its cloudy glitter, saw again the groove her shoes had worn away in the stool over the years, silently recited the blessing over bread and wine, seeing Manuel's face in the candlelight across the table. Was it like this for the children of Israel, abandoning home, leaving hurriedly, bread unrisen, fleeing from Egypt? No, not the same: they were bound for freedom, their flight fueled by hope. Today's children were not hopeful.

By now the decks were slippery with foul slime washed from dark corners so that the unsteady passengers fell and lay among the spreading filth they had themselves created. A woman gave birth, moaning somewhere, unseen. Later her body was cast overboard by two sailors while a rabbi hastily recited the prayer for the dead. There were more bodies—too many to pray for individually. People were succumbing to dysentery, scurvy, and fevers of various sorts. Below decks the rats grew fatter.

Esperança tried to comfort the children; each night she sang to them until her throat grew too dry. The old man was right: the voyage was being deliberately prolonged. As the sun rose on another day of agonizing thirst, with the stench from the hold rising through the hatches like steam, it seemed to her that her surroundings had been transformed into a phantasmal vision of hell. To left and right of her, bodies were casually fed to the waves by sailors clearing the decks of unwanted clutter.

She had exchanged her last ring for yesterday's food and water. She had only her clothes left to offer and she hesitated: two days before, a woman had bartered a few garments for bread. Later the sailors, their attention caught by her pale arms and shoulders, had returned to drag the woman away as Esperança distracted the children's attention with old songs. Out of sight, she could still be heard crying out for help, pleading for mercy.

Along with the wailing of infants, the shouts of the crew, and the subdued chanting of those who could still pray, there was another sound that now became familiar: the sound of women screaming.

Esperança tried to sing louder, her voice little better than a croak from her dry throat, repeating the songs she recalled her old nurse singing in the garden a lifetime ago. Some she avoided: songs of milk and honey, of fruit trees weighed down by baubles of golden flesh, and lullabies of happy children playing with dolls and spinning tops. But she could still sing of spring rain that brought flowers into bloom and of stars in the heavens—stars that could be trusted to guide you on a journey.

In the fetid air, wiping greasy sweat from the small, pinched faces, she found it impossible to believe that these songs described what had once been the everyday; that grass grew, that birds sang, that water tasted sweet on the tongue, and that children slept safely in their beds.

She tried not to think about Manuel; the pain was too great. She had imagined him stepping ashore, finding a place for them to live, preparing to welcome them. But could he, too, be afloat on some hellish ship bound for nowhere? Or—as she had heard it whispered—thrown out onto some African shore to die of thirst or be killed by snakes? Her heart twisted in her breast like a knife, tears stinging her eyes. She blinked them away and

smoothed the children's hair: a weeping mother was
no help to anyone.

A storm, rough seas, had driven them all below deck,
packed close. Years ago, one of Esperança's cousins—a boy
with a look in his eye she had found disturbing—had told
her about a cellar full of rats he came upon once in a house
collapsed into ruin. He described peering down into the
dank cellar teeming with the trapped rodents, the darkness
seething. The rats had outgrown their living space and the
stronger climbed on the backs of the weaker, slithering on
the living, shifting floor. So it was now on the ship. She
found, waking from a brief and troubled sleep, that the
children had wriggled from within her circling arms and
were lying on top of others, close to them. They had not
been pushed away or shaken off, because their human
mattress was composed of corpses.

She pulled them away fiercely and washed them down
with sea water, though as it dried, the skin tightened, itching. Isaac's face was rosy: astonishingly, he looked well,
until she noticed sores had broken out on his neck and
groin, his healthy color a feverish flush.

That day she sold her shoes for a mug of water, gave
them most of it to drink, and dipped a rag in the remaining drops to wipe their gummy eyes and cracked lips.

She had a sense of darkness descending and she found
herself wondering which God to pray to, the new or the
old—were they not the same God, really, and had she be-
trayed both by rejecting the one she had loved first? Either
she had left God or He had left them and she could no
longer find it in her to praise Him as the end approached.

By starting the journey in her father's coach, Esperança
had become separated from her neighbors, people she

156

knew, and since the accident had been among strangers. Adversity, she found, did not always bind sufferers to one another: mothers wanted their children to live; a son would protect his own rather than another's frail parent. Survival was competitive. But on the quayside at Lisbon she had found herself next to a young woman from Lagos whose sweetness of nature had moved her. She had seen Rebekah share her meager food with a stranger; had watched her help elderly men and women to find more comfortable resting places than she had herself.

"I can see why God might choose to punish me," Esperança said. "I am an imperfect soul; He might consider me a turncoat. But what have you done to deserve such treatment? And these people who have lived their lives in obedience to His laws? And the blameless children? While those who are oppressing us go profitably about their lives. How can this be?"

Rebekah was attempting to create a small breeze to cool Isaac's burning skin. She waved the hem of her skirt to and fro as they huddled in an inadequate slip of shade on deck. "You are asking Job's question. Why do the righteous suffer and the wicked prosper?" She managed a smile. "The rabbis would tell you man's mind is so limited that he is incapable of understanding the ways of God." And Esperança, stroking Isaac's blazing cheek, agreed angrily that she was incapable of understanding the ways of such a God as this.

Absurdly, she continued to say the daily prayers she had learned to live by, telling herself that at the least it comforted the children

Next morning when they woke, Isaac was no longer hot and flushed. Now he lay, quite pale, his hand cold when she touched it. She wrapped him in a scrap of cloth, carefully folding it round his small body. Before she covered his face she laid her cheek against his. She felt a leaping where her heart should be: sobs were fighting to escape and she held them back, hard.

Slowly, she climbed to the deck, lifting Benjamin before her. At the hatch she paused and looked up and down the deck. The ship had become a floating hell, the air filled with shrieks and moans. The doomed sprawled where they fell and before long the crew, who would by then have eaten and drunk in their quarters, would come looking for corpses to rob and women to beat into submission, to rape, and, when it fitted their mood, throw to the fishes. She held Benjamin's hand and led him along the deck so that they could feel the breeze on their skin. She had developed a skill at becoming invisible and should have slipped back below by now, but she rested for a moment and looked out at the sea.

The sun, which blackened their skin and blistered their lips, was scattering diamonds on the blue green water. She recalled a morning, long ago, when she had glanced out of her bedroom window in her father's house at the jeweled, undulating surface of the sea. Later she had instructed a seamstress to sew tiny gems on to a silken bodice so that they would sparkle like sunlight on water when she moved.

She had stayed too long—the moment's dream had delayed her and she saw that the captain was making his way along the deck.

The captain was looking well. He glanced around, smiling, though his cheerful expression had little to do with the welfare of the passengers. His eyes brightened noticeably when reflecting gold or jewelry. She drew Benjamin swiftly toward the bow. Out of the captain's sight, they might manage to get below. She glanced back and caught his eye. With a tired certainty she knew that it was too late to escape.

Catching her fear, Benjamin began to whimper and she hushed him quickly. A crying child would be struck aside with a backhand, bludgeoned to the deck. Whether the violated woman survived was a matter of luck. If she screamed too loudly or fought back, the encounter would be fatal.

She stooped and lifted Benjamin onto her hip, wrapping them both tightly in her shawl, binding them together. He sighed and tucked his head close into her neck. She felt his breath, like the touch of a moth's wing, against her flesh. As the captain came toward her, she waited calmly for the ship to roll, for the deck to tilt; then, as it dipped to its lowest point, she leaned out from the rail and allowed herself to fall backward. The cool green water closed over them both, her long, sinuous shawl slowly unwinding, swirling in the water above them like a pale flame.

LONDON | 2000

IN THE DARKNESS she is brought to a stop. She hears the jingle of a door and opens her eyes. She looks into a café behind steamed-up glass windows. They go in. The man in the leather jacket draws out a chair for her and she sits, dully, not undoing the zip of her anorak, keeping her hands in her pockets. The plastic tabletop is speckled red and black, the walls are like old custard. She has been here before.

She feels afraid. There is something peculiarly threatening about being lost in the familiar, like walking on a snowdrift: at any moment the firm ground beneath her feet might dissolve, or shift, leaving her in midair, falling.

He comes back from the counter holding two cups, the tea dark and steaming, and sets them down on the table. "Here you are, Pops, this'll put—" He stops and pushes the sugar bowl toward her.

She shakes her head. "I gave up sugar."

"I didn't know that."

"You said you know me."

"Yes, but not so recently. The last time we talked you said you'd given up guilt for Lent. I didn't know about the sugar."

Across the small table she can see a few silver threads, dramatic against the black of his curly hair. His eyes are dark, shadowed. He is unsmiling.

Can she trust him?

"Can I trust you?" she hears herself asking. Useless question. Would he say no?

"Absolutely."

"I'm frightened."

She expects him to ask "What of?" but he says nothing. She waits a moment or two, then adds, "I think someone wants to harm me."

"Drink your tea."

He has not contradicted her. Does that mean she is right? Someone wants to harm her.

As though reading her thoughts he adds, "You're quite safe. I'm here to make sure of that."

She has been skirting the question, deferring the possibility of an answer she might find painful. Now she takes a breath and plunges. "Who *are* you?"

"Just someone who knows you."

"And that means I know you."

The steamy air of the café, the plastic table. A voice — "Here you are, Pops" — the rest lost in background noise: laughter and shouting and music, filling the air, filling her head. She gives a quick shake of the head and folds into herself. She is crying again. He fishes a paper tissue out of his pocket and tucks it into her hand.

"D'you know why downmarket caffs always have useless, nonabsorbent paper napkins on their tables? It's to

161

discourage the customers from blowing their noses on them. An attempt to maintain a bit of class—"

"There's somewhere I have to go."

"Finish your—" But already she is pushing back her chair, heading for the door.

They walk across the bridge, toward central London. She knows the way. She knows other things, too: she knows glass is a liquid that behaves like a solid, though not when you draw it out of the fire, a globe spinning on the end of the blowing pipe, a bubble of clear flame waiting to be changed into something rich and strange . . .

As she feels her way through the darkness, here and there are pricks of light like stars, small areas of illumination: glimpses, no more. Close up, these stars are revealed as pinholes, grow larger, big enough for her to read a name, see a face, glimpse a child kicking a ball in a walled garden. Water, dull green, and the sound of chanting in an unknown tongue—yet one she has heard before—"*Shema Yisrael . . .*" Hear, O Israel, the Lord is our God, the Lord is One. . . . Some light proves too bright as she approaches, hurts her eyes, and she pulls away, shaking her head, shaking it all off. The light is the brightness of pain. Pull back, into the darkness.

She folds and unfolds a cutting from the *Times,* photocopied in the library:

> Experiments on zebra finches have shown it may be possible to repopulate the brain cells without having to transplant them from other sources. Such a method would be enormously valuable in treating degenerative brain diseases.
>
> Every winter, songbirds grow fresh brain cells, ready for the spring when they sing to attract mates. In the autumn, these cells die off again and the

birds fall silent. Zebra finches lack this seasonal cycle, so experiments have been carried out to provoke it by selectively destroying the birds' song-related brain cells. Within three months the cells had grown again; the birds were singing.

A degenerative brain disease could rob you of your memory. Was that her future? To have no past? Or could she, too, like the birds, repopulate her brain?

She tucks away the cutting, shuffles other pages, printouts from the enigmatic screen that offers limitless information but withholds the answers she needs.

There is somewhere she must go. Her checkpoints are bridges, embankments, public libraries; walking her way across London, she has trawled reference books, journals, terminals, searching feverishly. She is still lost. But now there is the man, someone who claims he knows her, intimate yet remote, following her patiently—or is *he* leading now?

Could there be, for each moment in our lives, an unimaginable number of alternatives, parallel possibilities? Could they coexist? Could there be an infinite number of universes, all of them real? Could she have fallen out of one and into another?

Or has she simply lost her mind?

Pull back, into the darkness.

There is a moment when she begins to run and he lets her go, knowing that the river on one side, a wall on the other, will contain her. When he catches up with her she is pacing between embankment and brick wall, to and fro, hands out in front of her as though to push away the obstruction. Above her, the arches of the bridge are dark against the sun.

She says, "I'm like one of those rats in a maze. I can't find my way."

"You will."

163

Resentfully: "You know all about me then."

"No one knows all about anyone."

She beats her fists gently against the high parapet. "When did we meet?"

"A lifetime ago. On Madeira. You came into Funchal harbor off a cruise ship—"

She came into Funchal harbor. Off the cruise ship—

She stands, blinking at him in the thin sunlight. "There was music—wasn't there music?" *A wheel turning, high overhead, and a statue, a man on a throne.* "There were people jostling. I saw fires burning through the trees. The flames rose into the air."

Close down. Close down. Close down.

LISBON | *1855*

LISBON | *1855*

THE FIRST MURDER was hardly noticed. After all, a washerwoman, one of the invisible cogs that helped keep the wheels of comfort turning, was a very small item indeed. No one could be said to be much inconvenienced by the killing, not even her employers, for she had delivered all the clean linen and was on her way home when it happened.

The second, third, and certainly the fourth violent death came up briefly in salon conversation. Someone was killing washerwomen, waylaying them on the aqueduct as they made their way home at the end of the day; a local scandal. A robber—some talked of a highwayman—had killed four women. Most respectable people were unlikely to be familiar with the aqueduct, although they relied on it for their clean drinking water. A landmark that had proved solid enough to survive the great earthquake, it was hardly the place for an evening stroll.

The bookseller had described to Esperança the aqueduct's dramatic survival as the city fell in ruins around it: "The arches were sunk deep into limestone from Jurassic times; with that bracing, it stood firm."

He enjoyed picking over details, the overlooked footnotes to great tragic events, the small ironies of history, and he passed along to her items that might be of interest.

She confessed to a curiosity that could take her down unlikely byways. "I am interested in women's stories. From different times. Women of different sorts: the overlooked, the unconsidered."

"You are speaking of novels."

"No. True stories. Women keep journals, write letters. Scribble notes."

She was indeed curious: it was a fault, her mother warned her. "To interest yourself in the activities of people outside your own circle can only lead to awkwardness. They will be encouraged into indiscretion, forwardness, presumption. It will end disagreeably."

So she would not have been pleased to know that Esperança talked to their washerwoman. Worse, there was a day when she might have been seen wandering down by the banks of the Alcântara brook beneath the aqueduct, where the women washed the intimate garments and bed linen of their well-to-do Lisbonian customers, shouting amiable insults at passing townsmen, occasionally breaking into song, one singing a verse, the rest joining in the chorus.

Serafina, who did their washing, appeared early each morning, gathered up their soiled garments into a deftly wrapped bundle and strode off with it balanced on her head, to return at the end of the day with clean linen neatly folded and ready for the pressing iron. Sometimes a child came with her, solemn and silent, trotting at her heels to keep up with her rhythmic, swinging stride. Esperança could see him now, sitting on a flat rock, waiting without impatience while his mother worked, a toddler about three, dark curls damp with sweat, big eyed and solemn.

The stony, shallow brook flowed down the valley, the women, bare kneed, skirts hitched up to their thighs, banged and rubbed the linen, the water clouding white with soap. The banks on either side dazzled the eye with linen spread out to dry beneath orange groves and vineyards. Olive trees turned pointed silver leaves to the sun. Small houses were scattered over the bare hills and, farther off, the distant mountains hid themselves behind clouds. Out of sight, downstream, lay the Almada shore, the waterfront with its brawls and big ships, where men gathered, prayed silently, and floated into the open mouth of the sea and the teeth of the wind.

Cupped between the widening river and the hills, this sheltered elbow of water had a domestic, comfortable dimension; here women worked, their steady, industrious movements giving the rhythm of a heartbeat to the passing hours.

The impromptu singing, the splash and bubble of the brook water racing over pebbles, gave the scene a festive atmosphere. Up on the hillside the sails of small windmills whirled dizzily, looking like paper flowers from a country fairground. Impulsively, Esperança removed her shoes and let the cool water swirl over her feet. Serafina saw her and called a greeting.

One of the women, tall and hawk faced, beckoned her to join them. "You could give us a hand with the washing!"

Another waved an arm derisively. "What? Wearing silken gloves?"

169

Esperança joined in the laughter. She wore a deep-brimmed hat to shade her face from the sun; the sleeves of her dress covered her arms. She was pale, protected, like a delicate fruit wrapped in tissue paper. Around her the women, skin gleaming with sweat and water, underarms fuzzy, bodies untrammeled by tight bodices, were all flesh and pulsing veins. She felt dry, artificial, a semblance of a woman, not the real thing.

They waded to the bank in pairs, carrying wet bed sheets to be wrung out between them, twisting the cloth into rope, and Esperança was struck by their slow, sensuous walk, an almost dancerlike quality, as though they were moving to music. Serafina, weighed down with wet linen, picked her way across the stream, the sharp-faced woman sharing her load. "This is my friend Paula. She works as fast as any two of us."

The other laughed, showing a mouth filled with stained, broken tusks. She gave Esperança a considering look. "Menina Esperança. The one that likes to read books."

"How did you know that?"

"You'd be surprised how much we know. You can learn a lot about people from their dirty linen!" She strode on, up the bank, arms already straining at the linen, winding it, squeezing the milky water from the sheets.

High above them, seeming to touch the sky, the aqueduct loomed: long, lean, a stone beast that loped across the valley like a great hungry lion. Esperança tilted back her head and gazed up at its bulk. A man, his face cast into deep shadow by a broad-brimmed hat, was looking down, watching them. Then, as though aware of Esperança, he stepped back from the parapet and vanished from sight.

The water stroked her feet, liquid fingers, soothing. She stooped, holding up her skirt, to pick a round white pebble from the stream, gleaming, smooth as an egg. It lay in her palm, cool, its weight comforting. They had begun to sing again, of the burdens of work, the sad destiny of women and the faithlessness of men, a plangent lament filled with *saudade,* the ancient Lusitanian yearning, their voices echoing in the hollow of the valley. She played with the pebble as a child would, passing it from one hand to the other. Then she slipped it into her woven cotton reticule and dried her hands on her skirt.

EVEN FROM THE house Esperança occasionally caught sight of the aqueduct playing hide-and-seek between the trees. Set on a plateau at the edge of the city, the terraced gardens of the family mansion overlooked the valley. Between the two slopes the pale stone of the aqueduct stood out against the green of treetops and the muddle of fields, gaunt arches receding to a vanishing point beyond the hills.

Her parents had created a shady, fragrant setting for their quinta: an avenue of poplars led in from wrought iron gates; another avenue, bordered by shaggy palms, ended in a grotto of statuary and richly colored *azulejo* tiles. At the apex of these walks the house sat comfortably, not elegant, but welcoming, the natural habitat of a wealthy, sociable family.

Here, at the appropriate time of year, balls, banquets, and entertainments took place; musicians played, several languages could be heard as foreign visitors were introduced and a mother's keen eye sifted through the guests for a suitable son-in-law.

At these events Esperança's face was rarely other than

cheerful. Her manner was agreeable. She smiled. Meeting her, people thought her happy.

And for much of the time she was, indeed, what passed for happy. Only occasionally did she sense a dipping of the spirits, a lowering. Her father would probably have said she was in need of a husband, an article that to him signified the proper state of affairs for a woman.

She talked pleasingly and dressed well enough, if a little plainer than was the fashion, her dark, angular looks set off by the somber linen and fine cottons she chose. Glimpsed reading in a quiet corner by a window, her hood of smooth black hair bent over a book, she could have been a nun.

She wore spectacles these days when reading. The tiny print, the yellowed pages, had strained her eyes and she needed help to distinguish the increasingly blurred letters. Her mother had hoped this reading was a temporary passion, something that would pass, the way other girls engaged a tutor or a dancing master to guide them in the intricacies of the latest fashion, the newest ballroom craze. But books, it seemed, would not go away. And Esperança would before long be thirty: her parents saw that they would have an old maid on their hands—one attractive enough to draw the widower or returning traveler in search of a bride for his mature years, less appealing to the young blood looking for a breeding partner.

But it was at just those times when suitable acquaintances were invited, when new faces were presented to her, when she found herself in conversation with the latest pair of fashionable trousers that she felt herself flagging. It was on such occasions that she would, after a while, slip away and renew acquaintance with a favorite book. And, in due course, go searching among the city's book traders for something new and special.

At one of these gatherings Esperança found herself being questioned by an English writer recently arrived in the city, an amiable young man with bright eyes and a high-pitched voice who declared himself "utterly *enchanted*" by every aspect of "this *fascinating* country."

She led him around the salon—"Here is Mr. Beckinsale, from London"—introducing him to the young men he would doubtless encounter at a different salon the next day, murmuring mischievous indiscretions to enliven the occasion. She thought he should meet Luiz, who was gambling his inheritance away, "although no one is supposed to know," and Diogo whose family had a port lodge in the north and who sampled the stock rather too generously; there was Ricardo who collected French paintings and Sancho who planned a career in politics, "if he can find a rich wife to enable him to do so." And others—Afonso, a rejected suitor, now a friend; Salvador, who had a reputation for being witty and unkind; Pedro who was kind but dull—in short, her circle.

"And now you must meet the ladies, who are waiting to welcome you—"

But he had questions that must be answered first: "I have been hearing about washerwomen being *murdered* on your aqueduct. And no one arrested? Details, please: are they young or old, these women?"

Sancho explained to the stranger that a washerwoman needed to be young: the work was strenuous; the distances to be covered daily were considerable. "It is not a job for the elderly."

"And indeed, if you watch them striding off to the river," Ricardo added, "their vitality is very evident: their walk, the poise of the head; Poussin could have done justice to those limbs—"

"We make a bargain with these women," Salvador said languidly. "They take our dirty linen and we keep them in food and drink—a fair enough exchange, wouldn't you say? A trade that suits both parties."

"But why choose exclusively *washerwomen* out of an entire city? And how are they killed? Are they stabbed? Strangled? *Bludgeoned?*"

The English were known to have a morbid imagination, but there was little here to nourish his: the washerwomen had been thrown from the aqueduct; nothing more was known, at least in the salons of the well-to-do. Esperança felt a twinge of dismay: the women had been felled as they walked, like animals knocked aside by a passing cart. Alive one moment, robbed and dead the next. No more to be said. New topic?

In general, what went on in the streets of Lisbon, on the Chiado, in the Bairro Alto or Belém, was of less interest to Esperança than what lay between the pages of a book. There were so many books, so many histories, the people she encountered there, spilling out from the confining leather covers across time into her own world, more alive to her than the flesh-and-blood men and women she talked and ate with. But this was different. She had heard these women singing.

"This aqueduct: you say it's visible from here?" Mr. Beckinsale raised his eyebrows inquiringly, eyes wide with anticipation. She sighed.

Walking in the garden in the heat of the day was to be avoided as a rule, but shaded by the tall trees and a silk parasol, she showed him round. He talked with passion, running his fingers through his hair, staring about him, noting plants, decorative windows and tiles, admiring the stream that flowed beneath flowering pomegranate bushes.

Now and then a scarlet bloom dropped on to the fast-flowing surface and some poor trapped ant, happily feeding on the pollen, was carried away to a watery grave.

"I mean to swim in the Tagus and pluck oranges from the trees like Byron!"

Her smile was not altogether benign. "Well, not everyone approves of Lord Byron's little excursion, as I'm sure you know, Mr. Beckinsale: the French called it *'sa regrettable découverte du Portugal'* and felt he should have gone straight to Greece."

He was not deterred: "He was happy here, and so shall I be! I must visit Cintra's glorious Eden, as he called it."

"Go on foot then, on the aqueduct. It will take you all the way. But perhaps wait until you have some friends to accompany you."

Mr. Beckinsale had received interesting reports of the social experiences available in this amiable country: beautiful boys, young Moors—he hoped to make some new friends here very soon. But this was not the occasion to discuss the exotic possibilities of the city.

He reached up to a branch of orange blossom and inhaled the scent. "Ah, Portugal! Ah, Lusitania, as you called it once! So much beauty! The poems will flow, here!"

Esperança was tempted to warn him that not only had Byron suffered attacks of dysentery and been horribly bitten by mosquitoes, but in her opinion had written some of his worst verses in Portugal. "The scent of orange blossom can be as heady as wine, Mr. Beckinsale. Be aware—"

But he had moved on into extravagant praise of her country, so small—"half the size of England!"—which had discovered two-thirds of the known world, mapped its seas, created the *first* and *greatest* maritime empire. . . . The hymn of praise died away awkwardly in midverse and she knew

175

what he was thinking: "What went wrong? Why did this great empire crumble?"

To save him from embarrassment, she pointed out a section of the aqueduct that could be seen from where they stood. The top ran level with their view; indeed, a slowly moving figure could be made out, probably a tradesman carrying cabbages or eggs to sell in the city, gliding along like the mast of a boat.

"I *adore* the stone sentry boxes—they look like shrines for weary travelers!"

"There are, alas, no sentries or watchmen, Mr. Beckinsale. Otherwise the women would have been safe. Those are simply water inspection points."

He gazed across the valley, his face intent. "The washerwomen: are they killed at night? Morning? When?"

"On their way home."

With the money earned that day tucked into their skirts. And no woman would cross by night, which narrowed down the possible time.

"Around sunset I would say. On the edge of twilight."

She pictured the narrow walkway soaring high above the valley, the inspection boxes punctuating its length like little temples. How would it feel to be a woman alone, the shadows lengthening, the flaming sun occasionally obscured by a shaft of stone, its red deepening? And then, as the woman walks on, radiance fading from the sky, the sun sucked beneath the horizon, the presence of another person, more sensed than seen, coming closer. Her pace quickens, though that will not save her. . . . Or does she suspect nothing; the attack, when it comes, as heart stopping as a hawk dropping on a fieldmouse?

The guests departed. She sat on in the open air as twilight

176

filtered through the orange grove. From the house she heard voices, a laugh, the closing of a door. She felt the silence deepen around her but with iron gates and walls for protection she risked no danger here. She was conscious only of a sense of solitude. Darkness crept in between the trees; the leaves turned from green silk to black velvet; glittering fireflies darted overhead like falling stars. Then the real stars came out and she was called in to dine.

SHE HAD HEARD about the bookseller soon after he opened his premises. Ricardo described the place—a room so small that it could hardly be called a shop—long and narrow, shelves from floor to ceiling holding books, "at least, the ones of lesser value," Ricardo said, "the old and shabby ones. The rare volumes and manuscripts he keeps in chests, wrapped in the finest silk from India." He smoothed his dark jacket. "I should have liked to buy not only a book but some of the silk for a lining. When he throws open the lid the chest looks for a moment as though it is filled with mist."

Esperança's imagination was caught by the idea of old sea chests billowing cloudy silk, among which nestled rare books like boxed jewels, and it seemed there were indeed jewels to be found—gems of literature and printing. She demanded to be shown some.

Afonso arranged a book soiree: "I want to look at old maps and charts. But he can bring some items of more general interest."

The young trader seemed withdrawn when Afonso led him in, his manner remote, eyes lowered. He bowed briefly to the room and turned away, unwrapping books and charts.

Esperança scrutinized him for a moment. Then she crossed the room and stood, fingertips tapping one of the time-rubbed volumes.

Without preamble she said, "Surely I know you. What is your name?"

He was looking down at a book. "I am called Manuel—"

She broke in, "But where have we met? When?"

Then Afonso joined them and there was no time to say more. She accepted a glass of Madeira wine and began to examine some of Afonso's objets d'art.

Her host was showing her a recent acquisition he took particular pride in, but she could hear only a roaring in her ears, like surf on the shore. She glanced quickly at the bookseller: he was looking through some pages, frowning, troubled. Afonso waved his guests toward the table; it was time for the expert to inform and entertain them.

Volume after volume emerged from its wrapping: glowing leather, kidskin with a bloom like velvet, pale vellum. He spread them out, carefully opening the pages, a magician of the printed word, releasing color and patterns from confinement.

"According to Suetonius, Julius Caesar was the first man to fold a scroll into "pages" for dispatching to his troops in the field. There is a story that Alexander the Great died with a copy of the *Iliad* in his hand. . . ." He glanced up to find her staring at him and faltered for a moment, before continuing.

After the books came the maps, leading the elegant company across the globe to dangerous, faraway places, building a picture of navigation and the spread of the known world as, inch by inch, the empty places on the maps were filled in. Where, earlier, one might read "terra incognita" or "here be dragons," on a later map there was a newly named country, an island, even a continent discovered, though he dryly made the point that America or the Indies had not, in reality, been discovered; "It was simply the sea route to that place that was discovered. America and India were always there, of course, inhabited by their people."

He showed them an early coastal *portolan,* a *Mappa Mundi.* "And here is a chart drawn by Abraham Zacuto, who was appointed Astronomer Royal of Portugal in 1492, the same year Cristoforo Colombo set off on his first voyage of discovery with one of Zacuto's charts on board." He paused. "By the time Colombo set off on his third voyage, six years later, Zacuto had fled from Portugal to North Africa in fear of his life."

"Why? For what reason?"

The bookseller was carefully wrapping up the chart, brittle and dark with age. Esperança watched his pale hands smooth and fold the silk.

"Because he was a Jew."

"Well," Afonso said, "we live in a more tolerant age today."

Esperança glanced up at the bookseller. His face was impassive as he bent over the chart. Tolerant? Was that the correct term, she wondered? Surely "civilized" would have been a better word?

"One hears little of persecution today," someone commented.

The bookseller rearranged some papers and gave the smallest of shrugs. "There are ways and means, as in all things."

Afonso, possibly to make amends for what he realized had been a clumsy remark, interjected, "I thought Pombal had put an end to all that." He glanced round the room. "I'm sure most of us know the old story about the Marquês de Pombal and the Inquisition. When the king was persuaded by the Vatican to issue an edict that anyone descended from the Hebrew race should wear a yellow hat, Pombal went to see the king with three yellow hats under his arm, saying he wanted to comply with the demand but didn't know a single Portuguese of any note who had no Jewish blood in his veins. 'But why *three* hats?' asked the king. 'Well,' said Pombal, 'one for myself, one for the Inquisitor-General, and one in case your majesty should wish to be covered . . .'"

As though hearing the story for the first time, Esperança clapped her hands, "Well, bravo for Pombal!"

"Yes, *après tout*," remarked Ricardo. "He may have been a despot but he did put an end to slavery and invite the Jews to return."

"I thought we were here to look at books," one of the guests said languidly, bored with the turn the conversation had taken. "I don't imagine there is much Jewish literature to discuss."

A gleam of amusement lit up the bookseller's austere features. "I think one could find a few examples: Josephus, Philo. There was Nehemiah, who wrote a hundred and forty years before Xenophon; Isaiah, seven hundred years before Virgil; the Proverbs and Psalms, a thousand years before Horace; Moses, a thousand years before Herodotus. Even before they reached the Promised Land, long before a Greek lawmaker could have given such an order with any chance of being obeyed by the entire population, the Jewish law stipulated 'These words which I command thee this day . . . thou shalt *write* them upon the posts of thine house and upon thy gates.' I think one might suggest it is a culture with some literary claims."

He had spoken lightly, deferentially, but the earlier ease had evaporated. Afonso signaled for more wine to be offered. Guests, suddenly restless, found reasons to move about the room.

Esperança turned to find the bookseller fastening his leather bag and making gestures of departure, bowing to his host. "My apologies. I have to go—"

Esperança broke in, "I, too. My carriage is waiting. May I drive you home?"

Politely but firmly he refused and was gone before she could say more.

There was a moment's silence. The others began to exchange gossip, sipping their glasses of Madeira.

Afonso said sotto voce to Esperança, "I feel a fool."

"He's a Jew."

"Of course."

"You said nothing offensive."

"Well . . . retelling that old story about Pombal. Clumsy."

She patted his arm reassuringly. Before she left she made sure she knew where the bookshop was—in a little street in the Jewish quarter of the Alfama.

———

HE OPENED THE door and stood aside for her to enter. The place was as Ricardo had described it: barely more than a corridor, the walls filled from floor to ceiling with books. On desks more volumes were stacked, perilously balanced. Chests sat beneath the desks.

She had expected remonstrance, reluctance on his part to admit her: unaccompanied young women, even today, did not lightly visit the premises of strange men, but he stood aside, bowing slightly, and she walked past him. He closed the door and cleared an upright chair of books so that she could be seated. Neither spoke.

She looked at him closely: thin, slightly built, black hair that curled close to his head. His clothes were plain; he wore nothing that would set him apart in a crowd and yet he was in some way different. He had a quality that at first she could not define. Then it came to her: it was a sense of holding back. His stance, his manner, his expression, even the way his hands hung by his side, proclaimed that he did not regard himself as at home.

It was a day of humid warmth. The air in the little room lay heavy, smelling of old paper and, oddly, of smoke, as though all these vulnerable possessions had been through fire and survived. She found it hard to breathe and pressed the flat of her hand to her ribs surreptitiously. He noticed, quickly opening the small window, though the air that flowed into the room was no less warm, smelling not of smoke but of jasmine.

She tried, calmly, to confront the conundrum: she knew nothing of this man and yet she knew everything. The situation was clearly absurd.

On a tabletop near her chair lay a fat Bible, the grainy black leather of its cover worn fibrous and gray at the corners.

"You sell Bibles," she said.

"A few."

Her palms were moist, sticky, and she reached into her bag for a handkerchief. Her fingers brushed something smooth and round: the pebble she had picked from the Alcântara brook the day she heard the washerwomen's songs. She brought it out and studied its form. Wet from the stream, it had shone in the light; now it had a flat luster,

like unpolished marble. The pebble lay in her palm: as
cool as though it held water, heavy. Comforting.

She said, firmly, "Rational people do not believe in
supernatural phenomena."

He inclined his head, waiting.

"It is therefore . . . disconcerting to be confronted by a
situation which cannot be explained by logic or science, or
the laws of nature."

Still he waited.

Suddenly angry, she exclaimed, "Why do you not say
something!"

"Not everything can be rationally explained. How would
you *explain* the Resurrection? Your Christian miracles?
Lazarus? The Kabbalah is filled with references to the hidden or inexplicable. . . ." He glanced about the room.
"Here, for example . . ." His hand hovered over some
books on one of the low shelves and he drew one from
the pile. "The *Sefer ha-Bahir,* a twelfth-century Kabbalistic
work, mentions . . . possibilities of one sort and another.
There is, for example, the idea of *gilgul.* Revolving."

"Revolving?"

He seemed embarrassed, reluctant to talk of such fanci-
ful notions.

"Tell me," she said. "I shall listen, but it is improbable
that I shall find this . . . revolving satisfactory."

As he began to try and explain the idea of lost souls,
sundered, thwarted from fulfilling their destiny, searching
across time, finding, not finding, her skeptical severity and
his rueful grimace—expressing something of a lack of
conviction in his own words—suddenly dissolved in an unexpected fusion: the shared release of laughter. They were
caught up, helplessly, in what struck them both as an unlikely situation. The laughter trailed away and he began

moving from one bookshelf to another, ill at ease again, turning away from her sharp gaze.

She dropped the pebble back into her bag and put out her hand. "For heaven's sake, Manuel, stop revolving. Sit down and talk to me."

THE WASHERWOMAN WAS at the house early in the morning as usual to collect soiled garments. She passed quite near to where Esperança sat in the shade, drinking coffee. She sniffed appreciatively and nodded at the coffee-pot. "Good?"

"From Brazil."

"Ah. Does it still belong to us?" Serafina shrugged. "I say 'us'; some of my family were sent off to work on the plantations early on. As good as slaves. None of them ever got back to Lisbon. But a lot of people got rich, didn't they? Ships using coffee beans in golden coffers for ballast, I heard."

Esperança poured coffee into a cup and held it out to Serafina.

The girl was tall, with strongly muscled arms and legs, burned almost black from the sun. Her face was coppery, dark as a coffee bean. Only her hands were pale: the skin rough, papery white from the water and the harsh soap, the rubbing and scrubbing. She lowered the bundle of clothes from her head and accepted the offer without comment, sipping, savoring.

"Do you ever walk across the aqueduct, Serafina?"

"The first bit, of course. I'd take half a day to get home if I went any other way. It's not much more than a mile. Otherwise I'd be running up to the Alto, down into the

184

vale, and up to the city again." She paused and gave a grin. "You've been hearing about the killings. It'll be some drunken sod, maybe a sailor who needs a few coins to keep him in liquor till the next ship sails. We're keeping our eyes open."

A few yards away the child waited; Esperança saw that he was staring at the small cakes by the coffeepot. She held out the plate and he came forward slowly, took one of the cakes, choosing thoughtfully, and bit into it with care.

"Say thank you to the lady, Fernando," his mother instructed sharply and the child removed the cake from his lips long enough to whisper his thanks.

The washerwoman finished her coffee, swung the bundle up onto her head, and continued on her way to the gates.

Esperança watched her go, the scuffed bare feet hardened by the stony tracks she walked each day, the upright body with the heavy bundle balanced so perfectly on her head. And her walk, that fluid, swaying movement, which gave the impression she was wading through water. There was an animal quality to the controlled energy, Esperança thought, like a lion's loping stride.

"Be careful!" she called out, not quite sure what she meant.

The girl half turned and smiled. "He'll take care of me!" she called back, giving an affectionate cuff to the curly head level with her knees. The child, too, looked back, laughing, a low, husky chuckle, and waved good-bye to the lady, as his mother told him.

From the house a maid came looking for the young mistress: instructions were needed regarding a dress, shoes, coiffure. Yet another formal evening lay ahead. Esperança sighed and gave her attention briefly to the details.

185

She was docile enough, continued to attend the banquets, balls, parties as required. She occupied her proper place in the pattern of the household life; it was mildly irksome, but it left her free to spend much of her time as she wished, though the family was unaware of this, seated at a table in a cramped, airless room, engaged in passionate conversation with a Jewish bookseller.

That night her mother glanced down the dinner table past the floral centerpieces and silver candlesticks to where her daughter sat, head inclined toward a guest. Esperança, looking up, caught her eye and smiled affectionately. She knew what her mother was thinking: the girl spends too many hours with her old books. In fact, it was not quite that: her mother was indeed thinking that she spent too many hours with books. But, the older woman was honest enough to admit, the girl looked happy. Indeed, she looked tonight as though a light shone within her.

Sitting in the garden later, as darkness painted its way across the sky, Esperança heard the squeak of bats above her head. A dog howled somewhere, yelped as a well-aimed kick hit home. Improbably, an African lion roared in the night. A family in a nearby mansion had bought it from an itinerant trader and kept it chained in a corner of the garden, fenced in with decorative iron bars, behind some orange trees. Occasionally guests would be shown the lion, as an amusement. Esperança heard it roar, heard in its hoarse, throaty snarl a sadness: this was a chained creature's *saudade*, a longing for his home, a yearning to be free of his shackles. Perhaps next time, if wild beasts enjoyed the privilege of *gilgul*, the lion might find himself back in Africa. She must remember to ask Manuel about the place of animals in the Kabbalah. Picturing him, with the frown of concentration he brought to her questions, the straight-faced reply, however absurd the enquiry, she began, without realizing it, to smile.

———✦———

SHE HAD BEEN thinking again about Mr. Beckinsale, the English writer, with his extravagant praise of "this tiny country," his admiration for the seafarers who created the "first" and "greatest" maritime empire. . . . She put it to Manuel: "He was about to ask the awkward question and then his English manners prevented him from embarrassing me, but we both knew what he was thinking: what went wrong? There we were in the fifteenth century, taming the wilderness, piercing the clouds of fear that obscured the horizon, and then this—what? Loss of nerve? This falling off, this draining of energy? What could I have said to him if he *had* asked? How do you explain what happened?"

He was diffident, showing her history books, tracing the rise and fall of reputations, decisions good and bad, Messianic dreams, the myth of Sebastian, the lost king.

"There are circumstances that encourage stagnation: give people too much wealth, slaves, conditions where corruption becomes a way of life—decadence follows. . . ." He paused. "And then . . . some people would say my view is bound to be partisan, of course, but I think the crucial step was taken when a Portuguese king faced with an ultimatum from the Spanish princess he was determined to wed confronted the Jews with an impossible choice: Christianity or expulsion. A few converted; some were killed resisting the violence of forced baptism. Most fled.

"Losing an ingredient diminishes a dish. Losing a part alters the whole. Individually, they seemed unimportant.

187

But when they left, something went with them. Some . . . energy departed, some odd aspect of the national genius was suddenly absent. Where there had been goldsmiths, cobblers, thatchers, doctors, there was a dearth. The gold poured in from across the sea, but there was no one with the skills to invest it, keep it moving. And there were other losses. Here an astronomer, there a mathematician. These were missed. Nobody, of course, missed the Jews. As such."

From one of his cluttered shelves he drew a battered tray holding old typeface, neat wedges of wood, each topped with a brass letter: ע . . . ם . . . ה . . . א. "This came from Faro. And here is a specimen of incunabula, their early work: the rarest, a few pages from a Pentateuch considered by bibliographers to be the finest specimen of Hebrew typography of the fifteenth century.

"They picked the type, set it out, pressed words onto paper, folded the sheets, and cut them, folio, quarto, octavo . . ."

He reached for another tray, holding typeface more familiar to her, and lifted a handful of the tiny blocks from the tray, laying a line of them out on his palm. Then he took a block and replaced it in the tray. "But take just one of those small shapes—an 'e' say—and remove it from your page. More noticeable than you would think? Now"—he took two more letters—"shall we say we'll do without these? J . . . E . . . W . . . The page is no longer the same: here a void, there an absence; the scene is changed. And so it was. A map remained incomplete, some boots lay unfinished. There were journeys untaken, merchandise lost, links broken. . . . Not a tragedy, you could say, those people were expendable. And yet."

As usual, the room was airless. As usual, he apologized

188

and she agreed that his premises did indeed have shortcomings.

She reached for her cooling pebble and pressed it to her throat. They were silent for a while as he checked a scribbled list and assembled books on the table. "I may look for new premises. Something—"

"—with a courtyard? I could bring you a lemon tree from my garden. Or if there were a roof terrace we could enjoy an occasional breeze. I might visit at sunset and watch the first stars appear."

"I shall consider those practical requirements when I search the city."

"Is this place too small now? Are you becoming successful?"

"To an extent. There is a fashion for the antique. Books and objects. I benefit from this new yearning for the old."

He was assembling a stack of richly bound volumes— "Desirable, though they have no particular merit but their beauty," he told her.

"Dear Manuel. Only you could regard beauty so lightly. Most of us long to possess it, if not, alas, in our persons, then in our possessions, as if some of that precious quality could be reflected onto our indifferent surfaces."

"Your surface," he said, "is as smooth as alabaster, golden as honey, as soft as the flesh of a peach—"

"And you are as silver-tongued as Solomon. What would my dinner companions say if they overheard such immoderate language?"

"They would banish me, of course. There is a precedent."

"We live in more civilized times."

Instead of replying, he passed her some handwritten pages. "You were asking about the earthquake . . ."

"Ah! Have you found me something?" She began to leaf through the pages.

The great catastrophe intrigued her: a mere hundred years before, yet the descriptions, written at the time, conjured up a world, a calamity as distant as Pompeii. She read aloud:

> All Saints' Day, 1 November 1755. Candles lit, the churches full. Women busy in their kitchens, preparing food . . . At about ten o'clock in the morning, I, Thomas Jacomb, merchant, in my country house in the Prazio in Lisbon felt the commencement of the earthquake . . . the earth shaking so much I could hardly stand and making so great a noise imagined it must be the day of Judgement. Two or three minutes during which through the falling of houses arises so great a dust that thought I should have been suffocated . . . In about fifteen minutes another shock, half an hour, another, about twelve but none so violent as the first. Many sick, many maimed and wounded from the fall of houses, some dead, women half naked . . . coaches, chaises, carts, horses, mules, oxen, some half buried underground, many people under the ruins begging for assistance. Many groaning underground . . . They say above forty thousand destroyed, buried, or burned alive. . . .

Manuel had found letters, eyewitness accounts of the event. Here, between the appalling statistics of death and destruction, lay the individual experiences; dead souls sprang to life as the city crashed about them:

> Yesterday several were hanged in Lisbon for robbing and plundering, in particular a Frenchman, an Italian, or Spaniard who confessed at the Gallows had set fire to the city in four different parts that they might plunder and rob the easier . . . fierce and scavenging dogs in the streets . . . the most populous street in Lisbon is now a mass of

broken ruins, a harbor for thieves, owls, and goats;
in short, the seat of desolation.

"There are others," Manuel said, "but this is for you,
one of your overlooked, unexamined women: it's the journal of a young girl, a novice in the convent." He handed
her a bundle of pages.

Esperança seated herself at the narrow table, put on her
spectacles, and brought the faded pages close to her eyes.

> I was washing up the tea things when the dreadfull
> afair hapned. Itt began like the rattling of coaches
> and things befor me danst up and downe upon the
> table, I see the walls a shakeing and a falling down
> then I up and took to my heells with Jesus in my
> mouth and to the quire I run, thinking to be safe
> there but there was no entrance but all falling
> rownd us and the lime and dust so thick there was
> no seeing. . . . Shakes and trembles all the day. The
> city nothing but a heep of stones. . . . Priests run
> wildly about the streets with crucifixes crying out
> repentance and confession.

The pages sprang apart, unbound, and Esperança
found herself searching, sifting through them, to continue the story. Instead, she found austere statistics:

> All prisoners set free and a general pardon, but in-
> credible the barbarity caused by Superstition, en-
> thusiasm, and bigotry. The Jews who were in the
> Inquisition and in a few days an Act of Faith was to
> have been published. For them to suffer now tyed
> on horses and sent with a guard to Coimbra . . .

"Even an act of God like the earthquake was not, it
seemed, enough to save the Jews from the toils of the Papal
workers," Manuel commented dryly. "In fact, it concen-
trated their attention; some Catholics began suggesting
that heaven had punished the city for suffering so many

191

heretics to dwell in it. But the English church was the only one undamaged. So they decided it must be the Jews and Freemasons after all . . ."

She read on.

> One moment has reduced one of the largest trad-
> ing cities to ashes and killed, maimed, and reduced
> to poverty and misery above five hundred thousand
> souls without a house to shelter themselves in.
> Lisbon in ruins, shrieks of buried people, and
> flames advancing down the street. In a jeweler's
> shop, gold and silver run together to create a new
> metal, a precious lava, and presently came a huge
> wave which carried away the quay with a hundred
> and fifty people on it.

As she read, Esperança in her mind inhabits the streets like a ghost among buildings that shift, collapsing onto themselves, every stone in the walls separating each from the other, some grinding like mill wheels . . . beams, masonry, a roof imploded so that it seems the jaws of the earth have opened and are crunching up the house from below. . . . Like the novice, she feels the heat of the leaping flames, smells the burning flesh, hears the cries of agony.

Tormented by the calls for help that come from all sides, the novice ventures from the cloister into the city streets. Terrified herself, she knows she must try and help others: this must be God's will. Around her lie broken bodies, severed limbs, remnants of clothing, smashed tables and chairs, scattered in the streets like some vision of hell. She helps a woman, trapped by wooden beams, to free herself, though the bones of her feet are broken so that she goes crawling on hands and knees down the street.

The man's voice is so faint that she might have missed it altogether but for a momentary pause in the distant uproar. Then, close at hand, she hears someone crying out—a

192

piteous moaning coming from beneath the ruins of a house—calling on God to end this new affliction, to deliver His people from their suffering and she calls through cupped hands, "Is there someone below?" and he answers, "Heaven be blessed! A living soul."

He is hidden from her, trapped in a black chasm under the ruins, beneath the shattered frontage of the house. She calls to him that she must get help but he stops her, gasping that he is killed already, crushed by the rock, but if she can stay with him till the end, it will ease his last hour.

They are invisible to one another, he trapped below, she kneeling at the edge of a pit filled with broken stone that groans, still moving. White dust fills the air between them. Only their voices connect.

"Shall I read to you from the Good Book?" she calls down, at a loss. "I have it with me."

"By and by," he says. "When the moment comes." He coughs, clearing his throat of the choking dust. A cobbler, he was on his way to deliver a pair of boots to a gentleman when the catastrophe struck. "No need for fine boots now." He draws a breath, a liquid bubbling sound that frightens her. For something to say she tells him she met a cobbler not long before, one who came to the convent to make boots for the nuns—

"But that was me! If you're from the convent by the hill. I came and measured you all for your winter boots—"

"You made us good boots," she says. "I'm wearing mine now. So soft it seems almost sinful. One Sister said boots should be rough to the skin, and ugly, to keep us from vanity."

When the cobbler was summoned to the convent a curtain had been drawn across the room, behind which the Sisters gathered. He knelt before the curtain and in turn the Sisters seated themselves on a wooden chair, only their feet visible to the cobbler, for measuring. This was a new refinement: the previous Mother Superior had simply ordered the requisite number of boots for winter, sandals for summer. Whether they fit or not was a worldly detail that did not concern her. Her successor, feeling pity for pinched toes and blistered heels, had called in the cobbler.

He took note of each pair of feet; some broad and flat, some bony, others arousing pity, swollen with bunions. And then, beneath the curtain, he saw perfection, set off by the stone slabs of the floor. Long and slender, the instep high-arched, each toe in perfect alignment, fine ankles, and below the ankle bone, on one foot, a tiny birthmark in the form of a crescent, like a new moon.

Reverently he took her foot into his hands, cupping the heel. "You have narrow feet," he murmured and she whispered back, "My mother's family . . . I hope it will not cause you extra trouble."

She must cause no one trouble. Life in the convent was hard: plain food and little of it, work, prayer. She was used to work and she found the prayers of increasing comfort. Certainly as a life it was preferable to the one she would have faced, drudge to some rich family or married off to a man chosen by her father, a man whose weight would crush her body as his authority would crush her will. God's wishes were more delicately conveyed: fear the Lord and praise Him . . .

The cobbler took the measurements, lingering over each calculation, awed by the harmony of muscle, skin, and bone.

Now, the words eked out with painfully snatched breath, he confesses he had loved the unseen nun for her beautiful feet. "On her boots only I fixed a small gold ornament, a crescent like a new moon, to echo the birthmark on her ankle; a tribute—hardly visible, for I supposed decoration would be regarded as vanity. I myself am a Jew and therefore the Catholic vanities are not something I understand."

The novice, kneeling by the pit, peers into the depths to try to see the doomed man, but can make out only the pale oval of his face. One arm is free, raised above the rubble, stretched out now, toward her. She lies flat alongside the crater, reaches down, and feels for his hand. When she touches it, the skin is hot, filmed with liquid, whether sweat or blood she is unable to tell in the flame-filled darkness. Through the uproar around them, she hears the liquid rattle of his breathing. "I am comforted by your voice." His own is a croak, barely above a murmur. "Read to me from the book, but from the old part, not the new. Isaiah, if you can find it."

Even with the light from the fires reflecting off the broken stone it would be impossible to find her way through the flimsy pages. She recites from memory: "'Terror, and the pit, and the trap, are upon thee, O inhabitants of the earth. And it shall come to pass that he who fleeth from the noise of the terror shall fall into the pit—'"

She stops in dismay. This will not comfort the dying man. But a muffled laugh filters through the dust. He tells her to continue.

"'And he that cometh up out of the midst of the pit shall be taken in the trap. For the windows on high are opened, and the foundations of the earth do shake; the earth is broken, broken down, the earth is crumbled in pieces, the earth trembleth and tottereth; the earth reeleth to and fro like a drunken man and swayeth—'"

His hand, still gripped in hers, begins to shake, like that of a man with the ague, then stills. His fingers slip out of her reach.

"Cobbler?" She peers into the blackness. "Cobbler! Your boots are the only beautiful thing I have ever owned. When I caught sight of the little crescent I thought you must have done the same on all the others, but then I saw it was on mine alone. May the Lord forgive me, I was proud of my boots."

She leans down, stretching into the darkness, trying to find his hand, distinguish his face. There is a movement below her: a sudden shift in the balance of the huge lumps of masonry and the whole gaping chasm collapses into itself. She leaps back, then kneels again, and recites aloud a prayer for the dead man. As a heathen he would not have been allowed in the graveyard, but she can pray for his soul.

The flames are spreading as she hurries away, back to the convent.

Among the papers on the bookseller's table, Esperança found the page she had been searching for, found her novice again: "The city is nothing but a heep of stones . . . the convent stands. We layde under a pair tree covered over with a carpett for eight days, giving thanks for our deliverance . . . and all this time the fires raged."

The print was blurred again, but the cause was not her eyesight.

※

SHE HEARD THE news from her maid Graçia: "A highwayman has been caught: a man from the south, a known criminal." The latest victim had, it seemed, fought back, kicking and screaming, and for once, others had been near enough to come running. The man was apprehended, jailed, awaiting trial.

The arrest set off a carnival of relief among the washer-women: the songs more cheerful, the women laughing. Only now did they acknowledge the fear they had walked with daily over the past weeks. In the big houses the linen was collected as usual; most people were unaware of the lifting of spirits, as they had been unaware of the gloom that preceded it. For Esperança, too, the episode receded: sad, shocking, but now resolved.

She accepted an invitation to Cintra, for a fête-champêtre organized by Ricardo in the gardens of the new Palácio Pena, a structure that Esperança found amusing, "but which those of more delicate sensibilities—such as I," Ricardo admitted with mock regret, "find vulgar, grotesque, and about as regal as a German brothel."

They drove through the outskirts of town towards Cintra. Esperança glanced up at the aqueduct, marching across the valley, the stone bleached pink by the sun. With the threat removed, it seemed now more graceful, less ominous, than it had. One of these days she might go down again to the brook and listen to the washerwomen singing.

In the palace gardens food was laid out in fantastical patterns on tables set beneath striped awnings; musicians wandered the shady paths dressed in minstrel garb, playing lutes and fiddles. Here and there Ricardo had set up *tableaux vivants* with actors recreating scenes from Watteau: through the trees came glimpses of eighteenth century satin and taffeta, fragile slippers, silk stockings, and floppy velvet hats, as beautiful women and handsome men lolled and whispered, laughed and dozed. Occasionally a ray of sun would pierce the frothy treetops and gleam on a glittering buckle, pearls on a slim wrist. Grace, elegance, sylvan setting; it all conjured up an idyll of ease and pleasure, where poverty did not exist and no one grew old or sick. In another clearing a group of anachronistically classical shepherds lounged round a stone monument. Somewhere farther off a musician strummed a mandolin.

Esperança shook her head admiringly. "*Et in Arcadia ego.* You are an artist, Ricardo."

He waved away the suggestion. "Watteau and Poussin are the artists; they said it all. I simply pay tribute." He took her arm and led her past a laughing group threading flowers into daisy chains. "Don't you think that in our way, we, too, are spinning away our days as though they will last forever? We are trapped in a very Lusitanian turmoil: local wars and sieges, uprisings and assassinations, tumult and unease, the empire slipping away, the monarchy—well, I think fragile is the word—but we sip our wine, our fingers hover over a ripe fig, and we take for granted our daily clean linen. Watteau was dead before he was forty. I wonder if I shall be as lucky."

"Ricardo!"

"We are all doomed, my dear. That is the way the tableau ends. Now: some sherbet? A daisy chain for your hair?"

As they approached the tables, she heard one of the guests, an Englishman, bemoaning the unrest, the country still quaking from political upheavals. . . . "Our man in Lisbon," she heard him exclaim, "told me—'Sir,' said he, 'if it had not been for the Inquisition, this country and Spain, too, would be overrun today with witches and Jews!' What do you say to that?"

SHE ALWAYS CALLED in to the little blue boudoir where her mother worked at her embroidery in the afternoon. It was a way of exchanging information, asking questions, and expressing preferences without seeming to do so. There might be a cushion cover or sampler to admire, some new silks to exclaim over, and Esperança would catch, between the spoken words, the inflection of her mother's displeasure or delight; a hint of her father's wishes; their reaction to her rejection of the latest approved suitor. Thus, confrontations were avoided and views aired. "Civilized," Esperança would have called the experience, if asked.

They sat for a few moments, the older woman placidly spearing the fabric, her needle injecting the somber cloth with brilliance. "You may find the servants a little . . . upset this evening. There has been another of those killings."

"But the man was caught!"

"So everyone thought. Well, it seems we were wrong—or rather, it seems there is another, who also preys on washer-women. Unfortunately, in this case, our own—"

"Not Serafina?"

Her mother looked surprised. "Was that her name?"

But Esperança had left the room, running down the wide stairs, through the hall, to the kitchen. She heard the babble of voices, stilled as she pulled up in the doorway.

Their faces turned toward her; they waited for some instruction, some order that must be carried out without delay. She saw tears on some cheeks, an expression of shock, dismay in their eyes.

"Serafina. . . ," she began.

The cook answered her unasked question.

"The aqueduct my lady. They found the bodies this morning."

"Bodies? More than one was killed then?"

"The child was with her."

Her grief took her by surprise: they had talked a few

times, she and the dead woman. She remembered the child, a small hand reaching out to pick a cake from the plate, the whispered thanks, teeth, perfect as pearls that bit into the pastry, his laugh. She remembered the song Serafina sang that morning by the stream: a song of yearning and the recognition of women's lot and the faithlessness of men.

It was her mother, needle stabbing at her embroidery panel, who murmured a comment about the inconvenience: someone new would have to be engaged to do their washing. For a moment Esperança felt a disproportionate rage: her mother had said nothing brutal; she had in fact expressed regret, dismay—particularly as a child had also been killed. What she stated now was nothing more than the bald fact that life must go on. A replacement washerwoman must be found. But the household was saved any inconvenience: next morning, from her window Esperança saw a tall figure, the familiar bundle balanced on dark, bushy hair, swaying out of the gates and down the road toward the river.

The cook, who managed most household affairs without needing guidance, explained that Serafina's friend Paula had taken on the job.

"But surely she cannot; she has so much to do already!"

The cook seemed amused by her concern—Esperança sensed an indulgent contempt behind the smile. "A good washerwoman can look after five or six families, my lady, not counting priests and foreigners, who don't go in so much for washing."

Esperança recalled something Paula had said that morning down by the stream: "We're not really human to those people. They use us. We're like animals who've learned how to pick up clothes and wash them, like you train a dog to fetch your slippers; they don't even see us."

"Some of them see us all right." Serafina had shrugged contemptuously. "I know when. I can feel it, feel eyes on me. I turn round and he'll look away."

And now Serafina was gone, carted off like a dead dog.

"Tell Paula to see me next time she comes," Esperança said and noticed the cook's mouth open in surprise.

The interview began badly. Esperança found it hard to say what she felt; words sounded mechanical, insincere. When she said, "I wanted to talk about Serafina," Paula's beaklike nose tilted suspiciously. "Are some clothes missing? Is that it?"

"No, no. I just wanted . . . to say—something. To remember her. I can still hardly believe—" She gestured helplessly. "The highwayman, or whatever he is, will be caught before long, I'm sure."

"This is not your business, Menina Esperança. You don't want to worry about it."

"You must not treat me like a child, Paula."

"But rich folk *are* like children. They are protected from the real world."

Esperança leaned closer, touched her arm. "What is it?"

There was silence between them for several moments, a troubled silence, balanced between fear and a desire to trust. "This was no robber, my lady."

"What are you saying?"

"Serafina's purse was not taken. Her clothes were ripped half off her. Bandits don't have time for that. This one wasn't after her money."

In the following silence Esperança rearranged her thoughts. Not a professional, picking off his victims, as devoid of passion as a tiger after a goat. This was a hunter with a darker purpose: his prey, selected, would suffer before dying.

"And there's another thing . . ."

The woman paused and Esperança caught an expression: *can I trust this person? One of the wealthy, the privileged.*

"Paula, I care about what happened. If there is something I can do . . ."

The woman thrust her hand into her blouse and drew out a scrap of cloth. She fingered it nervously, the fine silk catching on her roughened skin, and handed it over.

Esperança looked at it, puzzled: this seemed to be a fragment torn from a garment. "What is it?"

"She was holding it, gripped in her hand."

"But why would she have—"

"She was struggling with the murderer, fighting him off—" She stopped.

Esperança said, "How do you know that?"

The woman was sweating. She wiped her face with her forearm. "Because I saw it. I was well ahead of her on the aqueduct; she always walked more slowly when the child was with her. I decided to let them catch up with me. So I sat down to wait."

Her voice was flat, without emotion, as she described what happened that evening while the sun sank out of sight behind the rim of the hillside. She was tired. The air was cooling. She sat with her back propped against the aqueduct wall and closed her eyes. "I must have fallen asleep for a few moments. Then I heard voices in the distance. I thought I'd have a game with the little one. So I crouched in the open doorway and stuck my head round the corner like a dog—and I saw the three of them."

She saw Serafina, the child, and a man in a black cloak and broad-brimmed hat.

"Serafina said something; she sounded angry, and she was walking on when the man stooped and picked up the child. He threw him up, above his head, the way you do when you play with a toddler—I heard Fernando laugh, he had a special giggle—and then the man in the cloak turned and dropped him over the parapet. He didn't throw him roughly, just opened his hands and let him fall, like a bundle of clothes. And Serafina began to scream. She ran towards the man, clawing at him, and he hit her round the head but that didn't stop her. They were struggling and I must have yelled out something without knowing what I was doing—I was scared stiff. The man half-turned, then he grabbed Serafina and threw her over the parapet. I heard her screaming as she fell. I thought he'd come for me then, so I leaped to my feet and ran like hell and didn't stop till I got to the steps."

She was scrubbing tears from her cheeks, grief mixed with anger. She had looked back, she said, but in the thickening twilight she could see no sign of the man. "I got to the bottom of the slope and began to walk back underneath the aqueduct. The ground was all rough and I kept thinking I'd found them but it was just bushes. Then I saw them, lying close together, as if they were having a little rest on the way home. But when I got closer they didn't look so nice. You wouldn't have recognized the boy. Luckily it was dark. I went up very close to Serafina and I thought she gave a little moan but she couldn't have, she was dead all right, so it must have been me. I saw her hand, all clenched, and I could see she was holding something."

Esperança smoothed out the scrap of silk on her palm.

Neither spoke. This was an area of extreme delicacy. The barrier that Esperança had unwittingly crossed by her conversations, her visit to the riverbank, suddenly yawned between them. Despite everything they were on different sides of an unbridgeable gulf and neither woman could voice the unspeakable: that the murderer might not be a highwayman or a drunken sailor but a gentleman.

The silence lengthened. Paula's face grew pinched; she drew back her lips in an attempt at a smile, revealing the rotted stumps of teeth. "Well, I must get on with the washing. And I'm sure you have important matters to attend to, Menina Esperança."

There was a sourness in the air. Esperança's mother would not have been surprised: "To interest yourself in the affairs of people outside your own circle can only lead to awkwardness. They will be encouraged into indiscretion, forwardness, presumption. It will end disagreeably."

The washerwoman was at the door when Esperança said, "This is not the end of the matter, I promise you. I shall try to—" What? What would she try? To search the city for a gentleman with a scrap ripped from his shirt? To question her friends, to attempt to discover a possible culprit? Why should any of them even be acquainted with the man on the aqueduct?

Still: "I shall try to learn more," she said.

At the next soiree she moved with more than usual intentness through the guests, looking for faces that might be new to her, turning the conversation, whenever possible, to the murder. No one seemed much interested: the death of the child was regretted by the women, "but the mother should not have taken him on the aqueduct. The child should have been at home." And who,

204

Esperança wanted to ask, would have looked after him at home? In the real world children took their chances, as did their mothers.

Among the men the reaction was somewhat different: there was a veiled suggestion that the dead woman might have been at least partly to blame for her fate. From somewhere in the group came a dismissive comment from a voice she knew—Diogo, nursing an already empty wineglass—"One inevitably questions the circumstances; whether some sort of transaction might have been involved: favors offered for cash—which ended badly." And a foreign voice inquired whether washerwoman was a euphemism here, as actress sometimes was in his country, and there came a knowing ripple of laughter. But the laughter of the men had no gaiety at its heart. She recalled Serafina's comment: "Oh, they see you all right; I feel their eyes on me."

In the garden that day, as Serafina affectionately cuffed his head, the child had laughed. He had laughed, Paula said, as his murderer snatched him up. She was struck suddenly by the oddness of the child's laughter: that he had not cried out or protested when picked up by a stranger. Was that not peculiar? She heard again the boy's husky chuckle as he trotted off, clutching his mother's skirt. He had been shy, but with people he knew he was sufficiently at ease to laugh.

The thought had been nudging at her mind for some time; only now did she allow herself to acknowledge it: the child knew his murderer, of course, which was why he had laughed when the man picked him up and threw him in the air. It was a game that had been played before.

SHE WENT TO the bookshop next day; Manuel had something for her, letters written by a noblewoman to her secret lover at the time of the Great Discoveries, letters that dealt not only with endlessly postponed gratification and the minutiae of clandestine trysts, but also with dangers of a different sort, when old scores might be settled by false accusations—in some cases a hearing before a tribunal of the Inquisition.

The last letters made dark reading; an acknowledgment of despair: denunciation and treachery, a knock on the door in the night; an accusation of heresy, the necessary confession extracted by torture—colorful names describing instruments of torment: the Spanish Boot, lined with knives; the Necklace, for slow suffocation. What was it the Englishman had said, waving his wineglass, in the park at Cintra? "They tell me that if it were not for the Inquisition, this country and Spain, too, would be overrun today with witches and Jews!"

Esperança laid down the book of letters; she shook her head. Words were not easily found. She thought of Afonso's comment, "We live in a more tolerant age—" and her own substitution of "civilized," and repeated the phrase now, only to catch Manuel giving her one of his looks. But today the amused irony, the detachment, were missing. His face seemed shadowed.

"You haven't heard then? There's talk of bringing back the Inquisition. The times, it seems, are dangerous. Turbulent. Married clergy flaunting themselves—the British are being blamed for that. Too many heretics about. Freemasons everywhere." A pause. "And Jews, of course. You remember a few weeks ago I showed you some incunabula—early printing from Faro. There was something written by Samuel Usque that I thought might be of historical value. A vivid description of the Inquisition. This morning, with the talk of bringing back the Inquisition, I looked at it again with rather more personal interest."

She reached for her spectacles:

> They introduced from Rome a ferocious monster, of so strange and hideous a form that at its name alone all Europe trembled. Its body, covered with scales harder than steel, is formed of rough iron and venomous matter. A thousand wings of black feathers raise it from the ground; it moves on a thousand distorted feet; its countenance partakes of the ferocity of the lion and the horrid likeness of the serpent of the deserts of Africa. The size of its teeth is that of the strongest elephant. Its breath kills more speedily than the basilisk. Its mouth and eyes incessantly vomit devouring flames; it feeds on human bodies. . . . However bright the sun may shine at the time, wherever it passes it causes a sad and fearful obscurity and leaves in its track a darkness similar to that inflicted on the Egyptians as a plague.

Manuel read aloud from another sheet:

> "During the eighteen years that Torquemada was Inquisitor-General the number of victims of the Inquisition is stated by contemporary historians to have been 10,220 burned alive; 6,860 burned in effigy, persons dead, or escaped; 97,321 declared infamous and excluded from public office, with confiscation of property and imprisonment. . . .
>
> And the accusers remained secret, so there was no way of escaping or disproving the accusation."

She felt anxiety stir within her. Was this the way things could be going? In this "more civilized" age? "Is there really a possibility it could return?"

"I doubt it. Still, one hopes the political situation will settle down. Turmoil demands placation in strange ways.

When I hear a war or an uprising has been quelled, with an "accommodation" between victor and vanquished, I worry for my people. Also for Freemasons and gypsies. These are the times when scapegoats are convenient."

Partly to stave off the ache of anxiety that was growing inside her skull, she said, "I have been thinking about the murders on the aqueduct."

"Morbid interest?"

"I knew one of the women." She wanted to tell him her theory of the latest killing, but found difficulty in phrasing it. "This will sound absurd . . ."

When she finished, he sat thinking for a few moments. "Have you spoken your thoughts on this to anyone?"

"No. Should I, do you think? It could be useful—"

"Perhaps not." He shrugged. "What good would it do? You have no proof—"

"The piece of silk. From a fine garment—"

"A fragment. A cobweb caught on a hedgerow. You can only look ridiculous by raising this matter. And also"—a pause—"better, really, to let it rest."

She was surprised. Disappointed. She had expected him to be fired with her own wish to see justice done, to see a murderer apprehended, despite wealth and privileged position. She had not expected him to be circumspect. Discreet. Until on her way home she recalled the way he had hesitated, the odd non sequitur of his suggestion to "let it rest."

She would look ridiculous by raising the matter, he said. "And also." There had been a pause. Then he had continued, "Better to let it rest." And also. And also? What had he been about to say?

A man had been seen on the aqueduct the evening before

the murder. A mysterious stranger. No more was known and gossip embroidered the facts: someone knew someone who knew for a fact that he was a foreigner. Or possibly it was an aristocrat close to the royal family. Or an embittered exile returned from Goa, infected with tropical disease. Or a madman. Or—this one most frequently—a Jew. Soon everyone seemed to be in agreement: a Jew had been seen on the aqueduct.

Esperança heard the rumors and felt unease. With her friends she was straightforward at first: "Why a Jew? For what reason? Are they now suspected of killing Christian women in revenge for the Inquisition?"

"Nothing so straightforward. There was a rumor concerning the child." Luiz's sister looked uncomfortable and Diogo helped her out.

"The time of the Passover is approaching and there is that old story about the blood of a Christian child to be mixed in baking their unleavened bread."

Esperança began to laugh in disbelief and the others joined in, waving aside the rumor as a joke. Of course, no one of intelligence . . . these stories circulated among the ignorant . . . and in any case the murderer would no doubt be caught before long: the man would strike again.

"But won't there have to be a child," she asked provocatively, "so that the killer can get some blood for the unleavened bread?"

A ripple of laughter, but it was laughter to cover awkwardness. Of course, no one took these stories seriously, but there was no question that *someone* was stalking the washerwomen. An outsider? Well.

Her mother was starting a new cushion cover, choosing the silks, laying out the shining hanks to see which blended, which complemented or contrasted with the next. Esperança carried, as always, a book, which she set down carefully on one of the small tables in the boudoir. Her mother glanced over at the dark green leather binding, the gilded edges. "Something special?"

"Interesting, certainly."

"Your bookseller must be very successful if everyone buys as many books as you do—"

"Oh, he lends me most of them; he's very kind."

"Yes." Her mother picked up two blues, studied them, then set aside the darker. "Esperança, you know I never forbid you to do anything. I have trust in your good sense. Your intelligence." This time a yellow and a burnt ochre, the yellow discarded. "But perhaps a suggestion? . . . It might be better if you did not, for a while, see your bookseller."

Esperança was surprised. She also felt the beginnings of anger. "Why?"

Fingers dripping pink and crimson silk, her mother waved her arms helplessly. "These people . . . outsiders . . . foreigners . . . not belonging. They can cause problems—"

"Is this to do with the rumors? About the aqueduct?"

"It would simply be wiser . . . your father would appreciate . . . this will sound old-fashioned, but your reputation—"

"How sticky it is today. Humid. I must change." Esperança picked up her book and left the boudoir. She was becoming aware of the nuances of bigotry; she picked them up like a human weather vane caught by the passing air.

Even an act of God like the earthquake was not, it seemed, enough to save the Jews from the toils of the Papal workers.

Manuel had spoken with wry humor that day. Humor no longer seemed to be appropriate. She called for the carriage and drove at once to the bookshop.

210

She relayed her mother's carefully chosen words, her friends' skirting round the question of suspicion. He listened, his face impassive. The only reaction he displayed was to the word "foreigner."

"I have the keys to a house my family lived in four hundred years ago. The house itself is not there—the earthquake took care of that—but when I arrived in Lisbon, those keys gave me a sense of being part of the city, of belonging." His voice was colorless. "I think that is no longer the case. And I think that you should listen to your mother."

She took his hand and studied the palm like a fortune teller, tracing the fine lines with her fingertip. "I think you may be in danger."

"This will pass. Perhaps customers will no longer knock at my door. Perhaps my window will be smashed. Then all will be forgotten. Meanwhile, we must consider your reputation . . ."

He had a new book for her: a Brazilian novel. "You will enjoy the irony. This one is a gift. No need to return it."

No need, in other words, for her to return to the shop.

She saw what he was doing: distancing himself. She knew him well enough to know that to argue would be useless. He thought he was doing the right thing.

She watched him examining an old map spread out on the table, one that had taken Vasco da Gama round the Cape of Africa on the first stage of his voyage to the tapering point of India. Esperança touched a curling corner of the map. From her purse she took the pale pebble she always carried, her hand-cooling pebble from the brook of Alcântara. Placed on one corner, it held the map flat. When she left, from the door she could see the pebble, though Manuel had not yet noticed it. She made a silent promise: before long, she would return to reclaim it.

SHE BECKONED THE washerwoman to the shady corner where she sat pretending to read, and offered her a glass of lemon sherbet. "Paula, do any of you still take the aqueduct way home?"

"We all do, beggars can't be choosers, but we go in twos and threes, sometimes there's a brother or a husband to keep us company. Women don't go up on their own these days. Not with this grandee still on the prowl. They're saying it's a Jew now. To my mind that won't wash: they don't wear fancy silk, do they? But that's what they're saying."

The following day the decision was taken. Some practical advice from Paula, an hour of preparation, and she was ready. She made her way to the riverbank.

Seated beneath an orange tree, she watched as the washerwomen spread out the linen to dry along the banks of the brook. She took in the gleaming limbs, the swaying walk and, glancing up at the bony vaults of the arches, she thought she glimpsed a silhouette, a figure leaning on the parapet, watching the women below. But when she narrowed her eyes for a closer look she saw no one.

Later, with the linen dried and folded, the women dispersed to deliver their bundles and then gathered at the foot of the slope, climbing, calling out farewells as they split up into groups and drifted away, breaking into song, the voices growing fainter as they disappeared into the distance. The setting sun bled crimson, staining the sky so that the aqueduct stood out in silhouette as though carved from black stone.

In the sunlight, among the women, she had been inconspicuous in her pale cotton clothes. Now she waited in the deep shadows, her cloak pulled round her. She picked up a light bundle left for her by Paula. Then she began climbing the slope.

At the top she paused, regaining her breath, watching the last sliver of the sun peer over the horizon, the long shadow of the aqueduct flung across the fields, the arches fantastically elongated, reaching out toward the dark tangle of the vineyards.

She was unsure what to do next. She raised the bundle of clothes and placed it on her head. Mostly, the women went home without burdens, but she needed one, to give her the appearance of a washerwoman. Then, attempting their swaying, sinuous gait, she set off after the others, the gleam of a fine gold chain and cross at her throat. Ahead and behind her the narrow walkway was deserted now. The shadows cast by the little stone inspection boxes deepened and made her mistrust her eyes—was that a movement she had glimpsed or merely a flicker of her own eyelid?

Her shoulders ached already from the weight of even so light a bundle; how did the washerwomen support their heavy loads, day after day? Mouth dry, armpits wet, she was aware that she was frightened, but she already felt ridiculous. What did she think she was doing, exposing herself like some decoy bird to an unknown hunter who was almost certainly miles away enjoying the cool of twilight in a fragrant garden?

Sweat trickled between her breasts, into her eyes, and down her face. She blinked rapidly and licked her lips, tasting the warm, salty liquid, steadying the bundle with her right hand. As the light grew thicker, taking on a tinge like blue ink, she stopped again. Keeping her breathing slow she began to sing the washerwomen's song, plangent, yearning, turning her head slightly so that the sound drifted behind her like mist.

She was uncertain what to expect: sudden attack, the silent pounce of a wolf, or a voice calling, bidding her to wait, an invitation to walk together, a lull before the strike. Or there could be an anticlimax. Why should she be sure that the hunter would show himself? The decoy washerwoman might walk the aqueduct tonight till the moon rose and suffer no more than sore heels.

At what point did she become aware of a footfall? No click or slap of leather on stone, simply a sound that was more than her own movement. For the period of a long, indrawn breath, held, then carefully expelled, she walked on. The shaking started at her knees, spreading through her body until her hand, gripping the clothes on her head, jerked violently, almost dislodging the bundle. Her bare neck, her shoulders, shrank from the anticipated blow: was the follower even now raising his arm to strike?

She whirled as he reached her: a man in dark cloak and hat that concealed his face, moving fast, like a shadow, and instinctively, without knowing what she did, she swung the bundle from her head, knocking him off balance, dislodging his hat, and revealing his face. The movements, the sounds, were jumbled together as they both cried out in— what? Surprise? Dismay?

She knew him, of course, as she had known she would. One on the periphery of her circle, not a close friend: Salvador, who had built himself a social reputation for being heartless, which no one took seriously.

"Mamselle Esperança!" he stammered, attempting humor with mock gallantry. "How fortunate that just tonight I should have decided to admire the sunset from this high point!"

The strength left her limbs; she was overwhelmed not with fear but with a tired sadness. She found herself murmuring senselessly, "Forgive me! Your hat . . ."

Caught off balance, he had staggered as the bundle struck him and now he, too, was performing a parody of social intercourse—"Don't trouble yourself! No harm done!"

Retrieving his hat, bowing, smiling as he flicked dust from the velvety brim, he attempted at the same time to retrieve a position that might or might not be beyond salvation.

She watched him, heart thumping so loudly that surely he could hear the sound. Was this a bluff or a preamble to attack?

He looked at her more closely, took in her cold, undeceived eyes, and his smile faded. She saw his eyes flicker towards the parapet, judging the distance, then back to her face.

With genuine regret in his voice he asked, "Why did you come here?"

"Serafina was my friend."

He laughed then. "She was our *washerwoman*. We have no friends among the poor. To think so is a delusion. They despise and hate us. They fear us."

"With reason, wouldn't you say?" Keeping her voice light.

Her head was buzzing like a hive of bees: what is he thinking? Have I convinced him? Will we end this conversation with an elegant understanding, an unspoken agreement to let dead washerwomen lie undisturbed? Her hand, within the folds of the bundle, closed tightly, clenched, painful. He said conversationally, "This is most unfortunate."

With a speed that left her breathless, he spun her against the parapet, wrenching her free arm up behind her back. She weighed very little; one heave and she would drop from the arch like a stone. Like a washerwoman.

She gathered herself, pulling away from him, disregarding the burning pain as he wrenched again on her arm, forcing her over the ledge. She felt the stone bite into her flesh. She had been gripping the bundle; now it dropped from her arm and she swung up, backhanded, hard across his throat, her fist clenched round Paula's small pointed knife. Blood sprayed like a fountain, blinding her. He managed no more than a choked gurgle as he frantically wrapped hands to neck, staggering back. She struck him again, this time beneath his ribs, and felt the blade skid off the edge of bone.

Then she ran.

THE SERVANTS SHRIEKED at the sight of her: blood on her hands and face, clothes ripped and muddy, hair disheveled. She managed to reach the hall before her legs gave way. The butler caught her, contriving somehow to cradle her in his arms while giving the impression that he was simply carrying out an extension of his normal duties. He lifted her to the nearest couch, rapidly ordering the maid to spread a protective sheet over the Italian upholstery to safeguard it from possible bloodstains.

She heard all this, her eyes closed tight. She heard her mother's light footsteps, the indrawn breath. Her father's

216

voice; the terse instruction: "Fetch the doctor." Then she allowed herself to lose consciousness.

"What happened?"

Now that the doctor had confirmed the patient had been neither seriously wounded nor violated, merely bruised and lacerated; now that Esperança lay like a ghost between the smooth sheets of her own bed and had been coaxed into sipping a few spoonfuls of broth, her mother could ask the bald question, "What happened?"

She had known the explanation would be difficult: to make sense of it all, to make them understand why she would deliberately expose herself to danger—risk her life— she would have to present them with a situation beyond their imagining. Any connection between a murdered washerwoman, a Jewish tradesman, and their daughter was inconceivable.

She could say to them that an innocent man had been unjustly suspected; that his name and livelihood were threatened, indeed his person. And how then should she explain her own feelings? "He is very dear to me." No, that would not serve. "I care for him—" Worse.

Her mother, maternal anxiety sharpening her voice, said angrily, "You could have been killed!"

Her thoughts drifted, unwieldy, uncontrolled. Words surfaced, coming from nowhere—*love is stronger than death*— dramatic, quite unlike her, yet she was unsurprised.

She saw that they were still waiting for an explanation, so she told them, recklessly, that she had learned the identity of the person who killed their washerwoman and her child. Someone from their own social circle.

Their lack of interest astonished her. It was as though

217

she had changed the subject; it was an irrelevance. They simply wanted to know what had happened to *her.*

So she gave them what they desired. She described her walk, the attack, her defense, her flight.

From time to time her mother stifled an exclamation of dismay and pressed her lace handkerchief to her lips.

Her father broke in, "And none of these wretched peasants was close enough to help you?"

"Ah!" Belatedly she remembered the plan arranged between them. The scream that would alert them, bring them running. But there had been no screaming, she, breathless with shock, then caught in the duel of wills that followed. Fear had silenced her, and he, blood filling his throat, he, too, had been silenced. Then she had run blindly.

"It was someone we know," she said. A silence. "It is possible I killed him," she added and heard another stifled sound from her mother.

Her father stood up, said briskly, "I assume all this took place on the aqueduct?"

She nodded.

"This was foolish of you. Extremely foolish. Meddling. These deaths—"

"You think they're not our concern? I think they are. And moreover . . ." Choosing her words with care, she continued, "And moreover, an innocent man had been accused by innuendo, by a terrible rumor."

"The bookseller—"

"He has a name. He is a man."

A quick exchange of glances. Her father left the room, closing the door quietly behind him.

Time lost its usual shape. She lay in the shuttered room, dazed, her brow cooled by a damp cloth regularly renewed by the maid. Occasionally her mother was there, tilting a glass to her lips, murmuring that she must drink, rest . . .

When she moved, pain shot through her like a burning rod. She slept. Woke. Obediently swallowed some mouthfuls of soup. Slept again.

How long since she had collapsed, bloody and feverish, into the butler's impersonal arms? A day? Two? She was aware that occasionally she had staggered to the chamber pot next to the bed, supported by Graçia, to relieve herself.

Now she lay quietly, eyes closed, hearing her mother's questioning voice, the maid's answering whisper. Then, once again, her mother was at the bedside. "Esperança, raise your head, drink this—"

She pushed away the glass and sat up, conscious of an engulfing feebleness. "It smells disgusting."

"It will help you—"

"I want to get up."

"Nonsense. You must rest."

"I have rested enough." Her voice, at least, was firm.

Her mother sensed the change and shrugged. "Graçia will prepare your bath."

There was something she needed to know. What? Trying to think was difficult, like brushing aside cobwebs that clogged her mind. Her mother was at the door before the fog cleared. "Salvador . . ."

Her mother handed the glass to the maid. "Take this back to the kitchen, would you?"

She waited till the door closed. "He was found at the foot of the aqueduct. Of course the fall killed him. No one can say who pushed him to his death. Possibly some criminal, a thief. It is a dangerous place—"

"But I *stabbed* him."

Her mother gave a tight little smile. "Put it from your

219

mind. Such a small knife. Those wounds would scarcely have caused him serious harm."

Esperança stared at her, trying to see past the surface. Was she being lied to, for the best of reasons, to comfort her? Did they suspect that she might confess publicly to a killing? Bring scandal swirling round the family?

Bathed, dressed, moving with care, she made her way to the salon and ordered the carriage. She chose a time when her parents were busy elsewhere. She was aware of an atmosphere in the house, something almost audible; like a musical note too high for the human ear, which yet disturbs the air.

The carriage jolted her painfully. She wanted to call out to the driver to slow down, but she was anxious to reach her destination without delay: would anyone have thought to tell Manuel that the murderer had been unmasked? That he could no longer be under any suspicion.

She suffered the bumpy road without protest, rehearsing how she would break the news, what she would say to him.

When the carriage drew up she attempted to open the door herself, too impatient to wait for the driver, but the action sent pain shooting up her arm and she fell back, clutching her wrenched shoulder. When she stepped down from the carriage she stopped, bewildered, thinking for a moment that the driver had taken her to the wrong street.

The bookshop was closed and barred. The door was dusty; dead leaves clogged the step. The place looked as though it had been unoccupied for years.

At once she knew he must be ill. Who was caring for him? He had no family. Then she dismissed her foolish fears: of course, he was away on a business trip; he traveled from time to time in search of rare volumes. But when she moved closer to the window she saw that the shutters hung loose, the dim interior of the shop was bare, the shelves empty of books; no chests crowded the floor. A chair lay overturned. And stepping back across the pavement with its swirling patterns of black and white and gray, she noticed now that the discreet and decorative sign, painted in white and gray and black to echo the pavement, the sign announcing the presence of a bookseller, no longer hung by the entrance.

Seen through the grimy window, stripped of the clutter of paper, the glowing leather covers, the glint of gold-edged pages, the room was lifeless.

A wave of weakness, then rage, overwhelmed her. A sense of her own impotence.

She knew there was no point in questioning her parents. But a friend, someone who knew Manuel, might tell her more. She allowed the driver to help her back into the carriage.

Afonso embraced her with a curiously extravagant tenderness, making her feel suddenly fragile, vulnerable. "How thin you are! Well, you have been seriously ill. We were all worried—"

"Afonso. What has happened to Manuel?"

"The bookseller? Nothing, as far as I know. The rumors circulated for a while, that nonsense about the washerwomen, but there was never anything more than foolish gossip, of course."

"Not the rumors. I mean, where is he?"

"Not at the shop then? Ah. Well, of course, I knew him only at the shop."

She studied him for a moment, trying to read behind his smiling face. Her friend, her trusted friend, unaware that he had used the past tense about his valued bookseller.

Outside the sun still shone, the sky remained blue. But in the room the light had inexplicably dimmed; she felt chilled.

He would not have been killed, of course. *We live in civilized times.* But power and money could be used to destroy a life as efficiently as a physical attack.

"Why should anyone want to harm him? Where was the danger? He just lent me books. We talked and read."

"Ah! Books can be dangerous. Reading has led people to their doom—think of Paolo and Francesca. . . ." He paused. "A story that has no relevance whatsoever to the present situation, of course."

Somewhere, in some distant room, Manuel could be standing or seated at a desk. Opening the pages of a book. Looking up with that ironic raising of the eyebrows, the tilt of the head. The half-smile. She found she was weeping.

Afonso said gently, "It is natural you should be weak. You have been unwell for quite some time."

"Just a day or two."

"Come now. Nearly two weeks, my dear. We were worried. There was even a story that . . ." He paused. "That you—well, imagine the worst for yourself."

She laughed incredulously. "Rumors of my death; is that what you mean? Astonishing."

The more so since she had been little more than bruised and frightened. She saw it was possible that the useful sedative administered by her mother was what had kept her prostrate in her bed. Now it was her own weakness that sent her back to it. The helplessness spread through her like a new sickness. In the darkened room she lay, smoothing the sheets with her fingertips, allowing the maid to turn the pillow from time to time.

When her mother appeared they found it difficult to talk to one another.

"You must eat something."

"Perhaps some of that vile mixture you poured down my throat—Valerian root, was it?"

Perhaps she did have a fever. Graçia was concerned by the damp sheets: "If my lady would sit by the window, I can change the bed linen, give you clean sheets."

Like someone feeling her way along a guiding thread, Esperança thought carefully of soiled bed linen, clean bed linen, linen washed and dried . . .

Next morning she was up and dressed early, at her shaded table in the garden. It was not long before the washerwoman came into view, bundle balanced on her head, swaying down the path. She stopped. The blackened teeth showed briefly.

Esperança said, "I lost your knife."

"In a good cause."

"You heard?"

"They can't keep something like that a secret. The girls prayed for you."

"I would like to come down to the brook again one day."

The washerwoman looked pensive. "It's not easy for them, having someone like you sitting there with her shoes off."

So her mother was right after all. Intimacy across the barrier was not to be encouraged. She would hear the washerwomen's songs only in her memory. "Paula, you said once that you know what goes on in people's houses. I want to find out something. I want to know what has happened to a bookseller in town—"

"The Jew?"

Esperança stared at her. "You know him?"

"One of the girls did his washing. She likes him—"

"Where is he?"

"Who knows? She saw him a couple of days after that gentleman"—she paused—"fell from the aqueduct. The Jew was in a bad way. He'd been visited by some people. He seemed unhappy. Next day he was gone and all his stuff with him. A ship bound for Angola or Brazil, somewhere like that."

There was a pain sharper than the savage wrenching of her arm on the aqueduct; a pain that left her breathless, as though she had suffered a blow to the heart. The day see-sawed dizzyingly, now light, now dark.

Time spins.

She did not attend the formal dinner for the ambassador and she excused herself from the ball of the season. She had lost all taste for company, but more disturbingly, she found herself unable to read, the print blurring before her eyes. She removed her spectacles, polishing the glass with care, remembering with a small pang the time when she had glanced up from studying an old manuscript to find Manuel watching her, amused.

"I was recalling something I read, about Virgil wearing spectacles to study a rubricated volume, and thinking how much more attractive you look than he must have done."

"High praise indeed, Manuel, considering what we know of Virgil's appearance. Such flattery will turn my head!"

She dusted and rearranged her most cherished books, listlessly opening one or two. It was Manuel who had shown her how the early printers represented the title page as a door with portals, the first printed illustrations. Here was a centaur and a siren—what meaning could she draw from that enigmatic scene? Was the centaur about to carry off the siren to distant lands, or was it he who would be transported, caught in the siren's net, a helpless alien creature? On another, a lion guarded a shield of David.

The lion in the neighboring quinta garden still coughed and roared sadly in the night, perhaps when he caught some whiff of Africa carried on the wind across the sea, but he was safely caged, in no position to defend the shield of David when danger came.

She put the books away and sat, hands folded, regarding the faint gold letters on the spines, which, without her spectacles, were indecipherable and might as well have been in a foreign language, Hebrew perhaps.

She still called in on her mother in her blue boudoir, but the visits were shorter and the old ease was gone. No oblique references and discreet understandings these days; they confined themselves to embroidery matters, comparing a piece of rare Chinese needle painting with some domestic Madeira work, or discussing the relative merits of stem stitch or herringbone, Cretan or feather, on her mother's latest project. Her father she barely saw. After several months had passed, she agreed to accompany her parents to one of Ricardo's soirees. She had no expectations of enjoying herself; it was a sort of idle curiosity that drove her. She simply wondered how her closed little oyster world would cope with the grit of her presence.

Ricardo had a new passion: a Frenchman he had met on a trip to Paris. "Honoré Daumier. A Michelangelo in his own way—his shadows have more life than many a brightly lit canvas! He has no money and his eyesight is going. But what mastery!"

He had taken her arm and was leading her, talking all the while, to an alcove where a small picture was propped on a lectern. "I bought this; it's a study for a larger painting. Look: *La Blanchisseuse*—I thought of you, with your interest in our own *blanchisseuses*."

She looked at the small picture, the washerwoman, braced on her strong legs, skirt hitched up, the tilt of the head, the look in the eye. There was an insolent vitality to the figure: she would take no nonsense, this washerwoman, a word out of place and she would fling your dirty linen back at you. Or rather, Daumier's washerwoman would. The real-life model, Esperança suspected, would have the same look in her eye but keep the retort to herself. A girl had to eat.

"It's wonderful."

"I knew you would appreciate it."

Behind her, someone called her name. She turned to greet a couple, managing a smile. She and the woman exchanged kisses, cheek barely touching cheek.

"Esperança! Have you been collecting any of your interesting old stories lately?"

Ricardo flashed her a worried glance, but Esperança said cordially, "Why yes, Rosária, a most interesting love story, between a Christian and a Jew."

The woman shrugged. "I don't know why everything seems to be so difficult for Jews: the ones I have met look just like us anyway. Well, you know the old story about the Marquês de Pombal and the yellow hats—"

"Yes," Esperança said. "We all know that story."

"How does your love story end?" Rosária asked cheerfully.

"Doomed, presumably," her husband said, looking

round the room for more entertaining company. "Oil and water do not mix!"

Ricardo said, not quite managing his usual lightness of touch, "I must take Esperança away now. There are some people I want her to meet—"

He took her arm but she held back. "May I stay here for a little, Ricardo, and admire Monsieur Daumier's splendid washerwoman?"

"Of course." He kissed her hand and drew the other two away with him, to welcome a new guest.

Laughter from a passing group curled round her, like smoke, isolating her. She looked about, at the men clustered together, shiny faced, confident, the women with their pearly skin. The room became all at once unreal, the carved ceilings and pillars untrustworthy, trompe l'oeil, the guests assembled for a purpose: artists' models, posing. Some stood together, in a circle as in "Group, talking." At a table—"Still life with wine decanter and fruit"—a man in dark clothes leaned confidently over a mother and daughter, paying court to both. Two young girls sat together, backs to the wall, shy, their eyes on the men across the room, alluring in their worldliness and their private laughter. Two women approached each other, bending their heads in greeting, graceful as swans on calm water. Watteau would have painted the women's clothes with his brush dipped in butterflies' wings, gleaming, iridescent; their faces bright with gaiety.

Across the room someone waved, greeting an old friend. Flunkies circulated with champagne and in the next room musicians were playing against a descant of laughter: a lighthearted sound of merriment that seemed to her to come from very far away.

There was no room here for an outsider. Briefly, an outsider had entered their lives, but already he had been painted out of the picture. The remaining figures had regrouped, leaving no empty space. Which of these people had been involved? She scanned the smiling faces. Bookseller? What bookseller? Jew? What Jew? A closing of the ranks.

Esperança studied the small picture again. She met the washerwoman's gaze. There was a long moment of communion. Then she turned away.

LONDON | *2000*

LONDON | 2000

"I HAVE CHILDREN?"

There are patches of clarity, bits of a jigsaw puzzle, isolated sections of the big picture—a figure in a richly furnished room, a landscape, a rocky harbor—none of which makes sense to her.

"Children?" She sounds unconvinced.

They walk on. Sometimes she leads, walking fast, with that anxious, questing look—"There's somewhere I have to go"—then she will stop, turn to him. As now.

"Tell me their names." And then, almost as an afterthought, "You're not their father, are you?"

He laughs, "In my dreams. No, I'm not their father."

Without warning, with that quick shake of the head, she pulls away, back into the darkness.

Close down. Go blank. Cease upon the midnight.

He watches her, the thin, sallow face and thick black hair that stands out around her head like a shadowy aureole.

Her right wrist is bandaged and there is dark cross-hatching on her fingertips; the skin on her hand looks rough, calloused. "Have you been working in clay?" he asks.

"What? What?"

She looks distracted, fear sharpening her features. He knows how her face can look when she is happy, the way the muscles lift in a not-quite smile that sends upward curves to lips and changes the contour of her cheeks. Once, without skill or effort, he could achieve that change; he could make her laugh. He aches now for the magic wand he took for granted in the past.

She has closed herself again, unreachable.

She feels the pain begin somewhere inside her head: the first twinge, a toe dipped in icy water. She hesitates.

"Two children, you say. At school?"

"A bit farther on than that."

"Grown up. Of course they are. I knew that. I know that."

When did she see them last? A pinhole widens and she sees the children—two people she recognizes now—untidily elegant as only the young can be, but looking serious, angry even.

She is at least in part to blame; the children are making that clear.

Had she been firm, they say, had she resisted, refused to allow things to go the way they did, things could have been different—

The man in the leather jacket has remained silent, leaving her to lope on ahead, press her knuckles to her head, pausing now and then to rock to and fro like someone grieving. After a while he begins once more, tentatively, to throw out bait to draw her in.

Their first meeting, perhaps she remembers them meeting—Funchal? The harbor?

The harbor? Of course she remembers the harbor. Perhaps, as with the finches, her cells are busily rebuilding. Yes, she can see the harbor, at first faintly and then, as she concentrates, more clearly, like a photographic image developing, and there they are.

She examines them with a sad tenderness, seeing snapshots of people from another age, fresh and shining as puppies just licked clean, young and silly, full of plans and confidence—

"How embarrassingly juvenile we were," she says aloud.

Madeira, New Year's Eve, 1968. She stepped ashore into the curved arm of the harbor at Funchal, the cruise ship behind her, and stood, breathing in the smell of fish and woodsmoke, craving an hour or two away from grandparental surveillance and the relentless good cheer of staff and passengers.

The grandparents had been understanding: of course, they said, the younger generation needed to have freedom to spread their wings, do their own thing, wasn't that what people said nowadays? Adding, "Be sure you're back before midnight." They spoke in Portuguese.

"Yes, of course," she had replied in English. It was their normal method of communication. Each stuck to what they knew best.

The grandparents were disappointed with the cruise: in the brochure there had been talk of a visit to a village, inland, where the houses still had the old, traditional thatched roofs. But docking late, they were informed there was no time for the village. Instead, they were "at liberty" to enjoy the town "at their leisure." No thatched roofs, but there were traditional pavements patterned with black, white, and gray. Later, of course, there would be the

233

New Year's Eve dance on board. The grandparents decided to deny themselves this spurious liberty and leisure. They reserved an early sitting for dinner. Of course, young people must do as they wished.

So she stepped onto the quayside, the late sun in her eyes, hearing distant music: a combination of a worn Beatles tape from a backstreet café, a fairground cacophony from the far end of town, and, through an open window up the hill, the sound of a flirty, fast-stepping tango. The rhythms, cadences, cultures clashed, then merged into a sheet of sound that filled her head and stroked her skin till she tingled. She wanted to laugh aloud, dance in the street—she would have moved into the encircling arms of any stranger who stepped up and requested a spin across the promenade. She felt, briefly, free. To her surprise, tears pricked her eyes.

She could see flames through the trees. Huge grills set out on waste ground, logs beneath them crackling with fire and smoke, trestle tables, tree trunk stools, booths selling wine, voices shouting orders for food. A big wheel turned slowly. The statue must be Henry the Navigator, it was always Henry the Navigator.

A week of relentless cruise catering had left her bloated yet dissatisfied. She longed for something pungent, preferably not served from silver platters. Under the trees chickens sizzled and grew golden over the open fires, and round flat loaves like oversized muffins sat baking in tin ovens. She left the promenade behind her, heading for the trees across a squat stone bridge, the river gurgling below.

When did it occur, the transformation from generalized pleasure to the significant moment? The shock of recognition that could not be so; a sense of double vision, so that for a second she grew dizzy—as she felt dizzy now, seeing it all again as it happened—two identical figures with black curls and shadowy eyes; two thin, dark boys who beckoned her with a jerk of the head and quick flip of the wrist as they worked, chopping up chickens, flinging vast portions on to cardboard plates, sweating in the heat of the flames. Figures that she seemed to see as though in facing mirrors, endlessly receding.

The twins. And wasn't there a busker somewhere? Tangle-haired and vulpine, though not threatening. He had talked about danger, danger from fire, water, women. The sea, he had said, can swallow us all. Fire consumes what it touches. And women—he had given her one of his foxy looks—the sweetest danger.

The fairground at the far end of Funchal harbor. Two thin, dark boys; two figures in sharp focus against a swirling background.

Two figures in facing mirrors, endlessly receding, blurring into one.

They shouted across the heads of clustering locals, drawing her in, and as she moved toward them she had a feeling of returning to a place she knew.

Not that the meeting, when it came, was portentous. No gravitas or solemn statements. They were jokey, silly; Hope was a serious girl and unused to relentless banter.

"Dr. Livingstone, I presume!" From one twin.

From the other: "That's the *answer.* But what was the question?"

She shook her head, lost.

"What is your *full* name, Dr. Presume?" He thrust a cardboard plate at her. "Want some grub? Here you are, Pops; that'll put hair on your chest."

"My name's Hope," she told him.

"I'll drink to that."

"Get your wine at the counter when you pay," the second twin called. "We don't run to knives and forks."

Later, when she asked the first twin, "How did you know I was English?" he admitted that he had not been sure: "With that black hair and olive skin you could've been a local. It was the frock, Pops. I reckoned you were off a cruise ship."

By then she knew he called everyone Pops, male or female, a leftover from a boyhood worship of Sidney Bechet. At school he played guitar in a five-piece band, dreaming he was Django Reinhardt reborn. "And if you're wondering how a London lad finds himself slinging hash—or as it were barbecued chicken—in this place, it's a matter of economics. Otherwise known as a holiday job. Also nepotism. My brother knows the guy who owns the caff that does the chickens."

She found it difficult at first to distinguish between them: they talked in tandem, finished each other's sentences, knew each other's unspoken thoughts. Their voices were the same; they had the same mannerism of a fast Groucho Marx double eyebrow twitch when they were sending her up. Mel thought of himself as a musician. Dan knew he wanted to be a chef.

"Originally I thought I'd have a try at feeding the five thousand with loaves and fishes—there's a good precedent for my people—but blow me, the food just wouldn't go round, the crowd began to turn ugly and I realized the age of miracles *had* passed—"

"To misquote Gershwin."

"I want my own restaurant," Dan told her. "Food is like literature or music or painting: it can be beautiful; it can be important. It should move you, thrill you, give meaning to the moment—"

"—It can be a pretentious load of cobblers, as you'll have noticed," his brother said, mouth filled with barbecued chicken. "What he means behind the guff is that it should taste good. I'll drink to that."

Identical in so many ways, they were in this respect divided: one with a path mapped out, a goal. The other drifting with the wind.

"Mel can never resist the beguiling detour," Dan said. "He takes the byways, smells the honeysuckle. I envy that."

"No you don't. You think I'm a lazy sod and I'll end up sleeping in the gutter with the rest of the tramps."

"If you do, it'll be a better class of gutter and you'll be looking up at the stars. Right. Back to work," Dan said. "Chickens to cook. Fires to stoke."

The dreamer offered her a leftover drumstick. "You. Laura Ashley girl. Don't go away." She reached for the drumstick, but he held on to it for a moment, so that their fingers touched. "Don't go away."

They were nineteen, a year older than she was, and full of the ease that comes with being young and healthy and having parents affluent enough to cushion their offspring comfortably through the birth canal to the big world.

When the flames had died down and visitors had eaten all the available chickens, the three wandered through the town, climbing the steep little streets.

"Will your father buy you a restaurant?" She intended it as a serious question, but they rocked, sent into a spasm of delight by the idea.

"Like he'd buy me a jazz club?" Mel said. "Right."

Father, it seemed, believed in education as a serious

business. Had one of them expressed a wish to slice up bodies on a regular basis, or hobnob with criminals on a professional level, he would have stumped up promptly for the required number of years of law or medical school. If the twins chose to divert their intelligence into frivolous channels he would not throw them out of the house, but nor would he go out of his way to shield them from the realities of a harsh world. So Dan worked his way through fashionable kitchens, learning the trade, while Mel dipped into history at the LSE, not so much to please the parents but because it provided him with a regular program of London gigs.

"What about you?" Mel asked. "What's Laura Ashley girl going to do with her life?"

No one had ever asked her that. To do well at school had been all her parents required of her. When she mentioned art school they had been appalled: surely, like the daughters of their friends, she would marry before long and have no use for "artistic," possibly immoral, frivolity? But she refused their offer of secretarial college; it seemed she was determined to—as they saw it—waste her time on art. There were arguments, scenes. Her father banged the table to express his disapproval; this brought her mother out in tears.

Her persistence surprised them: she had always been a dutiful daughter; why now was she being so difficult? They called her stubborn; the arguments were followed by family silences. In the end, they gave way.

Now, in response to Mel's question, she said, "I want to make something that will last."

"What, like a building?" Dan asked.

"Buildings aren't meant to last these days," Mel remarked, "They don't make 'em like they used to. Now, music—that lasts."

"So does painting. And sculpture." Her hands cupped the air, moving as though forming a shape. "Clay . . . metal . . . stone . . . I don't know what exactly, yet, but I want to create something new, something different."

"And you will."

"Sure you will."

Taped Christmas carols crackled through bad amplification, cutting out the fairground music. The decks of the cruise ships were crowded with tourists waiting for the traditional New Year's Eve firework display. Beyond the ships, far out in the harbor, was moored a line of tiny skeletal caravels, outlined in colored lights, glittering ghost ships waiting for the time when the strangers were gone and they could catch the tide and come home. When the firework display began, the three of them watched it from a café terrace high above the harbor, an explosion of color and light, as though the town burned like Troy.

When the liner sailed at dawn, she was on the deck, waving to the twins. There were people in evening dress beside her at the rail, some in paper hats. The women gray faced, makeup worn off, hair no longer coifed, shivered in the cool air, rubbing their bare arms, laughing.

"You missed the party. . . . It was lovely!" one of them called to her.

A box of streamers left over from the celebration had been brought up on deck and people were throwing them from ship to land, calling greetings to any locals still awake.

Hope took a tightly furled spiral of yellow paper and threw the streamer toward the boys. One leaped forward and grabbed the spinning coil. It unspooled rapidly as the ship floated free of the dock and for a moment the frail link held, tautened. As the ship heaved on the swell, it seemed as though the streamer, strong as a steel hawser, was drawing them together. Then it snapped, the yellow paper hanging in the air before it dropped, the ends vanishing in the darkness.

On shore, one of the twins waved his remnant of streamer at her, calling, "Hold on to your end; we'll join up—it's a covenant!"

Which twin had reached out and held her in that miraculous grip?

On the quay they stood waving, side by side, blurring into one.

She remembers the moment, the ship lifting away from the harbor, the twins waving, the yellow streamer curling round her fingers in the gray light.

When they met again, Dan was running a café in the Charing Cross Road.

"So you got your restaurant, then?"

"Well . . . not so much a restaurant, more a greasy spoon."

He called it Fifty Million: "Mel gave me the jazzer's Good Food classification—fifty million flies can't be wrong. I thought we'd go with that."

She was at St. Martin's and Mel called her the new Bridget Riley; he suggested that since she was seriously into acrylic, she should do a mural for the Fifty Million.

The mural remained unpainted. She was working on a triptych—Unicorn and Virgin. It grew out of a question that Hope felt held a personal implication for her: had the virgin in the myth been a willing part of the exercise? Was she compliant? Reluctant? Was she, in fact, free at all? There were more ways to trap a girl than by putting her in chains: a sense of duty, too, could be a form of imprisonment.

She was not behaving well, in her parents' view—"Devoting so much of your time to this . . . art!" She should be at home, with them. They did not conceal their resentment. So hers was an inversion of the myth: the virgin, trapped in an urban cage, yearning for freedom, is rescued by the wily unicorn.

Hope was having problems with the third panel, where the captive and her rescuer escape.

"I don't want them riding off into the sunset," she told Mel, "but I'd like it to have a happy ending."

"I'll drink to that. But happy endings are tricky." He brooded for a moment. "How about a touch of Ovid, a bit of metamorphosis? What if she becomes a unicorn, too?"

"Have one of the gods dropping by on a Harley Davidson?" she suggested mockingly. "Sorting out the mortals?"

"No gods needed. You could call it 'The Power of Love.'"

"A love stronger than myth?" She nodded, considering the idea. "I'll think about it."

Because the café was so near the art school she took to dropping in most evenings. Dan would briefly abandon the steaming kitchen and chat with her. Usually Mel called by on his way to or from a gig and one hot night, when Hope had suffered her way through an experimental play at the Open Space, she arrived to find him behind the counter.

"Crisis in the catering area, Pops. No-show of paid staff. I'm helping out for a bit. Keep me company."

It was near to closing time; Dan came out of the kitchen and propped open the street door, and they sat on the step, convincing themselves they could feel a cool breeze. Mel picked up his guitar and gave them a few bars of "A

241

Foggy Day in London Town," and Hope and Dan went into a slow jive on the pavement. Soon a couple of others had joined them and a passing busker with a violin decided to pitch in.

Spinning, changing step, moving dreamily in warm air heavy with petrol fumes and the smell of fried food, Hope glanced over at the two musicians, linked in a musical dialogue—the busker's fiddle talking to the guitar, guitar replying: theme stated, picked up, played with, transformed. A perfect conversation.

She saw Mel, leaning into his guitar, face intent, absorbed, playing one of his own compositions. He seemed to shimmer in the light, waver, as though losing shape, and for a moment she felt herself to be weightless, floating toward him, part of a great continuum without boundaries or separation. Then he looked up, caught her eye, and gave her the ironical eyebrow twitch. She waved to him and swung back into the dance.

By the time the police arrived to move everyone on there was a sizable crowd.

The busker was complimentary: "You should get yourself organized, mate," he told Mel. He patted the guitar. "You could make a good living at this caper."

He had prudently picked up his cap from the pavement when the police appeared and flashed it discreetly, half filled with coins. "Never neglect an audience, my old son. They enjoy it more if they're paying."

She remembers the busker. Dark faced, with tangled red hair and an earring. He had called her "my love" and told her to keep her wits about her, look out for the Gemini factor; funny thing, twins, he said, shadow and substance. Twins are a double bind, he said, a two-headed axe, melody and counterfeit—surely he meant

242

counterpoint? Castor and Pollux, he said, one human, one immortal. Which one was immortal? Which one did she sleep with, finally?

"Did I go to bed with you?" She asks the man in the leather jacket.

"Just the once."

"I'm sorry, I should have remembered that."

"Why?" he says. "It obviously wasn't memorable," and sees with a surge of relief that he can still make her laugh.

They move on, the anxious woman who has somewhere she must reach and the man in the leather jacket, down Charing Cross Road. Who is leading now, and who is following?

Outside the old St. Martin's School of Art she stops. "I was here. Surely I was here? This is the building. But they seem to have changed the name." On, to the block where a short-lived café had served its clients with unfashionably strong coffee and homemade Danish pastry. She stops, as though searching for something.

There was a busker . . . and music.

They cross Piccadilly and turn right, under the arcades.

The name, spelled out in lights, looks dusty in the late sunlight; it needs darkness or a blue dusk to release its glitter. She stops, staring up at the sign.

Ritz Hotel.

He tries to read her expression.

She hears the discreet chink of cup on saucer, silver cutlery on porcelain. She fears she is not properly dressed for such a place. And facing her across the teacups—

"That terrible velvet suit!" Another piece slotted into the pattern. "Flares!"

She shakes her head, backs away from the Ritz, hurrying

243

on, walking blindly so that he is forced to grab her arm and steer her round people she would otherwise crash into.

He lets her choose her own path. Up Piccadilly, Park Lane, Sloane Street. Now and again she stops at a window and looks closely at a modish frock, a pair of flimsy shoes. It is almost dark now; they have been walking for hours.

The last of the light has left the sky and the city glows with lamplight from pub doorways and restaurant windows. She has walked her way to Pimlico, and now she turns down a side street and stops outside a tall period house, pale stucco, with wrought iron railings. The strip of bells and names gives away its status as a block of flats.

"I live here."

"You did, yes."

"I don't anymore. No. I live. . . ," she pauses. "I live in a house. I don't know where it is."

"Twickenham. On the river."

A riverbank. Music playing from an upstairs room. "Willow Weep for Me—"

"Eel Pie Island!" she exclaims, her face lighting up.

"Not quite."

She looks upset.

Surely she remembers Eel Pie Island?

"I have to go home."

"Maybe we should get something to eat."

"I want to go home." Her chin is set in the stubborn angle he knew of old. Her mouth firm.

"Right. We'll take a cab."

Almost at once she falls asleep, resting against his shoulder. He can smell her skin, her hair; a trace of something medicinal. He remembers the stuff she used in the past, health store shampoo and soap at the beginning, all herbs and plant extracts. Later it was designer products, musky and unsettling.

She had rested against him once before, worn out and close to tears.

"I'm tether-ended, Mel," she said then. "Non-ongoing." But she had rallied. "This too will pass. As the Arabs say." And then a shaky laugh, a change of subject.

The taxi swings left, throwing her sideways so that her face is close against his neck. She sleeps on.

After a while she stirs, sits up, and looks out of the window intently. "But surely this is the way to Eel Pie Island?"

"You remember it?"

"Of course. That Sunday."

THEY GOT TOGETHER on Sundays: the only time Dan was free, given the antisocial hours of the eating business. That particular Sunday they had driven to Twickenham and crossed over to the island where Mel knew someone who knew someone who was doing a gig at the yacht club in the afternoon.

The great days were over by then, he said, no more jazz Sundays at the old hotel, the ones his dad remembered from the 1950s. "In those days the audience crossed by barge ferry and got their wrists stamped with a number to prove they'd paid. Dad said the rot set in with the pop crowd—the Stones, the Who—that's when it began to change. Well, he's a purist so he's prejudiced, of course."

But after the hotel burned down, it seemed the spirit of the place departed. There were squatters and rumors of drugs. Occasionally the police came in. Dereliction hung over the burned-out shell. There were dances still, private parties at the yacht club, but the magic had faded.

Dan noticed a makeshift barbecue set up outside the club and went off to give it some informed investigation, confident he could parlay his way into getting them some nourishment. The other two stretched out on the grass under the willow trees overhanging the bank and listened to the music drifting from the club. A singer with a vibrato not always under control was attempting "Willow Weep for Me."

"So-so singers should never risk Billie Holiday numbers," Mel said sadly. "Even when her voice had gone and she was all over the place with the notes, nobody could do it the way she did." The song came to an end and there was some desultory clapping. He said, "That was the first song I remember hearing."

"Your dad?"

"Absolutely. Mum had taken Dan to have a haircut and Dad was babysitting, reluctantly. I must have been about three. The phone rang and it was one of his mates, he'd just got a bunch of new records in. . . . Dad strapped me into the car and twenty minutes later we were there. Of course, 'new' records in that context meant old."

Hope said drowsily, "My parents were so keen to be British they tried to convince themselves they liked Gilbert and Sullivan and Percy Grainger. Touching, really. In the end they gave up and sneaked back to listen to fado on Grandpa's gramophone."

Two swans floated downriver, riding the water like papier-mâché models, seemingly weightless. They paused and stabbed at the surface, snapping their beaks briskly with a hollow rattling sound, and inclined their necks inquiringly toward Hope's sandaled feet. She longed to reach

246

out, stroke the feathery neck turned so gracefully, drooping to the grassy bank, but a swan was deceptively fragile: it could break your arm with a blow of its beak. Without malice, merely protecting its territory.

"When Dad complains I didn't turn out to be his son the doctor, I remind him it was his jazz records that started it going. They got to me. I knew the names before I could even read the record sleeves. I heard the originals and then I caught the new boys. Humph, who played like Louis, and Melly who sang like Bessie Smith. There was a neo Teagarden, a so-so Mugsy, a passable Bechet, and a couple of Jelly Roll Mortons, though neither of them flashed a diamond in his teeth, all pouring out their guts in basements and upstairs rooms in pubs."

A clarinet solo spiraled from the window.

"As they still are."

"Ah, but it's not the same. They do it for the money now. Then, it was love."

Sun wavered on the grass and lay warm on her closed eyelids, and, half asleep, she felt Mel's hand circle her wrist, like a bracelet. He stroked her fingers.

"Your hands feel rough."

"That's because I'm working in clay; I'm having another go at the virgin and the unicorn."

"Still hung up on virginity? This sounds like autobiography, Pops."

"I'm a good Catholic girl, Mel, brainwashed out of my mind. Give me time."

"Oh, I've got time."

A breeze ruffled the willow tree branches and dislodged a few leaves, which floated down onto the bank. One landed on Hope's head and Mel carefully picked it out and tucked a lock of hair back behind her ear. She opened

247

her eyes to find him leaning on one elbow, looking down at her with the same expression she had seen on his face when he played.

Then Dan came back.

"Sorry I took so long. I went into the kitchen and had a look. They've got a guy in there doing salmon *en croûte* who knows *nothing* about fish. I gave him a few tips."

He was carrying burned sausages inside flabby rolls— "Don't you love the English idea of picnic nosh? Inspiring." And so the day passed.

As it grew dark she saw there were fairy lights strung round the boathouse garden, and through the open windows she could see people still dancing. A boat glowing with light came out of the darkness, glided past, and disappeared behind the trees. A faint snatch of laughter, voices, drifted back from the unseen presence of the boat, like an echo out of the night.

When they drove back, Dan was at the wheel as usual, concentrating on the road, while Mel sprawled in the back commenting idly on the intermingling patterns cast by lights from shopfronts, passing cars, and street lamps.

Dan informed him he was a dreamer and said he despaired of seeing him properly settled, and Hope saw that this was an ironic reenactment of a regular family ritual.

"Dad has finally twigged that even though Mel got a good Upper Second, there are going to be no fat history books bearing the family name. He's not altogether happy about having a layabout musician as his link with immortality."

"He's not particularly happy about having a son who stands slaving over a hot stove like some housewife, for that matter."

248

"Ah, but I'm going to have my own restaurant," Dan said.

Hope is awake. She pushes down the window in the taxi, letting the rush of air buffet her hair, eyes closed, riding the night. "Where are we?"

"Barnes."

Surely there was a restaurant in Barnes—

"I remember a restaurant—"

"Yes, I thought you might."

The taxi rattles on. She is curled into the corner now, away from him, gazing unseeing as the houses are left behind, trees taking their place, leading to the river. She tries to hold on to the threads, see where they lead. Words are returning, and scenes, brightly lit as stage sets, with people she recognizes. Teacups and silver dishes, a tabletop with light shining down onto flowers. But beyond the lights the room is dim and beyond the room there lies an area of darkness, like an unlit pool, that she skirts, wary.

A THREESOME IS a curious social animal with undercurrents of tension and opposing pulls of loyalty and betrayal. An emotional cat's cradle. She found it confusing to be with the twins, so like yet so unlike each other. There were moments of sexual electricity and fumbled encounters. Perhaps, had there been less laughter, less fun, less youthful profligacy, with time, the different paths might have been plainer. As things were, she was confused. *Watch out, the busker had said. Funny thing, twins*

There were times when, seeing them from afar, she was

249

still unable to distinguish one from the other. She kissed them both—how could she not? And felt even more perplexed. Now and then she caught that intent look on Mel's face. Give me time, she had said to him that day by the river. And he did. Mel never rushed things; life had its rhythm, he went with it. They continued in this bumpy, unsatisfactory fashion for some time and then one day Mel told her he was leaving for America.

It was the busker who called him away, reappearing unannounced, tracking him down to the Soho jazz club and making him an offer that seemed too good to be true—partnership on an album, all expenses paid and even a fee up front. The busker was much changed, with gold chains and a medallion, leather pants like a second skin, the matted red hair combed to a luxurious mane.

There were ironies to his success story: he had set off for India to find himself—a spiritual quest—and at an ashram he had met a young American group who told him they, too, were searching for something, without knowing quite what—possibly another hit record. In the end they went home, taking him with them, and the London fiddler became the new boy on the rock block.

"America discovered me!"

The New World, it seemed, was generous and work was plentiful. "It's a whole new, electronic scene out there, mate—multitrack, complex stuff," the busker told him. "Blow your mind. We'll work on it together; you'll love it. And they'll love you!"

"How long will you be gone?" Hope asked, aware of a hollowness, a sinking of spirits.

"Shouldn't take more than a few weeks. I'll be home for Christmas—or Chanukah if you prefer."

"Write me a postcard."

"I'll do better. I'll write you a song."

It was early December when Dan appeared at St. Martin's and announced he was taking her to tea at the Ritz.

"They won't let me in, dressed like this!"

"Yes they will. I've booked a table."

The waiter managed to avoid eye contact or indeed to "see" her at all. A woman so ill clad was more than his focus could cope with. Dan made up for her inadequacy in a velvet suit with flares and a voile shirt.

"The plus of not having Mel about is that the flat's so much tidier. I've actually got room for some new clothes in the wardrobe." A pause. "D'you think the shirt's over the top?"

She studied the heliotrope swirl print, the Byronic collar. "Just a bit."

Surrounded by pinkness: cherubs and swags and floral set pieces, she felt as though she had unwittingly stepped onto a huge fancy gâteau and was ruining the effect and the icing.

Dan was behaving unnaturally, shifting about in his gold and pink chair, checking the plates and silver, finding fault with the service sotto voce. Then he asked abruptly, "Would you consider getting married? To me?" He held out a plate of tiny sandwiches, "I'd see you never went hungry."

She laughed, as he had intended. But she did not take him seriously, which disconcerted him: surely she must know how he felt? He thought he had made it clear. She was the most important thing in his life—

"More important than having your own restaurant?"

He considered the question: "Close," he said.

She laughed again, as he intended.

Had Mel been present things might have gone differently; she could have taken refuge in banter, held Dan off. But Mel was away across the sea, kept on longer than he had intended by a burgeoning work scene. She felt abandoned. And Dan pursued her relentlessly: he knew they were right for each other. It was simply a matter of getting her to see it.

She threw up obstacles. His family: "You can't just wave away a Jewish background as if it were an unsatisfactory sauce. I'm a Catholic, Dan."

"Yes, but you're not *devout,* are you? I mean you're pretty relaxed. When were you last in church, may I ask? And you wouldn't reject me on racist grounds, would you, so what's the problem?"

He was not a bully; it was simply that when he wanted something he went after it. A restaurant. A wife. He always knew what he wanted. Like a boat taking the wind in its sails he surged ahead; she was drawn into the emotional wake he created, pulled along, slightly breathless.

"Tell you what," he offered, "as a goodwill gesture I'll name our first restaurant after your mother."

She gave him a skeptical look. "Conçeiçao? I don't *think* so."

He telephoned her that night. "Guess what I found in a drawer? Something long and thin and yellow and crumpled. I'll give you a clue: New Year's Eve. Madeira!"

In her own room, coiled untidily with unworn necklaces and laddered tights, was a length of bedraggled yellow streamer wrapped in a transparent shower cap. A small, insignificant object: a strip of faded, brittle paper. But it had held fast for a moment across an expanse of water. She remembered the words, reaching her above the noise of the crowd—"It's our covenant!"

The wedding was announced.

All four parents were distraught in their various ways. Dan's father was quiet, but he assembled his arguments with some force: had Dan considered the implications? There was the matter of contraception. Did he really want ten children who would presumably be brought up Catholic? That was the way *they* arranged things? His mother simply pointed out that he would be cut off from his roots. "Deracinated, Dan. Very sad."

"Come on, Ma," he said "What's with the roots? We're container plants: we pick up our roots and take them with us when we go. Fiddlers on the roof."

"I have to say I was pushing it a bit," he remarked later to Hope. "Ma and Pa are closer to Trollope than Tevye the milkman." The children of parents who had come to Britain from Fascist Italy in the 1930s, they were British-born, understated intellectuals, at home in tweeds and floral prints, "assimilated to invisibility," as Mel had once put it.

Hope's parents reacted more noisily: her mother made the sign of the cross and burst into tears, her father banged his fist on the table and strode about the room looking agitated, rubbing the sleeve of his dark business suit, staring at it accusingly as if discovering a stain.

They had arrived as refugees from Salazar's dictatorship and joined the nascent Portuguese colony in Vauxhall. The family business was conducted in Portuguese and when her father was displeased with his daughter he told her so—forcefully—in his native tongue. She, though she understood his words, responded in English: her A-level French

253

was superior to her fumbling grasp of the language of her forebears.

Her father was direct with the prospective son-in-law: "Mixed marriages create problems. Believe me, my boy, there will be conflict."

"We'll work it out," Dan said. "It won't be so bad. I mean, it could be worse: at least I'm a Jew, not a Protestant."

Nobody laughed.

The marriage took place at Caxton Hall with a hungover guitarist and a waiter for witnesses. They used a friend's address—"I mean, who actually *lives* in Westminster?" Dan demanded. "No one real."

"Are you pleased?" Hope asked Mel when he arrived, looking groggy, from the airport.

His eyes were bloodshot and the normal gaiety was not in evidence, but he rallied at the sight of her anxious face. "Of course," he said. "Any mate of my brother's is a mate of mine, though it's probably not legal. It couldn't have happened to a nicer guy—well it could, actually, it could have happened to me." Then, with a tight smile quite unlike his everyday grin, he added, "I didn't know things were moving in that direction quite so fast."

"Nor did I." She felt an ache, like the beginning of hunger, in the pit of her stomach and said, trying not to make it sound like a question, "You'll be around. We'll do things. This won't change anything."

Hope had expected the ceremony to be quick and casual: a bureaucratic procedure briskly dispatched, but the registrar was solemn, rolling out his words with unction, making the most of his role.

"Do you, Maria Esperança, take this man, Daniel, to be your lawful wedded husband?"

Do I? she thought, fear fluttering in her chest, taking her breath. For a moment she contemplated flight, crashing through the door, leaping on board a passing bus. . . . She caught sight of Mel's face: pale, tired, his eyes fixed on her. She found she was shaking so badly with nerves that Dan had trouble fitting the ring on her finger.

Afterward, Mel said, "I never knew your name was Esperança; it's beautiful!"

"At school they called me Essie. So when I left, I decided I wouldn't be Esperança anymore. I'd have the English equivalent, why not?"

Mel said, "Pity, though. Loses something in translation. And changing your name changes you."

"Oh, really?" she retorted. "Tell me about it, *Emmanuel.*"

He brushed the jibe aside. "I don't have a strong sense of selfhood. One of my teachers once said I was amorphous. I didn't make a decision *not* to be Emmanuel anymore, Mel was just less of a mouthful. But Esperança! It's full of guitar chords and shadows and swirling skirts. You should do a painting: 'Self-Portrait as Esperança.' See what you get. You might surprise yourself."

Self-Portrait as Esperança. One day she might do that. Find out who she was. She, too, lacked a strong sense of selfhood; perhaps it came of being the child of immigrants: a reluctance to stand out, be different, when already a difference existed. But then, perversely, her parents' friends clustered in their self-created ghetto, wore dark clothes, and clung to their foreignness and their *saudade.* Perhaps canvas and color would lead her to some answers, perhaps she could paint her way through the conundrum.

The bridegroom had arranged lunch at the Braganza in Mayfair, to please Hope's parents; unfortunately, they claimed to find the menu "on the rich side" and hardly

255

touched their food. Dan's mother and father, cosmopolitans who ate out regularly and spent their holidays abroad, pronounced the Portuguese dishes excellent.

The day after the wedding they drove Mel to the airport. He had to get back right away. The album with the busker had led to a commission in Los Angeles: the soundtrack on a low-budget art house movie. It could be fun, he said.

They stayed with him, laughing, joking, calling last minute messages, waving till he disappeared from view. A silence fell.

Dan took her arm. "I want to show you something. Premises."

"A new flat?" she asked.

He frowned. "The restaurant," he said. "My restaurant."

⚜

THE HONEYMOON BEGAN in Faro and, appropriately, with a recipe. They got off the plane and had lunch before they picked up their car.

"We'll start with *sopa de pedro*," she told the waiter.

Dan tried it doubtfully, brightened. "But this is good! What is it?"

"Stone soup. The way the story goes, a peddler knocks at the door of an old village woman and asks for some water. He says he's hungry. He knows she hasn't anything to spare, of course, but if she's just got a stone and a pan of water he'll prepare a soup that will satisfy them both.

"She gives him a stone and a pot of water and he puts the pot on the fire. After a while he says, 'A few beans would help the stone cook faster. And a potato, perhaps?' She finds him some beans, a couple of potatoes. Now the pot is bubbling, and the peddler says they're almost there.

'But an onion, a good slice of *chouriço* sausage, a bit of meat, a handful of parsley, would really soften the stone.' She gives him what he's asked for and soon a wonderful fragrance is rising from the pot. He serves them both, eats all he can, and leaves, with her calling her thanks. 'Not at all,' he says, 'it's easy to make a soup if you've got a spare stone.'

"That's the recipe," Hope said. "Or so legend has it."

"God," Dan said, "I hate legends." He took another spoonful. "But I like the soup."

Dan had told Mel about the Portuguese honeymoon before he left—"To educate me, I suspect. It's a present from Hope's father—"

"Don't you mean from her parents?" Mel asked.

"I've married into a patriarchal society, my son."

Mel had given him a skeptical twitch of the eyebrows. "Into a patriarchal society? So what's your take on Judaism, O wise one? You think that's gender equality?"

"Look, we all know the Jewish matriarch is the ultimate archetype."

"In the kitchen she's a matriarch. Outside the kitchen? Come on, Dan, you know the Law: does a woman's Morning Prayer include a thank you to the Almighty for not making her a man? No. Whereas every devout Jew begins his day with 'thanks again for not making me a woman.' . . . I rest my case."

The stone soup was a success. The *bacalhau* was not. "Well, if you think a plateful of salt with a mouthful of cod attached is fit for human consumption . . ."

They picked up the rented car and headed west. The almond blossom foamed white across the hillsides and Hope began to tell Dan a story her mother had told her as a child, about a young bride from the north who languished

257

for lack of snow in this sun-baked country, but he was concentrating on the road and the story tailed away unremarked. And in any case, his interest in old stories was limited—"I hate legends!" She went back to map reading, and ran her finger along the paper coastline to the final point: Cabo de Sao Vicente. Cape St. Vincent. Beyond it, the sea. And then . . . her finger ploughed the ocean, westward. America. In her mind she saw Mel, a faraway figure, across a vast expanse of water.

They spent the first night of the honeymoon on the edge of the world, in a room poised above the cliff, hearing the muffled roar of the waves hurling themselves against the rocks. Dan hurled himself at her with similar energy, enveloping her limbs, overwhelming her body with his. The first time, in London, she had blamed her inexperience as he attempted to spark a response from her like someone jump-starting an inert engine. She was learning to do better.

Next morning stepping from the shelter of the hotel's walled garden out onto the headland, they met the wind; it came at them with the ferocity of a thwarted deity. Once there were sailing ships here, square-rigged, whose canvases hung limp if the gods withheld their breath; whose masts the gods could crack when they wanted, whose men they could consign to coral and pearls. Columbus, shipwrecked, made it to the shore, clinging on to a plank. Now, cruise ships plowed past with no more than a pitch and a roll. But there were still men to be skinned alive. Leaning into the wind, eyes watering, Hope picked heads of wild garlic, ragged explosions of stamens and petals, which she wrapped in tissues and carried home to dry and hang in bunches from her new kitchen ceiling.

In Lisbon they abandoned the hired car and climbed

aboard an old tram. Hope dragged a reluctant Dan from monastery to cathedral, from castle to the vast water-front square, Praça do Commércio, arcaded walls glowing with a yellow rich as egg yolk. She took him from *rua* to *avenida,* following her father's injunction to "look at *os empedrados*"—the intricate paved mosaics—ships, waves, and symbols—black basalt and white limestone—that the exiles missed. Walking in Vauxhall, shrugging dismissively at the concrete and synthetic paving stones of London, her parents' voices lifted as they described the beauty of those they remembered from home—"*os empedrados!*"

"We ought to go to Cintra," Hope said. "Byron swam in a stream there—"

"He was *always* swimming somewhere or other," Dan said impatiently. "Still, let's, why not?"

They took the train. Sliding through the outskirts of Lisbon, Hope caught sight of the remains of an old aqueduct, gaunt limbs ankle deep in tacky suburban streets, a shabby behemoth stranded in twentieth century confusion. Here and there the grim muddle of grubby rooftops and traffic-clogged roads gave way to a stretch of undeveloped hillside running down to a brook and there she remarked how the stone of the ruined aqueduct stood out, soft gray against the green. Then she lost sight of it.

TEN MONTHS AFTER the honeymoon came Gideon.

Gideon was circumcised, Hope hesitant to break the ancient tradition—even though she, by what Mel referred to as her Gentility, prevented the child from being Jewish at all.

"Would you consider converting to Judaism?" Dan's

mother had asked her one day, when the pregnancy was confirmed. The tone was conversational. "It would be so much more convenient. And we're Reform of course: easier, quite human, really." She was doing the flowers, placing delphiniums in a tall vase so that they stood out against a white cloud of gypsophila. Her movements were unhurried. Occasionally she stood back to gauge the effect, narrowing her eyes, pushing her hair absently behind her ears. A big mirror at the end of the room reflected the two: Hope, with her bush of straight black hair, her olive skin, arched nose; Dan's mother, soft and fair, gently rounded. Of the two, she looked the more at home in the Victorian furnishings: a woman who knew how to keep a herbaceous border behaving properly; the tines of whose forks were never tarnished. Beside her, Hope looked exotic. Un-English.

Should she consider converting? As a Catholic she was thoroughly lapsed, but perhaps because of that she was reluctant to enter another controlled system and Dan discouraged her—"Funny things can happen when people convert: they go over the top; start checking if the mineral water's kosher, all that stuff." So things remained as they were.

A year after Gideon there was Ruth.

Staying at home with them was a treat to be savored almost guiltily because soon she would get back to work: to the easel and drawing board. Complete her degree and then . . . then what? She still cherished secret dreams; ideas for projects lay neglected in her subconscious, waiting to be revived, sleeping beauties hoping for the kiss of life. Meanwhile, domesticity was a new game and she enjoyed playing the part of a person who drove a double pushchair round the neighborhood pavements, was on first name terms with local shopkeepers, took the dogs for walks, and helped organize charity jumble sales.

She got a postcard from L.A., two lines scrawled in Mel's jagged black writing: "*Nu?* Yiddish, Pops, my latest affectation. It's the Americans, they're totally into it. They go on about 'schmoozing' and people being 'mavens' and how most movies are 'dreck.' And that's just the Gentiles. So how's life?"

She wrote back on a postcard of an Impressionist painting, a sunlit garden with an idealized family group, telling him she was busy making marmalade.

Fifty Million had been replaced by Dan's Diner, his first real restaurant, all scrubbed pine and Vivaldi on tape, occupying a leafy corner of Barnes. Prospering, highly praised, the Diner led on to Chez Daniel, very stygian, with lights made from lengths of drainpipe hanging just above tabletop level to illuminate the fresh flower centerpiece and leave everything else in modish darkness—"The Rocky Horror Room, I assume," Mel commented on his first visit, peering into the gloom. He placed his fingertips on the small round table and requested a Ouija board with his aperitif.

The art house movie had been an unexpected hit: first a cult, then a mainstream success that spawned a sequel.

"But do you like it there?"

"It's okay. They smile a lot."

"Better than a good old British scowl."

"I'll drink to that."

Dan came out of the kitchen and joined them, and within minutes the twins were at their old game of mutual destruction; the mood was buoyant and Hope was laughing.

When Dan went back to the kitchen, the other two sat on over their wine.

"You didn't answer my question on that postcard. How's life with Escoffier?"

"It's fine."

"Very English."

"Hardly. I'm a foreigner, remember?"

"You were never a foreigner. You were a Laura Ashley girl."

"Not anymore. Dan likes me in serious labels."

"Yeah. I noticed."

She was wearing fringed white silk with pearls tied round her brow and silver bracelets from wrist to elbow.

"The Tiffany's Pocahontas look. Nice. Well, you've got to live up to the food, haven't you." He reached for the hanging light and tilted it up, full into her face. "So how are you really? Remember, ve haf vays of making you talk."

She pushed the light away, blinking at him. "Dan works too hard. He gets up before dawn to do the marketing. He's here till after closing time so you can imagine when we get to bed. He's doing an eighteen-hour day and he's so drained he sleeps most of Sunday. I hardly see him."

"Can't he get himself off the hook? Hire another chef?"

"He happens to be brilliant at it. He's the reason all these people are here, Mel. 'Another chef' is not the same." She said, "You look so pale. What happened to all that Californian sun?"

"This is what they used to call a nightclub tan. It's the studio glow. We sit in this recording studio for eighteen hours out of the twenty-four, hunched over a console. Not a lot of time for sun."

She recalled for him a conversation they had once

about why musicians did what they did. "You said the old ones did it because they loved it, and you did it for fun. So?"

"Oh, I still do it for fun. Mind you, the more money, the more fun, I suppose. But let me swirl my wine and consider the question. The music's changing all the time; it's all technology now, different sound, very ornate but that's okay. I've learned to love the electronic world. And when I drop by some club and I sit in and it swings, it's as good as it ever was." He swirled his glass some more. "And I smoke a bit of grass and do the occasional line of coke and drive a vintage Cadillac, and I have a house and a pool with hot and cold running blondes. How much more fun can you have?"

Then he did the double eyebrow twitch and grinned. "Just kidding. I'm getting out as soon as the soundtrack's finished."

She wondered, with a lowering of the spirits, about the hot and cold running blondes. She remembered the next line of that old joke: luckily they don't run too fast.

Chez Daniel, with its dim lighting, got into all the good food bibles, and the prices got them to Pimlico and bought them the Jag. There were family gatherings at Passover, Chanukah, and Christmas—"We're nothing if not ecumenical," Dan's mother had remarked the first time Hope raised the subject of decorations and stockings hung up for Santa Claus. So the mantelpiece glowed with Chanukah lights and a Christmas tree twinkled in the window. But Dan's professional demands put strains on other people's calendars; festivals became something of a movable feast.

"You want us to have the Passover Seder on a Sunday because that fits in with the restaurant's opening hours?" His father looked bemused. "I never thought I'd hear myself sounding like an update of *The Jazz Singer,* but really Dan, I wonder if you've got your priorities right."

"They may not be right but they *are* priorities and I'm stuck with them."

"There's something I want to show you both," Dan's mother broke in. "I've planted some *Jackmanii clematis* in with the New Dawn roses. . . ." A practiced technique— pouring horticultural oil on troubled waters. "Masses of buds already. . ."

So the family celebrated Passover twice that year, once without Dan, once with him, and Gideon managed to get through the four questions in Hebrew—learned parrot-fashion in Sunday classes. Hope thought it might confuse the children to demand, "Why is this night different from all other nights?" when the same question would come up two nights later, until she discovered that traditionally there had always been two Seders, celebrated on successive nights, a leftover from a past when datelines could not be accurately calculated. To accommodate Dan, the second night had now simply been stretched even farther, to the nearest Sunday.

Later, when Gideon was older and more cynical, and he came to "Why is this night different from all other nights?" on the movable second night he would answer himself, "Because D's home for dinner. That makes it *really* different from other nights," before moving on to the more conventional response.

Sometimes the second Seder took place at Dan's and occasionally Mel got home to join them—"I hear you make your own matzah balls," he said to Hope. "Brave woman."

"Your mother's recipe."

"Well, that's what it's all about now. Judaism for people

like us is about chicken soup and bagels, a token peniten-
tial fast once a year and feeling slightly uneasy about eating
prawns—"

"That's Mel, not me," Dan broke in. "I have no problem
with prawns. Prawns are cuisine. As is lobster."

"Dan," his mother protested, "it's not all kitchen talk—"

"You're right! There's music—we're really big on
fiddlers. And Jewish jokes—"

"And of course there's the forgone foreskin. Though
even that's up for discussion now."

"Cue old Jewish joke . . ."

Later, with dinner over, the mood was more somber,
Mel edgy with the news from the Middle East: the
Palestinian refugee camp massacres carried out by
Lebanese Phalangists.

"Sharon's troops just looked the other way. Let them
get on with it. He seemed like good news in seventy-three,
forcing Sadat to talk, but we're ten years on and nobody's
talking. We're in the invasion business now; stuck in
Lebanon. With blood on our boots. What happened to
the Utopian dream? The whole idealistic, light unto the
nations bit?"

"It's the 'never again' syndrome. Twelve years of Nazi
horror have obliterated everything else—little matters of
Spain in 1492, Portugal in 1497. It's the Holocaust knee-
jerk. Young Jews today know more about Hitler than about
Moses."

"And most of them know even less about the
Sephardim!"

Hope said, "What about the Sephardim? I'm confused."

"As well you might be. Despite what Jews in London
or Leeds, in Brooklyn or Miami might think, not all of us
came from a Polish *shtetl*. We happen to be Sephardim. As

265

far as the Ashkenazim are concerned, we don't seem to exist. They've appropriated the Jewish identity—everything begins and ends in Eastern Europe. Who wants to talk about the Greek and Italian Jews—peripheral people."

"We've fallen into these absurd factions: secular, which just means guilt without the gingerbread. And the ultra-Orthodox. So which would we rather see? Jewishness gradually fading like an old stain until nothing remains of it but the shadow, or the rule of the black-coat brigade?"

"Is this the way it ends then," Mel said mockingly, "not with a Holocaust but a statistic: X percent marrying out? And would that be such a bad thing? But it's not ending, is it? The ultra-Orthodox will be the Jewish face of the future: bigoted, humorless, philistine sons of God. People I wouldn't want to have dinner with—and who wouldn't eat with me in any case, me being impure trash in their view. I met an ultra once. He not only wouldn't shake my hand, he wouldn't meet my eye—in case, presumably, I contaminated him with the secret weapon of my nonkosher gaze."

"Meanwhile," Dan said, "in due course, we have to face the matter of Gideon's bar mitzvah. What should I say to him? Let's do it for the grandparents?"

"What does Hope think?" Mel asked. "After all, he's only half Jewish."

"I think one should ask Gideon," she said. "I'm just the shiksa." At least that got a laugh.

When the time came, Gideon opted for a bar mitzvah: "Look, there's no *half* about it: if you've got a circumcised dick, you're Jewish. The otherness begins the first time you have a piss at school. The guy next to you takes a look and says, 'Oh, yeah. Right.' Or if he doesn't know the score he'll say, 'What's that, then?' So let's go for it."

Dan had in any case abdicated the authoritarian throne—"Life's too short and I'm too busy."

They are becoming archetypal permissive parents, crowded to the edge of the nest by their radiant offspring, beaks wide, demanding. Their identities, even their names have been changed: at home they are now Em and D, and seem of no great interest to their children: the incurious young do not ask to see her paintings, stacked up in her so-called studio in an attic room. Kicking a football about in the garden, they knock the horn off her terra-cotta *Unicorn with Virgin* and fail to notice the damage. They do not ask their father, how come you became a cook, D? The funky uncle is popular when he sends them the latest American album or when one of his songs makes it to the charts. She should get back to her work but she tells herself she needs to be here. So she is here, to see them through school changes, exam revision, the highs and lows and white-water rafting of adolescence. She can always take up her work again later. Can't she?

She does not much care for being addressed as Em, but Spock mothers avoid confrontation so she lets it pass. The children call each other sib and are casually foulmouthed as she had never been.

Ruth has inherited Hope's pointed chin, her cheekbones, straight hair, and nose. Gideon has glossy black curls and a bodily grace that renders slouching elegant. Ruth is jealous of his hair, his twelve-month seniority, his narrow hips, and his sex. She carries penis envy into new territory when Gideon announces he wants to be bar mitzvahed.

"It's so totally unfair; I bet he's only doing it for all the presents he'll be given, and the attention. Just because he has a circumcised nob he gets a bar mitzvah just like that."

267

But it was not, in fact, so simple at all.

Gideon's thirteenth birthday was still some way off when Hope went to see the rabbi, a man with a wry, worldly smile and tired eyes.

"Even in the Reform movement a Jewish mother is a necessary prerequisite for being, as it were, Jewish per se," he said kindly. "He'll have to convert."

Convert?

"Appear before the Beth Din. Answer a few questions, prove he has some knowledge of Judaism, the prayers, show them he can read Hebrew—"

"No problem. He's been going to Sunday classes for years."

"Good, good. Then there should be no difficulty." He hesitated. "And he'll need a ritual immersion. A visit to the *mikveh*."

Hope had gleaned a few facts over the years; she knew Orthodox women were required to have ritual immersions, to be cleansed of disgusting conditions like childbirth and menstruation. But Gideon?

"Oh, it's hardly a traumatic event. Don't worry. Just a dip in the pool, a prayer."

It sounded simple. "Where do we go?" she asked.

He hesitated again. "Cardiff."

"We have to go to *Cardiff*? That's about two hundred miles away. Surely there must be *mikvehs* all over London?"

"Ah, yes," he said, the tired smile briefly on view. "Orthodox *mikvehs*. Gideon is ineligible to use them."

The London *mikvehs* were restricted to the Already Chosen. Gideon lacked the maternal laissez-passer. Discussions had dragged on for years: one day, he assured her, Reform immersions would take place in London. But meanwhile the nearest pool was in Wales. One faith, one God. But different *mikvehs* to reach him.

She made the reservation, paid the required fee. Gideon took a day off school and they set off for Cardiff. On the train they had a British Rail breakfast. As the waiter swayed down the aisle toward them Hope suggested Gideon might forgo the bacon.

"Why?"

"Oh, Gideon, you *know* why. I do think that on the day you're taking the kosher plunge you should keep off the pig meat."

"D eats bacon."

"He had a Jewish mother. He doesn't have to prove anything."

In Cardiff the sun was shining. She checked the street map and they walked from the station.

"Will there be a rabbi?"

"I expect so." Certainly she felt she had paid enough for one to be shunted in for the occasion.

"Will it be like John the Baptist? That picture in the National Gallery. Will a dove hover overhead?"

"This is *Old* Testament time, Gideon dear. Different play. Different cast."

At the council swimming baths the girl on the ticket desk took their names and checked a list.

"Oh, yeah, love. You want the Jewish pool, isn't it? Hang on a sec."

She pressed a buzzer and after a moment the door behind her swung open. Hope had imagined a small procession, possibly a spot of chanting, even a touch of Israel in Egypt about the proceedings, a few Handelian chords, but it was a young man carrying a key, wearing a string vest, flip-flops, and cutoff shorts. He nodded in a friendly way.

Could this be the rabbi? Hope wondered. He *was* bearded. Just how progressive were these people?

He led them through a wilderness, a backstage pool world of pipes and filters and dank concrete; buckets and mops and a tangle of flexible plastic tubes lying in a corner like a stranded octopus. At the end of a dark corridor he unlocked a door and waved them into a small, windowless set of rooms.

"He can change in one of the cubicles. . . . The *mikveh's* next door." His Welsh delivery gave the word an oddly homegrown lilt. "Got to get back to the pool—I'm a lifeguard, see? Keep an eye on him, won't you? Lock up when you've finished." He handed her the keys.

Gideon observed the hair dryer and the pink nylon carpet.

"Hey, you could have yourself a quick shampoo and blow-dry while I practice my underwater chanting."

He put on swimming trunks and they peered into the neon-lit room next door: mosaic tiles in dull green. A tiny, L-shaped pool, the water tepid. He looked at her disbelievingly. "This is going to *change* me?"

"Qualify you. Shut up and plunge."

He walked down the steps and she heard him murmuring in Hebrew before he sank beneath the water. A stream of bubbles suggested that he was continuing underwater. Surfacing, he floated on his back, reciting various prayers appropriate to the occasion. He double somersaulted, agile as a dolphin, the water going *shh-shh,* like a disapproving monitor against the sides of the pool.

"Why don't you come in too, Em?" he called. "God can give us both the wink. Two for the price of one; a bargain!"

270

For a moment she contemplated stripping off and joining him to share the great transforming experience. On one level it would be a laugh, an in-joke; on another, she was aware of a flicker of yearning: she, too, might be cleansed in some obscure way, miraculously renewed. But this was Cardiff, not Jerusalem, and there was no pool of Bethesda to heal her, to wash away the callouses of life. The surface rippled gray green, dull as jade. He flicked water at her and she licked her lips—the taste and smell of chlorine was one of her earliest memories.

She was six when she learned to swim. Her father feared death by drowning—neither he nor her mother could manage a pool width between them and the presence of a daughter who stood some chance of survival in case of shipwreck, flash flood, or deluge reassured them; her prowess somehow held watery disaster at bay for them all.

Together the three of them would walk to the pool along the Thames at Vauxhall, breathing in traffic fumes while he conjured up for the girl a very different embankment: the Douro in Porto with its iron bridges like horizontal Eiffel towers spanning the river, the cliff face soaring from the *ribeira,* and, on the south bank, the pale stucco of the wine lodges—Cockburn, Campbell, Graham—"English names, like colonial flags, hung out for the world to see."

For her parents it had been the quayside on the north bank that glowed most brightly: cafés, open-fronted butchers' and fishmongers' shops; stalls selling almonds, dried figs, olives from barrels.

In her father's memory the waterfront and the city merged, the little flat-bottomed boats moored along the quay, the railway station whose vast walls glowed with frescoes and *azulejo* tiles—this was a city of hilly, winding

271

streets, of architecture that should have been dour, re-
deemed by graceful decoration. And there were the rattling
trams that led past the estuary bar to the open sea.

The river was always present, lying low and brackish in
summer, transformed in autumn by sudden violent flooding that could sweep away houses, drown men, women, and
children. England was no safer: the Thames, too, could
flood. And the sea was everywhere: "We speak of the earth,"
her father said somberly, "but nine tenths of the globe is
water!" So Hope learned to swim. The parental obsession
with her swimming achievements and the great past of the
mother country was synthesized in a phrase her father
often quoted: "God gave the Portuguese a small country
as cradle but all the world as their grave." So many young
men, sailing into the unknown, dying with salt water filling
their lungs, blind eyes no longer seeking a horizon.

Trade was what made a country great, he told the child.
Import-export, the movement of commodities, that was
what made the world go round. Tall ships carrying spices
and precious stones, sugar and gold. Later, when Portugal
joined the EEC, he was torn between pride in the achieve-
ment and lamentation that it should come to this: to go
cap in hand, to beg entry to a trading community where
once they had owned half the known world!

His face would darken as he gazed into the Thames,
seeing in its brown eddies the sweep and swirl of faraway
waters—beyond the Tagus or the Douro, he dreamed of
the Amazon, the Limpopo, the Congo, waterways that had
been part of their history. "The greatest maritime empire
the world had known. Gone, all gone."

Hope had no knowledge, then, of the condition of
yearning that forms part of the Portuguese soul. The

sadness, the plangent inner music, the sense of loss and distance that runs like an underground river through their surface lives. Their *saudade*. Later she shared it.

"Can I come out now?" Gideon asked. "Am I Jewish enough or d'you reckon I should give myself a bit longer, make sure I'm done?"

Hope licked her lips again. "The water doesn't taste of chlorine. I hope it's clean."

"They don't need chemicals: it's sort of divine purification; like manna from heaven."

When he was dressed they went back to the girl in the lobby, sitting behind the glass of the ticket desk. She was painting her nails but looked up briefly.

"I think we need an official stamp or something."

She smiled, friendly. "To prove you've bin yere, that's right, love." She waved her hand in the air, drying off the nails, picked up a date stamp, and pressed it carefully onto the form Hope had pushed across the desk. "There. All done, right?"

She went back to her nails and they walked out into the sunlight.

"Is that it?" Gideon asked. She suggested tea in a Cardiff café: toasted tea cakes and a Bakewell tart. Had she been a real Jewish mother she would have given him homemade honey cake and apple strudel. But of course, had she been a real Jewish mother they would not have been there in the first place.

Later there was the service; the synagogue full of Dan's relatives—the women elegant in hats and gloves, the men wearing top hats or bowlers. Gideon read the portion of

273

the Law in Hebrew with stylish fluency while Ruth glowered. Hope's parents were there, shaking hands stiffly, proud of their grandson but not knowing what to say when various in-laws bombarded them with *"Mazeltov!"*—and someone commented, "Our Sephardi Hebrew is so much more beautiful than that horrible Ashkenazi gabble, don't you think?"

❧

Routines are established. Yoga offers consolation for a while. Then, barely noticing, she abandons it for tai chi. Aerobics. She feels increasingly redundant; her meals no longer needed as the children graze at odd hours, moving seamlessly between deep-freeze and microwave. She becomes hesitant, uncertain, the habitual pause for consideration lengthens.

She puts forward plans for discussion, for consultation, to be examined in detail, decisions put to the vote. "Spontaneity is not an Em thing," she hears Ruth say once to a visiting friend. "She needs a show of hands to tell her she can have a shit."

There was a brutality about their mode of discourse that found its way, she felt, into their actions and reactions. By your verbs shall ye be judged.

So when they spoke of dumping and being dumped, that said something about the way they saw the world. When they referred to dick heads and wankers, that, too, established an overview.

Aggrieved about this or that, she might say she felt "upset"; they would be "pissed off." Under exceptional circumstances, "well pissed off."

Coming home from school one day, they found her "upset" by the presence of a dead bird in the garden, lamenting its bloodied beauty.

"Don't worry," Gideon said. "It'll be rats' breakfast by tomorrow."

"Oh, fox's supper before then," Ruth corrected him. They smiled down cheerfully at the winged corpse.

"Don't you care about *anything?*" Hope asked them. "Does nothing touch you?"

There was just too much, they explained. "You'd be eating your own entrails." And the law of the unintended effect came into it, too. "Give money to famine relief in one country and you find all you've done is extended the reign of a right sod of a warlord. Make a donation for humanitarian aid somewhere else and you've helped turn a localized uprising into a civil war.

"And all that dosh to help drought or earthquake victims that we drop into tins or send off to Sunday newspapers or television? Most of that ends up in numbered bank accounts in Switzerland.

"You want to help the planet, Em? Save the shark. Limit your ambitions."

At their age—the Swinging Sixties having failed to penetrate her corner of London—she had still been waiting to have sex. They did it. They did not fall in love, they fancied people; they shagged. She forced herself to raise the issue of safe sex with Ruth, to be rewarded with a pitying look and patronizing pat on the shoulder.

"Condoms, Em. We're not morons."

She did not, she decided, envy them. Their right-on vocabulary carried with it a penalty: liberated into frankness they were deprived of nuance, of the ambiguity that lay in "perhaps," in "possibly," in "perchance." Did no one yearn anymore? Or was she being too subjective, had her youthful yearning been nothing more than her personal *saudade*?

It was difficult to call a halt; it is always difficult, when each individual step seems perfectly reasonable. It was only when they were quite a way along the road that Hope looked back and wondered at what point she had lost her way—they both had. Where was the path that meandered, where they smelled the honeysuckle and went swimming in the sun? Then she remembered: that was Mel's path. The fun had stopped when Mel left.

A package arrived from Los Angeles, delivered by courier: an album with a cover in black, gray, and white mosaic—a close-up of a Portuguese pavement. Mel's latest, "Afternoon Sadness."

There was a scribbled card: "Sorry I can't be with you for the Seder; got to see a man about a tune in Havana. Forgive me: mea Cuba, mea maxima Cuba."

Dan was too busy and then too tired to listen to the record and she played it after the children had left for school. It was an offbeat take on the blues, with lyrics that captured the all too fleeting moment, the sunset touch, the evanescence of wood smoke rising through trees in an autumn dusk. The final track was a glancing look at the way the past and future clog up the present, with words whose aptness had become sharper with time:

> Keep a watch on the seasons,
> Time past and still to be;
> The pruning in the pod,
> Seed in the tree . . .

Ah, yes, propagation has its dangers: confidence breeds independence, which was what she had always wanted for the young ones, and then engenders solipsism, which she had not reckoned on. *They're flowering, reaching for the sun; we're the old wood of yesteryear, nice enough, but not to spend a whole evening with.*

His music filled the room, bringing back other times, other moments; his hand circling her wrist as they lay under willow trees on a riverbank; the way he cradled the guitar, drawing harsh sweetness from the glowing wood. She felt a chill as though someone had walked over her grave.

At what stage should she have cast off the knitting, pronounced the parental pattern complete, and let them get on with their lives? Got on with her own? When they reached double figures? After O levels? A's?

When they reached seventeen and it was they who were doing the leaving, off to university, off to art school, it seemed somehow too late. Filled with doubts, she took to questioning herself: *What of the day when you look at the creatures you hosted in your womb and see them with objective eyes, no longer trailing clouds of glory? When you fall out of love with them? What then?*

The moment passed, of course, but Puck's magic dust had fallen from her eyes and she saw the objects of her undemanding love without the shimmer that had blinded her, that brought the tears welling when she caught a glimpse of small fat knees or the vulnerable nape of a thin neck. It was no longer the love that requires only that the object of that love continue to exist.

And what of the moment when you look out of the window and see a stranger emerging from your own front door, leaping into the

Porsche and driving off without a backward glance, and know there was a day you took the wrong turn?

Dan grew ever more frantic, always on the mobile, tapping thoughts into his laptop, full of plans, projects. There was a television series and a book. They had made an arrangement, early on, that she would dine once a week at the restaurant. She would dress as if for a dinner party and he would join her at the table, taking a break from the kitchen, briefly relaxing into intimacy. Mel joined them one night, in London to record an album with a young African singer being touted as the next big thing in World music. He examined his architecturally assembled salad plate with interest.

"This is not a salad, this is a statement. I can't recognize half this stuff."

"It's the usual mix: *mizuna,* red mustard, ruby chard—"

"Ah, here's one I know: rocket—"

"Of *course,* rocket. Rocket is today's sun-dried tomatoes."

"So what are sun-dried tomatoes now?"

"Oh, sun-dried tomatoes are kiwi fruit. Forget sun-dried tomatoes." Dan broke off to scream under his breath at a passing waiter. "Enjoy," he said, squeezing Mel's shoulder and signaling furiously to another waiter with his head and eyebrows. "Got to get back to the kitchen. Catch you later, kid."

There was a silence.

"Done any painting?" Mel inquired. "Any work in clay?"

She wrinkled her nose. "Oh, that's all Dead Sea fruit. Dead kiwi fruit." She had not opened the door of the upstairs studio for years. "I'm learning to use a computer. Surf the Net."

Later Hope realized that it had been her last Saturday night date with Dan. The arrangement became difficult: the tables were all booked, there was a waiting list. And in any case the master chef was too busy to take a break at peak time.

She suggested they should go out for Sunday lunch instead and for a while they did, but Dan found the mediocrity of local eating houses unacceptable and if they booked at the Ivy or Caprice, or one of the new, smart places, she sensed an element of competitiveness that destroyed the day of rest.

He no longer discussed his plans; "the business," as he had taken to calling it, had grown too complicated: it was a matter of economics and expansion and marketplaces. He was still passionate, but these days he talked less of "the integrity of the plate" or the intricacies of sauce reduction, and more of interest rates and buy-ins.

Nor did she see much of the children. They, too, were busy, Gideon writing bits and pieces about his generation for magazines with incomprehensible names; Ruth creating polystyrene sculptures from discarded, unwashed burger containers. Hope sensed an undercurrent of impatience and, worst of all, objectivity when she spoke to them. She hungered for easy, unqualified affection; understanding. It seemed no longer to be on offer.

Gardening, she thought, could be an answer. Women talked of gardening with the sort of fervent seriousness the nuns at school had reserved for God. Planting the summer bedding was a sacrament: it brought them fulfillment, joy even; it was an innocent pleasure. Above all, it passed the time.

She studied the garden despairingly. She saw that it had been neglected for too long. The grass was cut, but husbandry went no further. Weeds flourished alongside the desirable shrubs, overwhelming them so that the seasons passed with no more than a token hint of a bloom here and there among the undergrowth. Her mutilated unicorn lay, unremarkable as any horse, next to a terracotta girl engulfed by weeds. Once, a mysterious force had ringed them: myth and the cunning of art had held the two together. Now the life had gone out of them.

She could have employed a gardener, but what would have been the point of that?

She was aware that her neighbor maintained flawlessly manicured nails along with a controlled display of color in her garden throughout the year. Visiting for coffee, Hope studied the warm reds, rich purples, cooling sprays of white.

"How do you do it? How does your garden grow?" she asked.

"You plant seeds, basically. And wait."

"But our soil is useless. Clay. Sour, ungiving. Things die on me."

"Masses of natural manure, that's what you need. Slather it on all winter. It improves the soil wonderfully. If you want a floriferous garden, well-rotted manure's the answer. And avoid garden-center stuff in sacks: useless."

Natural manure. Well-rotted. Where would one find it? Farms were probably knee-deep in the stuff, but she knew no farms. Yellow Pages, she thought, might suggest routes to the real thing. She looked up manure.

The headings went straight from Manufacturing to Maps

280

and Charts. No manure to be found in the Yellow Pages. She abandoned horticulture.

It was Ruth who, unwittingly, provided the answer. Reluctantly showing her mother round the end-of-term student show at art school, she paused to glance up at some shiny objects dangling from the ceiling. "Not bad," she said, "if you like glasswork."

Hope studied the glittering mobile suspended above them; she saw how the light was held at bay by some of the brilliantly colored shapes and allowed to penetrate others, so that the complex structure wavered, seeming both solid and fluid. Ruth read the caption aloud: "'Wave and Particle.' Yeah. Well. Of course."

This time there is no hesitation; no show of hands needed, no discussion. This time Hope knows what she wants.

From the fire she draws the invisible heart of glass. The paradox of a cool, rigid shape growing out of a furnace delights her. Transformation, alteration, the changing of one thing into another, these offer hope. So the process of turning a solid into a liquid that metamorphoses into a very different solid catches her imagination—"Though strictly speaking, glass is not a solid," the teacher explains. "At room temperature, glass can be regarded as a liquid so viscous that it behaves like a solid."

He works backward through history; he tells them of nineteenth century Bohemian glass, black as basalt; of the seventeenth century German glassmaker who created a new type of ruby red glass by adding gold to the liquid; he shows them fifteenth century Venetian *lattimo,* opaline white glass. The Romans worked in glass, he tells them, as did the Assyrians, "But the earliest of all were the Egyptians, who were creatively turning the apparent into the transparent fifteen hundred years before the birth of Christ. Now let's see what you can do."

Hope's first glass piece was a tree. Around her, other students began cautiously, creating small objects: a bowl, a plate, a simple vase or two. She embarked on an almond tree. The teacher suggested she might be attempting something perhaps too ambitious, but she persisted. From a trunk no more than ten inches high grew fine branches, delicate golden twigs topped with a cloud of tiny white blossoms fragile as snowflakes. She took it home and stood it on a table by a window. As the breeze touched the branches they shivered with a glassy tinkling sound.

Ruth hated the almond tree and called it literalist kitsch.

"It reminds me of the almond blossom I saw in the Algarve when Dad and I were on our honeymoon."

"Christ, Em," Ruth groaned. "Holiday snaps."

Ruth herself was working on a conceptual piece that involved telephone directories, pigeon shit, and a hair-dryer.

Gideon was now editing a modish quarterly magazine printed on dirty looking paper, the pages violently color washed more for dramatic impact than practicality. "I've written some lyrics," he told Hope one day. "A guy I know might use them in a multimedia thing he's doing. See what you think." He dropped a photocopied sheet on the table and loped off to the kitchen.

She was touched that he sought her opinion. They had been close once, laughing at the same silly jokes, fighting over the same licorice allsorts—the blue speckled aniseed disc, the fat pink coconut cushion. That long-ago day in Cardiff, immersing himself for the nonevent of the ritual bath, he had called to her to join him in the pool. "God can give us both the wink. Two for the price of one." The friendly girl painting her nails, pausing to stamp their official piece of paper "to prove you've bin yere, right?" But who, by taking thought, can be transformed?

She looked at Gideon's lyrics.

> Men lose their balls,
> Women their tits,
> Kids lose their sweetness,
> Old folks their wits.
> So come fill the cup with the last of the wine,
> Isn't it great to be just twenty-nine?

Her generation had expressed the same thought in different words: *I hope I die before I get old,* which several had managed to do, with a combination of drugs and drink and fast driving. And: *Never trust anyone over thirty.* Odd how thirty now seemed a remarkably youthful age; an enviable age, indeed.

Gideon called from the kitchen, "I thought you could ask Mel to take a look."

Ah. It was the famous funky uncle's view he really wanted. "Right," she said. "I'll fax him." But she forgot. She was busy now, learning to find her way through a miraculous new world; spinning translucent magic from the raw materials of frit and cullet—broken glass, limestone, and sodium; pouring, rolling, slumping, drawing.

There is heat and flame, and a fusion that changes everything while she watches: so might Daphne's smooth limbs grow leaves; a man's face melt into a pig's snouty features; transformation. And how satisfying it was, if a piece proved flawed, inadequate, unsatisfactory, to throw it back, consign it to the flames and make it afresh.

Might she, immolated, be transformed? Plucked from the furnace and remade?

But the flames are strictly for the blowing pipe, the heat

for molding, pressing, thinning. The glass is changed; she must continue as she is.

She was working on something new, a curious mixture of materials: a reclining figure shaped from a length of strongly grained wood, inlaid with blind amber eyes, glass veins, and nervous system in blue and green. Hope thought it looked like a piece of flotsam laced with glittering Sargassum seaweed, but when Ruth saw it she said, "Hey, it's you."

"It's not meant to be."

"Yeah, well it looks like you. See the way she's holding her own arms, as though she's cradling something that's not there. That's what you do when you're stressed out. It's a dead Em who's suffered a sea change. *Very* rich and strange."

"Is that a compliment?"

"What do you think? You've certainly come on since the comic almond tree."

The glasswork kept her busy. But not busy enough.

THEY WERE IN the kitchen when Dan came down the stairs, Hope making coffee and Mel leaning against the sink, eating muesli.

"Look who just got here," she said.

"The plane was early. I thought I'd call in en route—"

"Great to see you, kid." Dan was already punching in numbers on his mobile. He hugged Mel with one arm, the other holding the phone to his ear, and then he was out of the kitchen and into the study. They heard him demanding explanations for some unacceptable delay over a company report, questioning the result of a business study.

"Does he still cook food or am I out of touch?"

Hope smiled apologetically and put bread in the toaster. "Actually, most of the time he takes decisions. Has an overview."

The voice from across the hall was suddenly loud. "Fuck the lot of them!"

He came in, took a mug of coffee from Hope, gulped and handed it back. "Too hot."

"Sit down. Let it cool."

"No time. Got to go. Meetings all morning."

"So how's—" Mel began.

"Don't ask!"

As he reached the front door they heard him laughing. The door slammed and a moment later the wheels of the Porsche spun on the gravel as he gunned out of the drive. There was an instant's silence.

"Why did he laugh?" Hope asked.

"Old Jewish joke. Two friends meet after some time. One says to the other, 'So you don't ask how's business?' His friend says, 'So how's business?'"

Hope smiled faintly. "Don't ask! Right."

"This wasn't such a good idea. Bad timing."

"There is no good timing for Dan these days. Your coffee's getting cold. And eat your toast," she said.

"I see we've turned into a Jewish mother."

They had lunch at a café that could have been the original greasy spoon, except that while Fifty Million had offered fry-ups and apple strudel, now it was falafel in Lebanese bread wrap, or Thai fusion for light-diet clients. Hope noted the lack of background music.

Mel said, "It's a place for musicians."

Are you happy? she wanted to ask, but was inhibited. There had been women in his life: Ruth spent a week in Los Angeles and described a cool Californian beauty "with legs up to her armpits and teeth you need Raybans to check out." Adding, "Not a lot of laughs." Before her there had been a Japanese graphic designer, a record company publicity girl, and a retro-hippy New York lyric writer. An ongoing story of brief encounters, all history now. Just once, catching her in tears at a bad moment, when he discovered Dan was drinking too much, he had said bitterly, "You don't say what you think, Hope, do you? What you *feel*. You never have. You make it difficult."

To answer that would have been too painful, dangerous even: would have had her looking into the abyss. So she did her usual thing and changed the subject. "Dan's going to have this incredible restaurant in the Dome when it opens. High Concept, they call it."

"Is Dan happy about going in? Is a big tent the right place for a classy joint?"

"The backers seem to think so. You haven't seen it yet, have you? We could take a river trip. See how it's coming along. If you have time."

"Oh, I have time."

The riverside panorama slid past them as they stood, leaning on the rail.

"London seems to have changed its shape again every time I see it," Mel said. "I'm beginning to feel like a foreigner. Maybe it's time I came home."

Back in Soho as the sky darkened, he was on more familiar ground. They wandered through Archer Street, empty, lined with dot-com shop windows and offices, and he reminisced about the old Archer Street market for itinerant musicians, where the gigs were picked up, the wolf kept from the door. Where the all too available players waited hopefully for the fishers of men in their camel hair coats, with their notebooks and scraps of paper. On weekday mornings it would be buzzing, the pavements crowded with men, spilling over into the street itself, informally pedestrianizing the area. The musicians stood about smoking, chatting, looking bleary in crumpled suits, sweaters, unsuitable shoes. Some wore hats. Moving among them, the middlemen checked their notebooks, calling out the crucial words—"Trombone needed. . . . Sax and clarinet for Sunday wedding. Bring your own tux. . . . Keyboard and vocals for holiday camp week. . . . Any drums here?"

Now it would all be computerized, faxed, and emailed. A text message on the mobile. Voicemail waiting. Listen to these options. Speak after the tone.

"It's more dignified now, I guess. Better organized, this way. But the old Monday mornings were personal. Looked at objectively, I suppose it could have been humiliating. I was just a kid, a spectator on the outside, what did I know? But I seem to remember a lot of laughs."

Among the brash and shiny new shop fronts there were still shabby doorways, stairways clad in worn lino leading to grubby basements. There was still the occasional Italian deli or coffee shop, still the French patisserie—"parcels of our past," he said.

There was a new man on the jazz club door but the old boys were still there—most of them. They welcomed the prodigal with an unrestrained barrage of amiable abuse; they suggested he was slumming, or possibly desperate.

Had the Yanks finally kicked him out, or had he come to his senses unaided?

While he waited to get Hope a drink, someone at the bar—clearly not a regular—asked if coffee was available. There was a Bateman cartoon moment: looks exchanged, eyes rolling up, jaws dropping.

"Available?" The sax player's face sagged in deep shock. "*Available?* The coffee here is world famous. There are members of a South American tribe deep in the Amazon basin who cross the intervening continents to come here and dip their arrows in our coffee."

"I'll have a beer," the man said nervously.

The musicians looked much as they used to. Less hair, more paunch, and deeper wrinkles, but the *tristesse,* the *cafard,* the angst—all the silky, self-conscious worrying endured by the people who patronized Dan's restaurants—was not in evidence here. Here, the blues was on offer, but only on the bandstand.

When they first met, Mel had explained the blues to her. "The textbooks will tell you it's a diatonic major scale with added minor thirds and sevenths, but what it's really about is love and death; sex and betrayal." The inescapable sadness of things. And the magic. For the players, summer came nightly and they bloomed.

Hope sat at the back of the room, hearing again the way the musical conversation went on between one instrument and another, between the boys in the band: the ensemble, the riff, and, rising through it all, the irresistible beat.

"It don't mean a thing if you ain't got that swing," somebody muttered, croaky voiced.

Mel cradled his guitar, bending to it like a mother to a child, as the number built, threads weaving the group into a single entity, emptied of sorrow, disappointment, fear, regret. Swinging to a cleansing climax.

This, Hope realized, was what kept them young: the ritual immersion in the music.

Afterward they went on to the restaurant. As Hope pushed open the kitchen door, Dan was having a seizure over a spoiled batch of lavender crèmes brûlées: he slammed a cleaver down on a chopping block with a force that embedded the blade deep into the wood. There was a pause, a hush; even the bubbling pans went silent. Nobody moved. Then he hurled the entire dessert tray—ramekins and contents—into the nearest dustbin, screaming curses. The pastry cook burst into tears.

"Bad timing," Mel murmured.

Glassy eyed, his face flushed dark red, Dan registered neither their arrival nor their departure. They threaded their way through the tables, through the social laughter of people confident that they were in good hands here, through the questioning voices of waiters and the discreet clatter of plates and cutlery. When the front door swung shut behind them, they stepped into the silence of a sleeping street.

"Jesus," Mel said. They walked on. "If that's what it's like at work, having you and the kids must keep him sane."

"Since he never sees them, and me only when he's on the point of collapse, I'd say that was an overly optimistic comment. We have a boat we never go near, we have a swimming pool he hasn't used for six months; he bought a camcorder, a set of drums, and an exercise bike and I don't think they've even been unpacked. It's a treadmill."

He drove her home to Twickenham, by way of Eel Pie

Island. They walked across a new bridge and found their way to the bank with the willow tree. The place was much changed: where the burned-out shell of the old hotel had stood were neat rows of terraced houses, manicured gardens running down to the river. There was an almost full moon and the grass glittered as brightly as the water. Bushes shone like silver. Interlopers in a suburban enclave, they crept under the willow tree and sheltered in its shadow.

It was then, with the past nudging them so sharply, that the protective barriers she had built and reinforced over the years gave way. She leaned against his shoulder and wept. "I can't face going home. Not yet."

"It's okay," he said. "I've got time."

At the wedding ceremony, when the registrar had launched into the portentous "Do you, Maria Esperança, take this man . . ." Mel had run a crazy movie moment in his head, breaking in, shouting out that the marriage could not take place. "She's chosen the wrong man! He won't make her happy!" But the ceremonial words had flowed on, uninterrupted to the final knell: till death us do part. Hope was not a practicing Catholic. But she had promised to cleave to the man in question. He found it impossible to ask her to break that promise.

The closest he could come was to tell her now that she was not alone. "I'm here whenever you need me. We made a covenant, after all."

"What?"

"You probably won't remember. On Madeira, when the boat was leaving, we were waving good-bye and you threw—"

"A streamer."

"Right, a yellow streamer. It lay in a drawer in the old flat for years, mixed up with cough sweets and train timetables and passports. When Dan moved out it must have got lost in the upheaval. Whatever. Or maybe it just disintegrated and, anyway, by then it seemed irrelevant, you being married. But when I grabbed it that morning on the quay, I wanted to make sure you kept your bit of the streamer, so I yelled out, 'It's our covenant, Pops!'"

"No you didn't!" Her voice was sharp, panic-stricken. "You couldn't have!"

"But I did."

"If you had, I'd have heard you, I'd have known. You *didn't* say 'Pops.'"

"No? Maybe not. Does it matter?"

The river slid past, ripples catching the moonlight in an endless ribbon of silver.

"Not now." Her voice was lifeless.

"Well. It still holds. If there's anything I can—"

"Comfort me, Mel."

And in the shadow of the willow tree, its weeping bulk blotting out intrusive moonlight, he comforted her.

THE SECOND HONEYMOON was a sort of ultimatum. Not that the words second honeymoon or ultimatum were used. She simply told Dan they could not go on the way they were. They needed to get away, spend some time together.

At first he refused to take her seriously. "Don't be ridiculous! I can't take a week off—"

"Two weeks."

"Even more insane. I'm not a company director, Hope. I've got restaurants to take care of. I have to *be* there. Keep an eye on them. I've seen what happens to absentee chefs. Business goes pear shaped."

"Have you considered what happens to absentee

husbands? Have you considered you might end up with a pear-shaped marriage?"

He laughed. "I'll try and get home early next week, I promise. Tell you what: I'll take you out to dinner."

That was when she brought out the ultimatum: either he took two weeks off and they had a proper holiday or she was leaving. He took refuge in a music hall response: "'I say, I say, my wife's gone off on her own.' 'Jamaica?' 'No, she left of her own accord.'"

Hope was standing by the window. A slight breeze set the glass almond tree tinkling. Without turning her head she swung her arm, hard, and swept the tree off the table. It flew across the room and shattered against the wall, scattering the floor with a thousand glittering pieces.

There was a silence.

He bent down and picked up a tiny white disc; a fragment of almond blossom, pebble smooth, and nodded as though in response to a statement. "When d'you want us to go?"

He called in a favor from a top Paris restaurateur and arranged a French season: internationally renowned guest chef; rare wines. The PR people took over.

"Two weeks," he said. "I'm all yours."

"Really? You won't be taking your mobile, then?"

"Well, *obviously* I'll be taking my *mobile*," he said. "There could be an emergency."

"Dan," Hope said. "This is the emergency."

The children billed it the second honeymoon, sending them up, but supplying a subtext of support that surprised Hope. On board the plane, they discovered that Gideon had organized a bottle of champagne.

When they disembarked a bouquet of red roses was waiting for Hope at the car check-in. She glanced at Dan, surprised, pleased. Then she looked at the card and saw that the flowers were from Ruth.

There was an old aunt in Faro who had stayed on when Hope's parents left for England and wrote occasionally to her mother, but when they went looking for her the street seemed to have vanished into a hospital complex and a parking lot. The Faro Hope's parents talked about no longer existed. It had been swallowed up into developer land: raw cubes of concrete, shopping malls, and multi-story car parks.

They were studying a street map on a traffic island between a supermarket and a block of flats, when Hope noticed the little pedimented entrance a few yards farther on. Shielded by cypress trees, it was flanked by white walls that appeared to enclose a hollow square, and the numbers 5638, blurred with time and pollution, were carved above the entrance gates. At one side was an unobtrusive plaque in Hebrew.

They walked up the tree-lined path and Dan pushed open the wooden door. Beyond it lay a small cemetery, an unadorned space with stark white walls, floored with a mosaic of pale stone. Laid flat on the ground in neat lines were about fifty marble gravestones and, haphazardly placed nearby, some smaller graves, simple mounds of pebbles set in cement.

In the pitiless sun the graveyard had the stark look of a Foreign Legion outpost. Two trees set close against the wall provided patches of shade.

Dan went from grave to grave, crouching to read the names, the dates—the last 1932—"Or 5692 as they have it"—and a rededication plaque dated 1993: *In memory of Dr. Aristides de Sousa Mendes, the Portuguese consul in Bordeaux,*

*who saved thousands of Jews from the Nazis by issuing transit
visas after he had been instructed not to continue.*

"I remember now," Hope called from beneath the tree.
"My aunt wrote us about a derelict Jewish cemetery somebody bought up, to stop it being turned into flats. They
must have restored it."

Beyond a small door marked "Museum" was a tiny
room, the exhibits amounting to little more than a few re-
ligious artifacts and sepia photographs of a community that
no longer existed, though the vivacious woman in charge
did her best to engage their interest. "We have something
rather special here," she said proudly, "a facsimile of the
first ever printing in Portugal. Samuel Porteira Gaçom did
it in his shop in a street quite near here." She gave Dan a
sharp look: "You're Jewish?"

"Yes."

From a cupboard she withdrew some large printed
sheets gripped in a plastic folder and held them out to
him. "It's an edition of the Pentateuch in Hebrew, with the
Targum paraphrase of Onkelos, and the commentary of
Rashi in two volumes. The original is in the British Library
in London."

He took the folder and turned the decorative pages
politely while Hope looked over his shoulder. Then he
handed it back and they left.

"You're very quiet," he said. "Are you okay?"

"Yes."

She felt dizzy. A combination of heat, the fierce sun
beating into the enclosed cemetery and the aftereffects of
too much champagne, she decided. Staring at the ornate
black and red printing scrolling its way down the page,
she had felt a stab of familiarity, a sense that she had seen
these pages before. She could feel the texture beneath her

fingertips, smell the ink. *Dragon's blood.* She shook her head to clear it and reached into her bag for a bottle of mineral water. "I must be dehydrated."

Dan had told her once that Portugal did not have a cuisine; it did not compete for inclusion in the pantheon; it was, so to speak, *hors concours.* He left his critical faculties at the airport and expected nothing.

Dinner consisted of grilled sardines at a wooden trestle table overlooking the port: plump fish with blackened skin, tender white flesh, served with half a lemon and coarse local bread. Dan pronounced it a triumph.

Hope leaned her elbows on the harbor wall, watching the movement of the water, the surf curling, breaking on the bottom of a flight of stone steps. Waves had always fascinated her: eternal and ephemeral at the same time; the surf surges and dies, endlessly renewed, at the same time constant and fleeting. Like love, perhaps?

Had she ever really loved Dan? Or had she been swept away by his energy, a force that admitted no opposition. The problem with an overwhelming life force was that it fed on others. With a pang she recalled a youthful dream: to create something of lasting worth. But she had not carried within herself the ruthlessness of the true artist prepared to sacrifice self and all others in the greater cause. An overactive conscience had disarmed her; she had temporized, put herself on hold. She had been supportive wife, good mother. And now she found herself without a role.

Wrong turns had been taken, she saw that with painful clarity. What was needed now was some determined navigation, not to discover terra incognita, but the way back to herself.

The aunt, when they found her, was a surprise: a thin,

fierce woman living in a tiny flat crammed with books. She had stayed on when her older sister left, risked imprisonment during the dictatorship, never concealing her political views.

She fed Dan tiny, lurid yellow sweetmeats, which he nibbled in dazed acquiescence while Hope crouched at the bookshelves, studying the worn covers. She realized that she knew nothing about the writers filling the shelves—Camões, Almeida Garrett, Fernando Pessoa—she knew nothing of her own literature, she could at best experience it secondhand, in translation. Would she hear the author's voice? How authentic could a translation be? She had long ago read Pound's Cathay poems and she had wondered then: were these in truth the words of the Chinese poet? Seen through the prism of a double translation, would Rihaku recognize his own work? Looking into Chapman's Homer, whom had Keats really discovered? She felt a gnawing frustration that only now, so late, had she become aware of this. To disregard your own heritage was to lose a part of yourself. She should learn Portuguese properly, learn to read its subtleties, not just the menus and guidebooks. She would teach herself. Get a CD-ROM.

The aunt had a set of engravings on the wall: the Great Discoveries, the far-flung empire, exotic imports from the Orient, a caravel. Vasco da Gama. Magellan.

"Such a little country, such a huge empire," Hope said. "It must have been painful, the decline. The loss."

"Would you not say, rather, a return to reality? Like Rome. Like Britain. All empires fall in the end. We have regained, perhaps, a sense of proportion."

It was the aunt who told Dan about the restaurant in a village a few miles inland from Faro: "A simple little place, not at all expensive, even the locals eat there, but he has a way with herbs. . . . I would say you could find it of interest."

Hope saw how curiosity sharpened Dan's features, the precise way he noted down instructions for reaching the village. Something told him the aunt had taste—despite the egg and sugar sweetmeats. In Hope's view this was unfortunate: unrealistic expectations might be built up and then dashed. Cuisine was an unreliable password.

They drove through hills still bright with flowers, though the heat foreshadowed summer. Dan switched on the air-conditioning so that they were sealed in coolness rather than open to the fragrant warmth outside.

The aunt's directions led them to the village, the turning off the main street, and the small, insignificant house that advertised itself merely as Ricardo, offering home-cooked food.

"Have the herb fritters," the aunt had instructed. "Specialty of the house."

The dining room was small, with an open terrace at the back overlooking a river. Hope watched children playing at the water's edge, throwing in fishing lines, skimming pebbles across the surface, spraying each other with refilled plastic bottles, shrieking, falling over in the grass. A young mother sat, shoes discarded, bathing her feet in the water and singing.

When the fritters came they were dark green globes the size of golf balls, crisp, light as air, piled into a ceramic bowl. Dan helped himself. After a moment he paused, looked more closely at the fritters.

"What's wrong?" Hope asked.

"Nothing's wrong. The texture's remarkable: as fluffy as a good soufflé and the outer surface"—he tapped it gently with his knife—"the thinnest layer of crispness. And the flavor . . . it's clever; it's subtle. I can't single out the specific herbs yet."

He asked to speak to the chef, and a young man in jeans and white T-shirt came out of the kitchen. He said, in English, "You're enjoying the herb fritters."

Dan said, "They're extraordinary. I'm trying to tease out the ingredients. There's spinach, of course. Possibly coriander. I think I can taste mint, perhaps—"

"No coriander." The young man smiled. "Thirteen herbs altogether. It's an old family secret."

"I'll get there. I'm working on it." Dan savored a mouthful slowly, holding it on his tongue, eyes half closed. "There's . . . egg and . . . courgettes?"

"Bravo."

"And presumably a soufflé base."

"No flour." Ricardo cocked his head thoughtfully. "You a chef?"

Dan nodded.

Ricardo's smile widened mischievously. "Ah. I've had chefs in here before. It drives them mad." He raised a hand in an ironic benediction. "You'll never get it. What makes it fluffy. And all the herbs." Laughing silently, he went back into the tiny kitchen.

Hope knew the day was ruined. All the signs were there: Dan was now carrying out a tasting operation, a laboratory experiment. He broke open one fritter, chopped up another, he nibbled, chewed slowly, he flattened some of the mixture on to his plate to distinguish individual ingredients. She sat across the table from him, silently staring out of the window at the children playing on the riverbank, at the woman singing.

The lines in his face had tightened into what Hope had

298

once described as the kitchen clench, and when they drove through the next village and she pointed out a Manueline window in a little church—a graceful stone rope encircling the opening—he drove past without pausing.

The millennium took place elsewhere, it seemed, with its anticlimactic fireworks and the Y2K computer meltdown panic that proved groundless. She watched it all on television, Dan busy with staff problems and VIP guest lists.

Meanwhile, she switched channels and tried to summon up appropriately millennial thoughts. Once, she might have gone to church; the very idea of a millennium was bound up with Catholic hopes and fears: St. John of the Cross and his picture of Christ returning, to scoop up his saints and carry them off to heaven as a reward for all their suffering. As a child she had read how the saints endured martyrdom: dismemberment, blinding, decapitation. . . . But later she had realized that life itself was something to be endured—an interesting word, endure, meaning at the same time to suffer and to survive. Life was a war zone: you endured what it threw at you, and battled on.

A week after the big night she was woken by Dan screaming in his sleep. She shook him awake gently, soothing him. He sat up, flung himself back on the pillow, rubbing his eyes, breathing heavily. "Bad dream. I'll make myself a cup of tea."

"I'll do it. I'm awake anyway."

There were more bad dreams, more broken nights, and a refusal to accept that anything was wrong. Or rather, to discuss anything.

"It's business. Don't worry yourself. I'll make some tea."

Coming up from the kitchen, carrying the mugs, he must have tripped: she heard him crash to the floor. When she reached him he was lying sprawled on the turn of the stairs, unmoving, his cheek flat to the carpet. She saw his eyes blink and thought: it's a stroke, he's had a stroke. But then he spoke, quite clearly, sounding puzzled, "I can't seem to move my legs. Perhaps we should call the quack."

Stress, the consultant said; prolonged anxiety and tension. A temporary glitch in the nervous system. Within days he was walking; a week later, disregarding all advice, he was back at work. The restaurant near St. Paul's was breaking even; the one in Chelsea was busy but costing too much to run. Hampstead had always been a question mark; and the newest, brightest hope, Fishing for Compliments at the Dome, was a disaster. The idea—Hope had always suspected it was too cute, too self-conscious—of having live fish and crustaceans occupying a vast, picturesque aquarium circling the room, never took off. Had the Dome itself been packed, the place might have worked, but there were too few customers for the restaurant, as well as the underpopulated tent in which it sat. Those who did come admired the fish but—presented with a long-handled net—balked at being, as it were, the executioners of their chosen prey.

"Wrong sort of punter," Dan said wearily. "Too down-market."

And not enough of them.

That same week Dan had agreed to do a TV cookery show: appear as one of two guest chefs judging the efforts of amateur but ambitious cooks. It should have been easy, he had done many such programs: he could be witty, rigorous without being unkind; a good advertisement for his own trade. But this was a turning point. Hope, watching at home, saw the reality of the generation gap yawning beneath Dan's feet before he was aware of it. He spoke with passion, as always. He drew attention to the nobility a sauce could attain, he lauded the integrity of the plate, the importance of the correct balance in a dish; the combination of the visual, the olfactory, and the gustatory. The presenter was respectful.

The other judge was a new star chef in her twenties, a larky girl filmed zooming up to the studios on her motorcycle. Confident in torn jeans and trainers, she talked of preparing a dish in terms of ease and fun—"Throw it together, have a bit of a laugh. Grab a few fresh herbs, throw in the oil and garlic, chuck on a handful of rough salt, and whack in the chicken. Fling it in the wok for a quick sizzle and you're there. It's a doddle." The audience reaction was rapturous and Hope saw Dan's face go dark.

The two star guests examined the amateur cooks' efforts, tasted, pronounced judgment. Dan liked the first presentation, he found it well-balanced, pleasing to the eye, perfectly seasoned.

The young co-judge took a forkful, held it on her palate consideringly. "Yeah," she said with a one-shouldered shrug. "Nice. A bit Seventies."

That night Dan watched a late show with a bottle of whiskey. Hope went to bed. Next morning, when she got up, Dan had already left for work and the bottle was empty. It was the first of many such nights.

She wrote to Mel, voicing fears. The letter was not posted.

She wrote to Dan. The letter, rewritten several times, lay on her desk, covered with charity appeals and a council announcement that the refuse collection day was to be changed. In the end she abandoned lengthy explanations and on a single sheet she told him she was leaving. She would prop it on his answering machine when she left the house: there, he would be sure to notice it.

She was upstairs, going through her wardrobe for the things she wanted to pack, laying them out on the bed, when she heard the sound of a car.

⸱⸱⸱⸱⸱⸱⸱⸱

SEDATION. SHE HEARS the word swimming toward her; hears sedation, and also calm and quiet being recommended.

"Keep an eye on her. See how it goes."

Swaddled in darkness, she senses cool liquid. She sips. Darkness envelops her.

Eyes open, she sees a window, pale green walls, a door with a glass porthole. The walls are scarred by many glancing encounters with sharp objects.

She is in bed, or rather in a bed, narrow and with iron bars at its head and foot. She finds she is wearing a curious garment: a cotton robe, loose sleeved and bulky, like an overall.

What is this place? Voices and clattering footsteps beyond the door are muffled. She analyzes the pervading smell, looks closely at objects on view and attempts to assess the conclusion. A problem presents itself: there seem to be few words available for use. Her mind, too, is fragmented, with blank patches, like a picture daubed with obliterating paint, or rather, like a film where the action every now and then blacks out. Areas of emptiness. But now she reaches for the word she needs and finds it: hospital. This is a hospital.

A woman entering is . . . *nurse,* she discovers, yes. The nurse is brisk and unsurprised. "You're awake. Good. Lunch will be coming round soon."

What's happened? she wants to ask. Why am I here? But

the nurse has gone, the door sighing closed behind her with a soft, rubbery thump.

She sleeps again, the spinning darkness a comfort. She wakes to find Lunch has arrived. Lunch is a large, cheerful Caribbean woman pushing a big steel box full of covered dishes. The smell is not encouraging.

When Lunch has gone, calling loudly to someone in the corridor outside, she gets cautiously out of bed and explores the room: a table, on which sits a plate of fish pie and white wallpaper paste; pills in a small, dark brown plastic bottle; a clipboard hanging on the end of the bed, mysterious words jotted below a name she does not recognize; a tin cupboard and inside . . . she touches various garments, feeling the texture of the fabric, trying to arouse a sense of familiarity with these clothes. She is stroking a jacket questioningly when another nurse hurries in and glances at the plate beside the bed.

"You should try and eat something, that's a good girl."

"My clothes—"

"Don't worry. They'll be bringing you clean ones next time they come."

They? She sifts the darkness. She knows it is populated. Shadow people are out there, waiting to be reached, to be called into life, summoned to step forward and declare themselves. *They?*

"Can I get dressed?" Another word she knows, another action described.

A bit soon, the nurse says. Better to have a rest. The door closes. Sigh. Shh.

She tries to take off the cotton robe, briefly panicking when there seem to be no buttons or zips—*buttons and zips. She knows buttons and zips*—then finds the way to untie the robe, free herself.

Clothes: she knows the names as she touches them, dons them. The last item is a sort of jacket . . . *anorak,* she savors the word, an anorak made of some dark green material. A small purse in one pocket. Pleased, she nods at purse and pocket. She places the anorak on the bed and reaches for shoes, *trainers, yes.*

She can hear Lunch still clattering and laughing her way in and out of rooms. The door with the glass porthole gives a view of the world immediately beyond: corridor, table, a couple of tubular steel chairs with worn canvas seats. An elderly woman passes the door with painful slowness, gripping a steel scaffolding frame, pulling herself forward step by step, straining like a climber conquering a cliff face. Farther away, a bell is ringing.

She steps into the corridor. At the far end is a double door. She knows this is the way out and walks unhurriedly toward the doors. Locked. No visible handle. Behind her she hears Lunch approaching; the bang and clatter, the rich laugh. She seats herself on one of the tubular steel chairs as though waiting for someone. She reads signs. "In Case of Emergency Break Glass." "Ring Bell for Attention." Lunch rolls past her, ample in a green nylon— *nylon*—overall. She stops at the doors, presses a button high on the wall, and with a click the lock is released.

A button. Of course. She waits till Lunch has gone through. Two nurses hurry past, talking. They pay no attention to her.

She picks up some leaflets lying on a plastic table, stands, presses the button, and pushes open the door. She walks down the corridor glancing at the leaflets. She feels instinctively that the leaflets give her a sort of validity, a purpose. She negotiates her way through temporary blankness to familiar territory, her vocabulary expanding: lift, exit, street.

Fugue. As in Bach? Why should a musical composition be referred to on a hospital clipboard?

Hope reaches the street and sets off at a fast pace. She has a journey to make.

In the first public library she consults a dictionary.

Fugue: (1) A composition harmonized according to the laws of counterpoint, with various contrapuntal designs. (2) Flight.

Why should the pathology of flight appear on a clipboard in a room with green walls where Lunch comes calling with a big steel box? She would like to look up more, but she knows there is somewhere she has to go. She replaces the dictionary on the shelf and makes her way out of the library.

She finds her way to the Thames. It is as though she knows the route, but this part of the river is unfamiliar to her. She wonders if there is a way people can smell the river, sniffing their way to it like a dog or a wolf. She walks on, sometimes leaving the waterside, taking roads that lead away, or seem to, until again she catches the gleam of sky on surface. There are gray buildings and yellow stone. Red brick. Some, she can see, are old. She feels she should recognize one street or another, but when she looks more closely she feels pain begin somewhere behind her eyes and she hurries on, away from the embankment.

Another library. For a modest fee, she notes, she can log on to the Net. A terminal is made available.

Click.
"Who am I? Where have I come from?"

Unable to find "Who am I? Where have I come from?"
   Please try again.
"Where am I going?"
An error has occurred. This program is not respond-
   ing. It may be busy, waiting for a response from
   you, or it may have stopped running.
"Search. Search for me."
Click.
This program has performed an illegal operation and
   will be shut down.

She abandons the terminal: there is somewhere she has
to go.

The river has found its way to her again. She crosses by
one bridge, back by another. She knows this bridge.

Beneath her the water swirls, a murky brown, an unsatisfactory element, insubstantial, ambiguous. A body, dropping from the iron above, falling through the air, would it
be buoyed up for a while in the soupy stream, or swallowed
in its thousand liquid mouths? A body, falling, could test
the waters. Unobserved, she is invisible.

"Looks like soup, doesn't it?"

A man, invading her space, bothering her with a pointless question, a man in a black leather jacket.

The taxi turns right, leaving the river behind, and pulls up
at a pair of ornate wrought iron gates that stand open. In
the darkness beyond the gates lies a curving drive, a double
garage, and an Edwardian house with a portico.

She stands staring at the house while he pays off the cab.
She hears it drive off, the distinctive rattling engine sound.
She is already walking toward the gates. Her feet crunch
loudly on the gravel drive.

She remembers the sound of the gravel.

She reaches the front door and stretches out her hand

to the heavy brass knocker. As she touches it, she turns back toward the drive, to call out, to ask about a key.

Mel, walking toward her, sees awareness flood into her face, her mouth stretch open in an O of pain.

She screams "No!" into the night and then she crumples, eyes shut tight, arms flung up as though to protect her head, ward off a blow; a small, huddled figure pressed into a corner of the portico, humming tunelessly to blot out all sound.

He kneels next to her, holding her, murmuring non-sense, rocking her gently.

Hands over her ears, humming frantically, she tries to obliterate the sound of a car.

SHE HAD HEARD the car turn into the drive and assumed it was a delivery of some sort. She carried on taking clothes from the cupboard, folding them, laying them out on the bed, to be transferred to a suitcase. After a minute or two she registered that the car's engine was still running and no one had knocked or pushed anything through the letter box with that metallic rattle she knew so well. She crossed to the window.

The Porsche was parked in the drive and she could see Dan slumped in the driver's seat, his hands resting on the wheel, like a waiting chauffeur. While she watched he suddenly doubled up as though in pain, his head hitting the steering wheel. She dropped the jacket she held and ran down the stairs, across the hall, and out to the drive. Her shoes crunched loudly, heels sinking into the gravel. She had never liked that surface.

He was still bent over the wheel and she opened the

door, calling out to him anxiously, asking if he was all right, stepping back as whiskey fumes hit her. She thought, detached, that he should not be driving in this condition.

She slid into the seat and touched his shoulder. He flinched and pulled away, then straightened up. His face was streaked with tears.

"What is it?"

"Everything. It's over. All over."

In her mind she turned over words that had, until now, been abstract, unspecific: bankruptcy, receivership. And those Dickensian characters, the bailiffs. She saw them arriving in bowler hats, breathing heavily. They would list his assets. Take away his restaurants, the tables and chairs and light fittings; the French plates, the Swedish cutlery. Presumably they would take the house. She had never liked it anyway. She felt the guilty stirring of a sense of release.

He leaned across her and reached for the door, slamming it shut. She heard the central locking system click in. He said, "We could go together. You're always saying we should do things together." He was rocking to and fro, in the grip of an overwhelming agitation. She felt a twinge of unease: he was overwrought; he had been drinking. But he had always been a good driver, careful.

"Go where?"

"Go. Finish it. Off a cliff. Brick wall. Whatever."

People said silly things under pressure, things that should not be taken seriously. But she found she was having difficulty breathing. She said, firmly and carefully, the way she used to speak to Gideon or Ruth when they threw a tantrum, "Dan, please unlock the door."

He turned the ignition key and the engine sank into silence. She said, "Come in and I'll make us some tea—"

He screamed, "There's no *point*. No point in anything.

You're like those people on the *Titanic*. The fucking ship's going down. We're *drowning*. So let's have a cup of tea."

"I want to get out of the car. It smells of whiskey."

He touched a switch and she heard the locks click open.

"Thank you." She opened the door and began to get out. Turned back. "Don't be an idiot," she said. "Come inside." Coaxingly, again as though to a child, "Come on, then."

For a moment they remained as they were, he at the wheel, she half out of the car, leaning in toward him. Then she got out.

He switched on the ignition and pulled the door shut. The locks clicked. Through the closed window she called, "Please don't drive. I'll worry." He heard her and his head went back in silent laughter. He was crying again.

She walked back over the gravel to the house and pushed open the front door. She paused, her hand on the heavy brass doorknob. Looking back she saw that Dan was holding up a container of some sort, upending it so that liquid poured over him. He raised his head to the gush, eyes closed, like someone under a shower. For a moment the action seemed meaningless. Then she screamed "No!"

She began to run toward the car but before she reached it the windows went white; there was a roaring sound and flames engulfed the Porsche. Like the finale of some mad fireworks display, the car appeared to be made out of fire.

The white windows crackled into crazed patterns and bulged outward, as the glass broke free of the restraining rubber and exploded into the road. Flames leaped out of the windows, reaching for her. She heard a neighbor calling and yelled, frantic, "Get the ambulance! Get the police!"

The handle burned her hand and the door was locked anyway. She tore off her cardigan, wrapped it round her arm, and tried to open the door from the inside, but she was beaten back by the heat, the wool catching fire so that her arm was sheathed in flame.

She could smell burning rubber and then the flames shifted, blown back by the wind, and she saw Dan, a thing that had been Dan, his skin blistered and blackened, splitting like pork crackling, his hair blazing like straw. One window had remained intact and now seemed to be melting, liquefying as it flamed. Dan's face, too, seemed to be melting, his eyes boiling in his head. She wrenched and kicked at the door, sobbing, screaming for help. She smelled flesh burning.

Blinded by the smoke and heat, coughing, she heard a police siren in the distance.

<hr />

IN THE AMBULANCE she was calm. Afterward there seemed a great deal of administrative detail that needed attending to and she filled in the requested forms, signed on various dotted lines.

She organized the funeral. Mel—in Africa on a tour raising money for famine relief—could not be reached, but a Jewish funeral waits for no man. Forty-eight hours later what remained of Dan was deposited in the ground and the family gathered at the graveside to cast their individual handfuls of earth on the coffin. What finality there was in that thud of soil on wood. The charred, grinning corpse that leered at her from the flames, the sheet-wrapped body, the discreetly covered form of the deceased in the undertaker's parlor—all those seemed temporary conditions. Now, as the shovels dug into the mound of mud and the pit was filled, the reality of Dan mingled with the dust he would return to. "As for man, his days are as grass," the rabbi had intoned, "for the wind passeth over it, and it is gone." And then, offering a sort of consolation prize: "May he come to his place in peace." Later he commiserated with Hope on the "tragic accident," which was the way he preferred to describe the death.

Dan's mother was calm, only her red, swollen eyes giving away her true state. "This sort of thing is easier for the Orthodox to deal with," she said. "The ritual: rending garments and going unshaven, sitting on low stools, being comforted by mourners—it all helps, I suppose. We're not trained for it anymore, most of us. Death takes us by surprise." She took a sudden deep breath. When she spoke, her voice shook. "It's hard to outlive one's child."

After the service there were refreshments at the house, platters rapidly emptied of bridge rolls and sandwiches, second cups of tea requested, a buzz of muted conversation, the occasional indiscretion of a spurt of laughter from across the room as cheerfulness broke in. Life reasserting itself.

Ruth and Gideon passed plates round and behaved with unexpected grace, and one or the other of them was at her side the moment she showed any sign of drooping. They stayed till the last guest left.

"Now," Hope said, "I think I would like to be left alone." They argued, bullying her for her own good. "I have your mobile numbers," she said, "if there's any problem."

She watched them go down the drive, the two siblings, thin and black-haired, elegant in their unstructured dark suits—Ruth never wore a skirt. Walking away they looked identical, the two blurring into one as they hugged briefly before fishing out car keys to drive away.

The house seemed darker than usual; it was a cloudy

day, and she switched on the landing light as she went upstairs to change out of her funeral outfit. The built-in cupboard was full of neatly arranged clothes, rows of shoes on racks, one above the other, like seats in a grandstand. She looked them over with some surprise: these flimsy dresses from Armani and Gucci; these cashmere, velvet, and silk confections, seemed to have nothing to do with her. Surely the tiny shoes would never fit her feet? The high-heeled boots looked absurdly impractical. And fur hats. When would she wear a fur hat? She put on a pair of comfortable jeans and a sweatshirt.

She walked slowly down to the study and switched on her computer. The screen swam into pearly life, the cursor blinked encouragingly. She logged on.

So much information to download: how do you read your way into the past? A shape scratched on a flat stone; the Aztec codex; the Rosetta Stone; the decoding of Linear B. The shilling life will give you all the facts. Dates of birth and death, wrong turns taken. A yellow streamer thrown across the water. . . . How do you decipher the mystery? Unravel the thread? When do you deal with the importance of love? What—

She recalled an old game Mel and Dan used to play years before: "Okay, here's the answer. What's the question?" But she had questions that needed answers and she began, fingers flying, to tap in the words, but in midsentence she became aware of an overwhelming restlessness, a need to leave the house, to go out. She took her old gardening anorak from the hall cupboard, grabbed her purse and went to the front door.

She opens the door, puts her hand on the brass doorknob to pull it shut behind her, and turns toward the drive. As she turns she feels the heat; it burns her face, blackens her skin, flames reach out—

She screams, "No!"

Blankness descends.

Sedation. Green walls, a door with a glass porthole. In case of emergency break glass. A river, the water slow running, brown. A man in a leather jacket, rocking her gently back to consciousness. They spin together, in the darkness. More information needed.

Dissociative fugue: a flight from an intolerable situation. A condition in which the distinctive feature is the patient's inability to remember important personal information. A mechanism that allows the mind to compartmentalize certain memories from normal consciousness.

A disorder in which the subject suddenly goes on a journey that has no apparent relation to what he or she has been doing, with amnesia for the past.

Traumatic memories are not processed or integrated into a person's ongoing life in the same way as normal memories. Instead they are "compartmentalized" and may erupt into consciousness from time to time without warning. Over a period of time the two sets of memories—the normal and the traumatic—may coexist as parallel sets without being combined or blended. It may be regarded as a normal defense mechanism.

"So that's what I am: an example of a defense mechanism. Not something I'd want on my gravestone." She clicks the cursor, and disconnects from the Net and its flood of information. The screen goes blank. A bright light shines down on the desktop; the rest of the room is dark, but familiar to

313

her. This is the study, cluttered with Dan's papers, household accounts, back numbers of Gideon's magazine, books bought but left unread.

It has been a long night. First the paralysis, unable to move from the portico as he rocked her, murmuring soothingly, as to a child; then the tears, the shaking, the fear of falling. She has felt her way back, inch by inch, testing each step as though treading a minefield. Now, like those laboratory finches, she seems to have rebuilt the lost cells, though it may be too soon for singing.

She sees that Mel has made tea and she reaches for the mug with her left hand, gulping the hot liquid.

His fingers touch her blistered palm, circle her wrist. "The bandage . . ."

"I thought maybe I could open the car door, pull him out. I stuck my arm through the window . . ."

The smell of burning rubber, plastic, flesh. Heat ballooning from the interior, the flames driving her back. Glass, windows melting, his face—

She gives a small shake of the head. The gesture will remain with her, but she will learn to live with it.

"How did you come to be there, on the bridge?"

"Ruth managed to get through to me via some African sculptor she knows—she and Gideon were frantic when you collapsed; they thought the doctors were stringing them along, talking about fugues and dissociative states. They thought you were in a coma. And then you vanished."

Police, it seemed, had been alerted; people had been looking for her all over London.

"I had a funny feeling you'd find your way to Vauxhall. The old *saudade.*"

She notices, with a pang, how his hair has grown gray— in streaks, not distinguished at all. But the curls are still

thick and wiry. He is not tall; when they stand she rests against him for a moment with an extraordinary sense of belonging. It is an epiphany of an odd sort, a long-delayed acknowledgment. No need now to say she has always loved him. She is a storm-battered craft clumsily coming to rest after a tortuous journey, blown off course, getting lost, mistaking shadow for substance, at last dropping anchor to discover, in the shelter of a familiar harbor, the prize of a newfound land.

They walk through the house and she notices to her surprise that it is in need of decoration, the woodwork chipped, paint showing signs of age. Neglected. For so long she had been in the house, but not of it, not seeing it, she and Dan, both blind in their different ways.

He helps her into the green anorak and, after a momentary hesitation, he opens the front door. She, too, hesitates, hanging back, then steps forward, bracing herself. No shock, no flames, no crackle of burning. She breathes out.

She says, "What now?"

"If you'll let me look after you I'd see that you manage a laugh at least once a day—for purely therapeutic purposes. We could visit that country of yours, catch some fado. You could tell me a few of the old stories—"

"Dan was bored by old stories."

"In thirty years nothing you have said has ever bored me. Try me on the 'Once upon a time' and 'happy ever after.'"

"I'm afraid old Portuguese stories tend to have unhappy endings."

"Well, you know what Orson Welles said: If you want a happy ending it depends on where you stop the story. This could be a good place, two people walking away from a

house together. You could stop the story here. If you were an optimist."

They come out of the house into the early morning light. Mist lends the wrought iron gates a poetry they normally lack. Virginia creeper cascades over a brick wall, the leaves green, bronze, crimson, clinging to the surface like glossy leather paneling. In the grayness the colors glow with unearthly brilliance. Autumn lies about them at the roadside: small fallen apples, wrinkled and rosy; horse chestnuts gleaming within their split, prickly husks; yellowing leaves from bushes and trees pile up in drifts along the gutters. Unpicked blackberries have shriveled on bramble stems. Ahead of them, where the river curves close, a thick white mist hovers like frozen breath.

In the road, a flat pebble gleaming with a sheen of dew catches the light, silvery. He stoops and picks it up. Hands it to Hope. She weighs it in her hand: smooth, hard, a fragment of something ancient that has survived through time, changing its form, its shape. And he, too, has been touched and changed by time. But she has no doubt that a gray haired man in a creased leather jacket can be an instrument of the sublime.

They walk on, a man and a woman somewhat the worse for wear and tear, though intact apart from two wisdom teeth and an appendix. In the vast empty spaces that make up the bulk of the human body lie cells which, one day, examined under a microscope, will reveal—("Not good, I'm afraid")—that joy is finite. This is the mortal condition: bad news always lies in wait. But that time is still to come, ten thousand dawns away, spinning toward them. Tides turn, suns rise and set. Meanwhile, two people walk toward a riverbank, his hand holding hers.

316

ACKNOWLEDGMENTS

Distant Music is a work of fiction. The historical material interwoven with the story is a blend of fact and imagination. Real people mingle with fictional characters, but do not step beyond the bounds of their biographies.

Christopher Columbus did visit Madeira and spend some time there, but it is unlikely that he encountered Esperança, who is my invention. Fires were lit on the island, as I describe, and according to some sources they burned sporadically for several years.

The decision of the King of Portugal to expel the Jews to clear the way for a royal marriage with Spain is fact, as is the later edict on forced conversion. The conditions on the boats carrying the refugees away from Portugal were, in some cases, worse than I have described.

A novice from the Lisbon convent did experience the horrors of the earthquake in 1755 and wrote of it in her journal. The encounter with the cobbler is conjecture.

319

Serial murders of washerwomen took place on the Lisbon aqueduct in the mid-nineteenth century, though not necessarily in the year I have chosen.

Several people gave me the benefit of their special knowledge while I was writing this book. I would like to thank Professor Michael Alpert; Dr. Jean Curtis-Raleigh; C.A.R. Hills; Professor Helder Macedo; Dr. Colin McEvedy; Rabbi John Rayner; and Simon Richmond. For her perceptive and sensitive nurturing of the book, many thanks to my editor, Penelope Hoare. And to the London Library for its patience: some volumes rested on my shelves for much of the three years I worked on the novel.

Any errors that have crept into the text are, of course, my own responsibility.

The book was inspired by the history of Portugal and the beauty of its landscape. Its kindly and hospitable people made research a pleasurable labor.

LEE LANGLEY was born in Calcutta, of Scottish parents. She traveled widely in India during her childhood. She has written eight critically acclaimed novels and a much praised volume of short stories, as well as poetry and television screenplays. She writes on travel and the arts for leading British newspapers and magazines.

Her novel *Persistent Rumours* won a Commonwealth Writers' Prize for Best Novel and the Writers' Guild of Great Britain Best Novel of the Year Award.

She is a Fellow of the Royal Society of Literature and has served on the British executive committee of PEN, the international writer's organization, and the literature advisory panel of the Arts Council of England.

JOIN US

Since its genesis as *Milkweed Chronicle* in 1979, Milkweed has helped hundreds of emerging writers reach their readers. Thanks to the generosity of foundations and of individuals like you, Milkweed Editions is able to continue its nonprofit mission of publishing books chosen on the basis of literary merit—of how they impact the human heart and spirit—rather than on how they impact the bottom line. That's a miracle our readers have made possible.

In addition to purchasing Milkweed books, you can join the growing community of Milkweed supporters. Individual contributions of any amount are both meaningful and welcome. Contact us for a Milkweed catalog or log on to www.milkweed.org and click on "About Milkweed," then "Why Join Milkweed," to find out about our donor program, or simply call (800) 520-6455 and ask about becoming one of Milkweed's contributors. As a nonprofit press, Milkweed belongs to you, the community. Milkweed's board, its staff, and especially the authors whose careers you help launch thank you for reading our books and supporting our mission in any way you can.

Interior design by Christian Fünfhausen
Typeset in New Baskerville 10.5/14
by Stanton Publication Services
Printed on acid-free 55# Sebago 2000
Antique Cream paper
by Maple-Vail Book Manufacturing